The Traveler

ALSO BY JENNA LINDSEY,
QUEST FOR EVIL: THE MAGIC
OF THE KEY

THE TRAVELER

JENNA LINDSEY

iUniverse, Inc.
New York   Bloomington

The Traveler
A Novel

Copyright © 2010 Jenna Lindsey

All rights reserved. No part of this book may be used or reproduced by any means, graphic, electronic, or mechanical, including photocopying, recording, taping or by any information storage retrieval system without the written permission of the publisher except in the case of brief quotations embodied in critical articles and reviews.

This is a work of fiction. All of the characters, names, incidents, organizations, and dialogue in this novel are either the products of the author's imagination or are used fictitiously.

iUniverse books may be ordered through booksellers or by contacting:

iUniverse
1663 Liberty Drive
Bloomington, IN 47403
www.iuniverse.com
1-800-Authors (1-800-288-4677)

Because of the dynamic nature of the Internet, any Web addresses or links contained in this book may have changed since publication and may no longer be valid. The views expressed in this work are solely those of the author and do not necessarily reflect the views of the publisher, and the publisher hereby disclaims any responsibility for them.

ISBN: 978-1-4502-0697-6 (pbk)
ISBN: 978-1-4502-0699-0 (cloth)
ISBN: 978-1-4502-0698-3 (ebook)

Library of Congress Control Number: 2010900330

Printed in the United States of America

iUniverse rev. date: 02/19/10

For my husband, Jerry

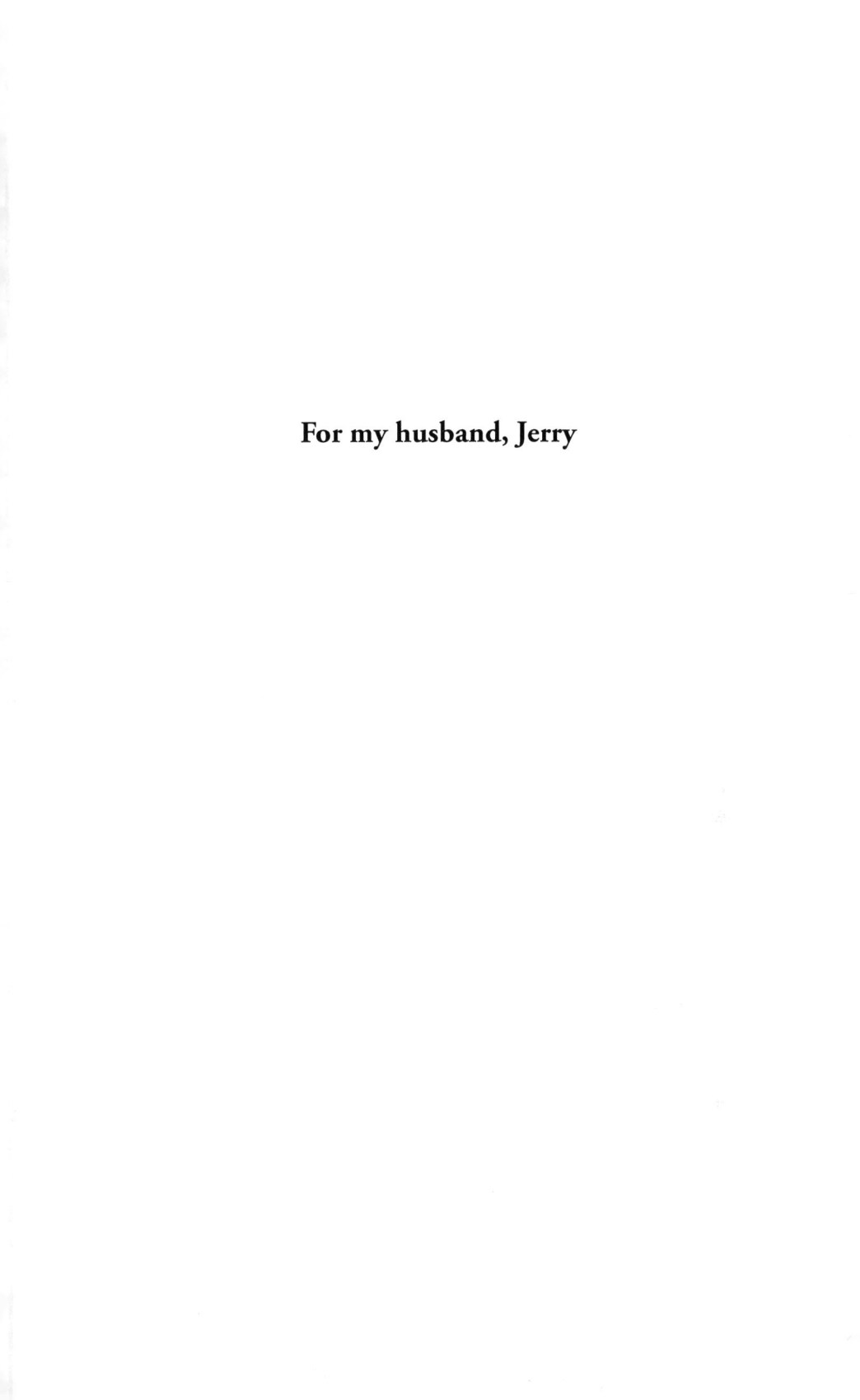

Acknowledgments:

Thank you, Sarra, Jade, and Amy.
Special thanks to Tomi and Helene.

Prologue

The Machine was ready. The Traveler examined the final data again. After centuries of traveling from world to world, she felt afraid. After mediating political disputes, preserving treaties, and preventing wars, the Traveler felt small, uncertain, and alone.

Facing the opportunity to cross Time and Space artificially, she hesitated. Was she certain this next destination would be her final lifetime? If she had miscalculated or misinterpreted the data, she would Travel again without hope of ever returning to him.

The Traveler backed away from the Time Machine she had created, as if seeing it for the first time. Bumping into a chair, she sat down abruptly, eyes on the Machine.

It was a frightening decision to make, more difficult than any other of her long life. But if she was right, if it worked, if …

She focused inward, remembering the first time she had Traveled.

"I looked out the window," the Traveler said, "and he was there."

Part I
Ispell

O N E

What miracle had drawn him across time and space to wait for her in the street below? And now that he was here, why did she hesitate to go to him? Wasn't this what she'd always wanted?

I should feel excited, not anxious, thought Jinnie.

Her hands trembled, and she clenched them to her sides.

It's not as if he's a stranger, Jinnie told herself. *He's been the most important person in my life for years. He's everything to me—the only real love of my life—My other life.*

She had long since stopped telling friends or family about her strange dual existence—how she felt that she lived in a doorway, with half of her life on one side and half on the other.

No one understood. They told Jinnie to put aside her "vivid imagination" and settle down.

She had tried to fit in. Jinnie had let her roommate, Karen, set up a few blind dates. Jinnie's deep blue eyes and dark brown hair made her a pretty companion. But Jinnie always felt uncomfortable on these dates, as if she were being unfaithful.

Kisses and warm words fell flat as Jinnie longed for the familiar embrace of the man in her other life. The man she knew loved her beyond small gestures of romance, sex, and the occasional weekend in the country. Every touch, every kiss, only made her miss him more. What was his name? Griffin?

Recently Jinnie had felt a pull toward her other life stronger than she had ever felt before. As if something important, perhaps something terrible, were about to happen.

Peeking out at the street below, Jinnie remembered finally telling Karen her secret. It had been hard to find the words. The darkness of the bar didn't help. It made Jinnie feel uncertain. Who would she see if she looked away from Karen? Who might be waiting in the shadows?

"Even sitting here with you, Karen, I'm somewhere else."

"Where?" Karen asked, accustomed to what she believed was Jinnie's romantic nature.

Jinnie focused inward for a moment. "I'm in a conference. At a long table with heads of state. But that's not what they're called. And I'm in charge. I'm settling a border dispute."

Karen laughed. "Jinnie, you avoid politics like the plague. True, you've always been organized, but now you're rearranging state lines? What are you? A queen?"

"No. But I am someone important. I know that there, in Ispell, I'm so much more. Better somehow. More certain of myself. Beautiful and strong and …"

Karen signaled the waiter for another round of drinks. "And?"

Jinnie fidgeted. "And loved. Really loved."

"Really?"

Jinnie blushed, glad of the dim light now. "Yes. Real love. More than true and better than everlasting. Real love: incomprehensible, passionate, peaceful, and life-fulfilling. And I know I'm everything to him and always will be. Now and always." Jinnie played with her swizzle stick. "That's what he says."

"This is too much," Karen said.

"Don't you think I know how it sounds?" Jinnie leaned forward. "All my life I've been told that I'm making it up, but honestly, Karen, I'm not."

"What makes it so real to you?"

"I can feel myself moving there, when I'm motionless here. Sometimes my other life is closer to me, sometimes farther away. Like the orbit of the Earth from the sun. Once I woke up feeling his arms around me. I opened my eyes, and I could almost see him. And I hear people talking. I have conversations with people who are my friends there, and when I come back, I'm typing some businessman's report on economics and wondering why I'm here."

Karen looked alarmed. "What do you mean, *here*?"

"Here." Jinnie looked around her. "In this reality, this world. I've always felt out of place, like I don't belong here. I should be in Ispell. With him." Jinnie's face became a perfect oval of resolve. "I belong there. I belong with him."

"Well, it sounds like you're there already." Anxiety pricked Karen's words, making her attempt to be teasing sound accusing.

"Only part of me," said Jinnie. "It's not enough. I need to be completely in Ispell."

"Jin." Karen put a hand on her friend's arm. "What you need is another drink." She paused, thinking. "And maybe a psychiatrist."

Jinnie remained silent.

Karen tried another tactic. "Why are you telling me this now, Jin? We've been friends and roommates for over a year. I always knew you were a romantic—a dreamer—but what's changed?"

Jinnie looked away for a moment. Her voice dropped to a whisper. "Because I feel like I'm finally going there."

Jinnie saw the fear peering out from Karen's eyes and pushed a smile at her friend. "I'm sorry, Karen. I shouldn't have said anything. You're right; I'm just a silly romantic with a vivid imagination."

That talk had been two months ago.

Jinnie looked at the man outside. He was still waiting. She wondered if anyone else could see him. The fading sun cast last tendrils of light through his body, as if he were a ghost.

"You're really here at last," Jinnie whispered. But for how long?

Panic seized Jinnie. She yanked her housecoat from her thin shoulders and jammed herself into jeans and boots. An oversized sweater followed. Digging behind the pillows of the couch, she found her purse. What more?

Jinnie ran to the door and then turned back. Impulsively she dashed to the kitchen and snatched up the grocery list from the counter. She turned it over, grabbed a pen, and wrote, "Karen: He's here at last. This is my chance, and I'm taking it. If I come back, I'll tell you all about it. Love, Jinnie."

Leaving the note on the counter, Jinnie locked the door behind her and hurried down the stairs. She pushed the outside door open carefully. The cold autumn air made her hesitate.

Across the street, he smiled at her and waved.

Jinnie took a deep breath and crossed the street to join him. "Griffin?"

"My liege." He bowed his head, but when he looked at her, Griffin's eyes sparkled with love. "I feared you would never descend. Are you ready to return?"

"Return?"

"To Keldonabrieve. The sun is setting. We must hurry. The Chill is coming."

Jinnie nodded, not understanding, but unwilling to question. "Then let's go."

Griffin smiled and took her arm just above the elbow, guiding her steps.

A drunk, propped in a doorway across the street, saw a man and a woman talking beside a lamppost. He blinked, and they were gone.

It began to snow.

Two

Jinnie gasped as a white light pierced her heart. She stumbled forward, feeling something peel from her entire body like a snake's skin. She fell.

"Tessajihn!" Griffin dropped to his knees beside her. "What is it? What's wrong?"

Jinnie lay face down in the cold snow, afraid to move.

Gently Griffin turned Jinnie over, sliding a warm hand beneath her head and smoothing her hair from her face.

Jinnie opened her eyes. Stars stabbed a black velvet sky. She focused closer and saw Griffin.

"Tessajihn," he said again.

That's me, thought Jinnie.

"Are you all right? Can you rise?"

"I think so." Jinnie pushed gingerly against the ground, expecting the movement to hurt, but the pain was gone.

Griffin helped her to stand.

"I'm okay." Jinnie's voice wavered, like her smile. Straightening her purse on her shoulder, she brushed at the wet snow clinging to her sweater.

The world blurred for a moment.

Griffin kept one hand on her arm to steady her.

"We can return to the Tower, Tessajihn." Griffin stopped himself from taking Jinnie's hand. The Dardidak could be watching. He let his hand drop away.

"We can send for help, my liege," he said formally.

Jinnie looked to the gray stone tower looming, grim and ominous, against the forest. She shook her head.

"The Dardidak are far too perfidious. I will not trust their hospitality further. Besides, I'm fine now. Really. Let's get away from this place."

Griffin still looked doubtful, but he obeyed.

"The horses are not far. I hid them in that copse of *burna* trees."

Following Griffin, Jinnie nodded. She remembered the thick aroma of *burna* trees, like oily cloves, and how the Sunadin used the sap to obscure the scent of their horses when traveling in Dardidak lands.

Quarrelsome and complaining, the Dardidak were one of the more civilized sub-species of Troll. Although their numbers were increasing, they lacked the organization and leadership to threaten the Alliances. They were hazardous, however, because of their taste for horseflesh.

Jinnie wrinkled her nose, recalling the Dardidak's squat, fetid bodies, yellow eyes, and protruding lower lips. Truly they were a detestable race, yet she had to make truces with them again and again. The Dardidak were always looking for a better offer or an excuse to break faith.

An oath broke Jinnie's thoughts.

"The fiends!" Griffin cursed. "They've killed my horse for their supper."

Peering around his shoulder, Jinnie shuddered. Griffin's horse had been eviscerated. A black gelding pranced nervously nearby, pulling at his tether.

"At least they spared your horse, my liege. No doubt as a courtesy."

Griffin led Jinnie around the corpse. "Steady, Nightfall," he said, patting the horse's neck. "We'll soon be away from here."

Boosting Jinnie into the saddle, Griffin handed her the reins. She kept Nightfall still as Griffin swung up behind her and slipped his arms about her waist with a comforting familiarity.

Jinnie hesitated. She didn't know how to ride. Did she? She clicked her tongue.

Nightfall needed no urging. Certain of the way home, the black horse threaded his way through the trees, heading north to Keldonabrieve.

The Traveler

Clutching the saddle horn with one hand and the reins with the other, Jinnie was grateful for Griffin's supportive hold. She let herself lean back against his chest.

Griffin was her Sheninn, her personal guard, but he also loved her. That certainty made her smile with an indescribable happiness. Griffin loved her.

But how long has he loved me? Jinnie asked herself. And do I love him? *Yes!* But I'm married to someone else. *Why?*

She felt like an actor in a play who knew the story, but had forgotten the lines. Intimate knowledge of people and events eluded her, while the immediate circumstances seemed natural and familiar.

Jinnie couldn't remember the details of the truce talk with the Dardidak, yet she knew who and what the Dardidak were.

She knew she was married, but she didn't remember to whom. Only that it wasn't Griffin. Why hadn't she married Griffin?

Jinnie frowned, confused. She shivered as the penetrating cold deepened, making her wish she had brought her cloak. Cloak? Didn't she mean coat?

She noticed that Nightfall's trot no longer jostled her, and she rode with more confidence. *And why should that seem strange? I've ridden since I was a child*, Jinnie thought. *It was there, in that other life that …*

A sharp pain danced behind her eyes. The forest, eerie with falling snow and pale moonlight, clouded before her. She swayed slightly in the saddle.

"My liege?"

The world took shape again. Jinnie straightened.

"I'm fine. Just cold." Her breath fluttered in the air, as if her words had become visible, hanging in the night.

"It is the Chill, my liege," Griffin said. "It seduces the mind. At first you cannot think clearly, and then you cannot think at all."

He pulled her closer against the warmth of his body. "You must keep warm, and we must keep moving. The Chill is worsening."

"The Chill?" The term evoked a memory of danger.

"Yes." Thinking her confusion an effect of the Chill, Griffin continued. "The night gives Ispell's heat to the sky; the sky gives it to the stars, and we suffer the Chill until the sun rises."

"Of course," Jinnie nodded with a vague remembrance. Snow covered her like an unwelcome blanket. Her hands and ears were growing numb. "How far have we to go?"

"Too far." Griffin's voice sounded uneasy.

Jinnie twisted in the saddle to see his face. His reddish-gold hair was shrouded with snow, and his brown eyes were worried.

"I should let you go on alone," Griffin said. "Nightfall might outrun the Chill with only one rider. You could reach the lakeshore and Keldonabrieve."

"No! I won't leave you. We'll find shelter."

"What shelter is there between Keldonabrieve and the Dardidak's First Tower?"

I don't know, thought Jinnie. *But I should know. Think! What shelter is there?*

"Escabel's!"

"Will the witch let us in?"

"We have no other choice."

"Very well, my liege."

Griffin took the reins now, turning Nightfall to the left. In a few minutes, the trees thinned, and Nightfall sprang forward, galloping across a clearing.

They hastened west, the coming Chill chasing them like a wolf. The snow glittered with ice, and frost stiffened trees. Nightfall's breathing grew labored, and his pace slowed.

"There!" Griffin pointed to a flickering, distant light. He slapped Nightfall's haunch, urging him back to a gallop, making the deep snow fly around them.

All around them now, the air crackled with the Chill. To their right, a hundred yards away, a sapling exploded from the quick-freeze. Nightfall stumbled, gained his footing, and galloped on.

The flicker of light grew brighter. Soon they could see the shadows of a house.

Jinnie's cheeks burned. Her thighs were numb against the sides of her horse. Snowflakes froze upon her eyelashes, blurring her vision.

Nightfall faltered again. He skidded in the wet snow, then fell to his knees. Jinnie was flung over his head. Griffin was pitched to the right.

Struggling to rise, Nightfall staggered, collapsed awkwardly, and then lay still, dead.

A piercing wind swooped down on them. Beneath its abuse, Jinnie, too, struggled to rise. She fumbled for her purse, trying to see through the gusts of snow.

"Griffin? Nightfall?"

As she grasped the strap of her purse, Griffin grasped her left arm and yanked Jinnie to her feet. "Your horse is dead, Tessajihn. We must run!"

"I can't!"

Ignoring her words, he dragged her after him, shouting, "Run! Run for your life!"

The wind snarled and snapped at them. Icy air seared Jinnie's lungs with each gasp. Her feet were frozen. She felt like a marionette, disjointed, no longer with a will of her own.

Griffin held her against him, supporting her as they lurched down a slope toward their sanctuary.

Jinnie thought she heard his voice in her ear. They were there? Where? Did it matter? Anywhere warm. Anywhere with Griffin.

The door swung open, and they staggered gratefully into the cottage.

Three

Griffin and Jinnie slumped against the nearest wall. Snow and wind roared in around them, rousing Griffin from his stupor. He pushed the door shut and searched the room.

The low roof dripped herbs and upside-down bouquets of flowers. Shelves, crowded with books, jars, and bottles, crouched haphazardly along the walls.

To his left was a narrow window flanked by an armchair and table. Across the room, a low wooden bed offered furs and blankets.

To his right, a woven rug stretched like a cat in front of a large, stone fireplace. A fire beckoned.

"Escabel?" No answer.

"Are we safe?" asked Jinnie, aware only that the brutal wind was gone.

"For now, yes." Taking her hand, Griffin led Jinnie to the hearth. "Sit here. I'll bring you a blanket."

Jinnie sat down on the rug, focusing on the fire, feeling as if she were waking from a long, restless dream. A minute later, Griffin knelt beside her.

"My liege?"

Jinnie looked away from the flames to find Griffin's eyes equally mesmerizing. What was it she saw there? Her past? Her future?

Whichever it was, Jinnie felt she belonged to it completely and that anywhere that Griffin was, she had to be, too.

"Where are we?" Jinnie finally asked.

"Escabel's house."

Jinnie dragged her gaze away from Griffin. "And Escabel?"

"It would seem she is elsewhere," Griffin answered. "But why leave a fire burning?"

Because she knew I was coming, thought Jinnie. Aloud, she said, "Does it matter?"

She slid her purse off her shoulder, stretching cold fingers to the fire. "I'm just glad to be warm."

Griffin placed the blanket beside her. He wanted to warm Tessajihn with his body. To say "I love you" again and again. To convince her to run away with him.

For months she had been withdrawn, silent. To protect him, he believed, but it had been a torture to endure. Tonight was his chance to change her mind. Tonight, while they were alone, isolated, with only the storm outside to bear witness against them, he must try. Would she still pretend not to love him?

He watched as Jinnie plucked at her sweater. It was now a cold, soggy mass that clung to her like a living thing. Silently Griffin reached around Jinnie's waist and carefully freed her of the heavy, wet material.

As he drew the sweater away, Jinnie wrapped the blanket about her like a sarong. Familiar feelings of love and desire competed with a sense of danger.

What happened between us? Jinnie wondered. *How long have I felt so much love and trust for Griffin? When did we meet, and why did we agree to part?*

Griffin arranged her sweater on the hearth, gently, as if she might still be within its confines. Then he undid his shirt and laid it next to hers.

The symbolism was not lost on Jinnie. She stood up and retreated to the chair. Perching on its edge, Jinnie pulled off her boots and socks, watching Griffin as he sat on the rug and did the same.

Why can I only remember feelings and not circumstances? Jinnie questioned herself.

She shivered, wanting to be next to the fire's warmth, next to Griffin. Jinnie wrestled free of her jeans and drew the blanket over her bare legs.

I remember someone's arms about me in the night, her thoughts continued. *But whose? And when? Where?*

The questions roused a sharp pain behind her eyes, and the room blurred.

"Griffin," Jinnie said, heart beating too fast. She felt disoriented and afraid. Lost. She couldn't remember her life.

"Yes, my liege?"

"Say my name."

"Tessajihn." An ache etched his voice.

Griffin rose and walked slowly toward her. Naked to the waist, the firelight dancing across his body, he looked like a wild fairy king.

"It has been too long since you asked me to call you by name." Griffin's voice dropped to a whisper. "Tessajihn. My *jinnie*."

When had Griffin first called her that? She wondered. *Jinnie*, the Kabada word for "best loved." It must have been a very long time ago. To hear it now was bittersweet. It left her wanting to hear him say it again.

She got up from the chair to meet him. Seeking reassurance that she wasn't imagining him, Jinnie put a hand on Griffin's chest, recognizing the feel of his skin against her fingertips.

"I feel so strange," she confided. "Like I'm not real. Like you're not real."

Griffin took her hand and kissed it. "The Chill sometimes clouds the mind, Tessajihn. But not for long."

Jinnie pulled her hand away and returned to the fireplace.

Griffin shadowed her. "Tessajihn." He said her name as if it were a prayer. "I have missed you so very much."

Jinnie kept her back to him. "Missed me?"

"Yes." Griffin touched her arms lightly. "I have missed your soft words in the morning, your body close to mine through the night."

His fingers drifted up her arms to her shoulders. "I have missed your smiles, your kisses."

Griffin lifted Jinnie's long brown hair and brushed his lips against the nape of her neck. "I have missed your breath in my ear and your lips against mine."

Jinnie hoped her voice would not betray her longing. "You mustn't speak to me like that, Griffin," she said. "Not now. Not yet."

"Tessajihn," Griffin's breath was warm against her ear. "I love you, now and always. Run away with me. We belong together. I love you."

Jinnie turned to face him, glimpsing a memory of the first time he'd said those words. She searched his beautiful eyes.

"How can you still love me?" she protested. "I married another."

Griffin stepped closer. "You married for politics, not love. It cannot be said you did not try to save the Alliances, but let it go now, my *jinnie*. Run away with me. I love you." He leaned toward her, and Jinnie let him kiss her.

"You love me," Griffin whispered.

"Yes," she whispered back. "I love you."

Jinnie reached up to caress his cheek and run her thumb along his lips. "I love you, Griffin. Now and always; I love you. But—"

Griffin lifted Jinnie into his arms and carried her to the bed.

"We can't begin this again," Jinnie finished her sentence even as Griffin undressed and lay down beside her.

"Begin what? I have never stopped loving you, Tessajihn. And I have waited so long a time for you."

Griffin kissed her, and she parted her lips slightly, feeling a familiar thrill between her thighs as he slid his tongue into her mouth. They kissed passionately again and again, Jinnie shivering with pleasure as Griffin pulled open the blanket she was wrapped in and caressed her breasts.

For long minutes they kissed and touched. Jinnie lifted her thigh as Griffin began to press his hips against hers. She whispered his name and reached for him, guiding him into the warmth of her body. She watched him as his breath grew faster.

They kissed hungrily and, hip to hip, belly to belly, they began the slow, rhythmic push and pull of lovemaking.

Jinnie let her head tilt back against the pillows as Griffin kissed her cheek, her throat. He spoke softly in her ear, telling her he wanted her, he needed her, he loved her.

"Jinnie," he whispered, "my *jinnie*."

Jinnie smiled, feeling as if she'd been away for a very long time and now, at last, she was home again. She was her true self, and nothing and no one else mattered. She belonged with Griffin.

Wrapping her arms about his neck, she urged him to move faster, lifting her hips to meet his thrusts. She reveled in his hoarse groans, the pounding of her heart, and the delicious impact of their bodies against each other. Their lovemaking intoxicated, overwhelmed, and addicted her.

"I don't want to move," Griffin murmured at last.

Jinnie sighed. "And I don't want you to." She gave his shoulder a gentle shove. "But you're getting heavy."

Griffin pulled her with him as he rolled onto his back, holding her close.

"Tessajihn."

"Yes."

"I love you."

"Yes."

"You and I belong together."

"Yes."

"Run away with me, my *jinnie*."

Jinnie didn't answer. At last she raised her head from Griffin's chest. "No."

Griffin started to speak, but she pressed a finger across his lips. "Don't spoil tonight with too many words. I love you. Let that be enough for now."

"And tomorrow?"

"Will be here too soon."

"Yes." Griffin lifted his head and kissed her. "I love you."

Smiling, Jinnie laid her head back on his chest. "And I love you."

She hugged him. Somehow everything would turn out all right. It had to. She belonged nowhere that he was not.

Jinnie listened as Griffin's breathing grew slower and deeper, his heartbeat loud in her ears. Becoming lovers again placed them both in terrible danger and placed herself in the role of adulterer She frowned. The thought of her husband made her uneasy. Jinnie lifted her head. Griffin was asleep.

Withdrawing from his embrace, careful not to wake him, Jinnie wrapped a fur about her shoulders and went to sit by the fire.

She looked back at Griffin. *I don't recall when I first knew I loved him, but I remember the summer we spent together. We were happy. In* love. *The future was ours to face together. Then I married someone else. A political marriage.*

But why? Jinnie frowned. Memories danced on the edge of her mind.

Griffin mentioned alliances, she thought. *Alliances between the Dardidak and someone else? No. I feel it's more than that. But how much more? And why me?*

Jinnie looked back at the fire, finding no solace in its heat, no answer in its light.

Is it really the Chill that's made me forget my responsibilities, or did I choose to forget, until tonight, how much I love Griffin? Everything and everyone seems unimportant compared to that. Why not run away with him now, when we have the chance?

Jinnie plucked idly at her purse. *This is a strange satchel,* she mused.

Picking it up, Jinnie dumped the contents onto the hearth. She stared at them, bewildered. Except for the brush and the keys, none of the items were immediately familiar.

What is this? Jinnie held up her wallet.

Pain echoed in her head. Resolutely she pushed it aside, trying to concentrate. The leather was unusually soft, folded in half. She opened it.

Paper lined one pocket. And there was a picture of someone who looked like her. Not a painting. A ... photograph?

That's me, she thought. Jinnie stared hard at the picture. *This is a driver's license, and the folded leather is my wallet.* She held it up to the firelight.

The pain writhed behind her eyes. Jinnie dropped the wallet into the fire, forgetting what it was the moment it left her hand.

She picked up a small, round disk. Its surface was hard and smooth. Two circles were stuck together with a thin line of metal protruding on one side.

The pain was a dull throb now, pulsing louder as she concentrated. Impulsively Jinnie pushed her thumb against the metal tongue, and the disk opened a little. She carefully pulled the two pieces apart. One side held a smooth powder. In the other side of the disk was the smallest mirror she had ever seen.

Her mirrored compact! Holding the compact at arm's length, Jinnie saw pieces of her reflection. It was the same as the small picture and yet slightly different.

Her eyes were still a deep blue, but the nose seemed straighter, her cheekbones a shade higher, and her mouth, thin-lipped in the picture, now looked fuller and redder.

Jinnie fingered her long, thick hair. It fell in soft waves of dark brown flecked with gold, over her shoulders and down her back.

She snapped the disk shut, forgetting it was called a compact, and returned it to her purse. Next, she held up a small, narrow cylinder.

The name came to her through a haze of stabbing pains in her forehead: lipstick. Wrestling with the pain, she put the cylinder back in her purse.

There was one item left. The pain made Jinnie's fingers tremble as she examined the little book with the lined paper.

Curious names crossed the pages in her handwriting, some vaguely familiar, some completely unknown. Yet, as she looked at the words and saw the people in her mind, the language became strange, incomprehensible. Frustrated, Jinnie threw the address book into the fire and tossed the keys in after it.

She huddled deeper into the fur and looked again at Griffin. The pain faded as she turned her thoughts to his love for her and the peril in which their tryst placed him.

I love him, thought Jinnie. *I love him, and if it shows in my face or can be heard in my voice, Lancin will kill him. Lancin? My husband.*

No face formed in her mind, but a memory awakened. A memory of a dangerous man: possessive, ambitious, insanely jealous. A Sunadin of a respected House, true, with a violent passion for her. A good political choice for a marriage. A House to lend weight to her pursuit of peace for the Alliances.

Is that why I married Lancin when it's Griffin I love? Jinnie rose and paced the shadowy room. Thinking of Lancin stirred no feelings of warmth or desire, only dread.

Jinnie stopped in front of the window. She scrubbed at the frost with a corner of the fur and looked outside. The sky was at its darkest, fat with cold and night, gorged with stars now dull and glassy.

Looking out at the frightening loneliness, Jinnie knew she could never again relinquish Griffin. Whatever tricks her mind was playing on her, she would remember how much he loved her, now and always.

I won't give this up, Jinnie promised herself. *I can't.*

She moved to the armchair and sat down. *What can I remember? I am Tessajihn-rika-Lancin of the Sunadin. I am without child or kin, but I have many friends.*

I can see their faces, I know their names. Peesha. Deva. Koldin. Karen. Karen?

The pain sprang back. Frantically, Jinnie tried to think of something else, but the thoughts cascaded into her mind.

Karen, her friend. "If I come back, I'll tell you all about it. Love, Jinnie."

Jinnie? That's what Griffin calls me. But I was called that somewhere else, too. Somewhere. Somewhere unhappy, so why think of it? This pain is like a vise.

"Stop!" Jinnie cried aloud.

"Tessajihn?" Griffin rolled from the bed to his feet, ready to slay any intruders with his bare hands.

Jinnie ran to him, clung to him, shaking with pain and fear.

He held her close. "What is it? What's wrong?"

"I don't know. I can't think clearly, and my head hurts terribly."

"Come back to bed, my *jinnie*. You've suffered more greatly from the Chill than I realized. It will pass."

Jinnie returned to the bed, and Griffin lay down beside her.

"I'm afraid, Griffin."

He kissed her. "Don't be afraid," he soothed. "I'm here, my *jinnie*. Now and always. I love you."

Jinnie relaxed into his arms. Everything was all right. Griffin loved her. Even now, the pain was receding.

"Kiss me more," she whispered.

The pain sputtered, faded, vanished.

Four

A gray light sifted the shadows of the room. It ran pale fingers over the cold ashes in the fireplace and brushed against Jinnie's eyelids with gentle insistence.

She turned away, snuggling closer to Griffin, unwilling to abandon sleep.

A long whinny, followed by several answering neighs, penetrated Jinnie's dreams. She opened her eyes. The room was cold, unwelcoming.

Had she been dreaming?

A distant shout brought her wide awake.

Not knowing what she feared, Jinnie grabbed a fur and ran to the window. A group of horsemen rode from the north. Though they were still a mile away, Jinnie knew at once who led them.

"Griffin!" She dashed back to the bed. "Griffin, wake up. Lancin has come to find me."

Griffin hurried from the bed. Snatching his breeches from the hearth, he jerked them on. He hopped on one foot as he pulled on a boot and saw Jinnie still rooted to the floor, eyes wide.

"Get dressed," he ordered. "Quickly. You slept in the bed. I stood guard." His eyes shot around the room. "The chair! I slept in the chair."

He stuffed his shirttails into his pants as he seized Jinnie's arm and hurried her to the hearth. Numbly, she dressed.

The pounding of hooves grew closer, louder. There was another shout. "Tessajihn!"

Jinnie looked at Griffin, unspoken questions in her eyes.

He kissed her. "Don't be afraid," he whispered. Turning her away from him, Griffin gave Jinnie a gentle push toward the door. "Run and greet him."

Jinnie hesitated.

"Go!"

She went. Throwing the door wide, she went out and stood there, dazzled in the early sun, her breath clouding her like a veil.

Then she saw her husband. He was flinging his leg over the shoulder of his horse, dropping to the ground. Jinnie hurried to him.

"Tessajihn! Thank all the gods you're safe." He hugged her to him.

Jinnie felt as if she had been swallowed whole. He was a giant of a man: six feet four, with broad shoulders and a thick torso. Black hair stung with gray framed his bearded face, and his eyes were blue and fierce.

Lancin stood her back from him. "You look well enough, but where is that dog, Griffin, who let you tarry so late with the cursed Dardidak?"

Jinnie opened her mouth, but nothing came out.

"Here!" Griffin, calm and smiling, stepped from the cottage and closed the door behind him. He approached them at a leisurely pace.

He's not afraid, thought Jinnie. *Perhaps there's no reason to be.*

Griffin offered Jinnie her purse. "My liege." He bowed his head slightly.

Taking it, Jinnie murmured her thanks.

Lancin reached out to Griffin, and Jinnie paled, thinking he would strike him. He slapped the smaller man on the back.

"Well done, you motherless toad." Lancin laughed. "When the Chill began, I knew you would find shelter for her."

Lancin pulled Jinnie to him, crushing her against his side. He gestured to one of the riders behind him. "Ornack! Share your horse with this worthy fellow."

Griffin, not even looking at Jinnie, bowed his head to Lancin and mounted behind Ornack.

Lancin lifted Jinnie to his saddle, swinging up behind her. His deep voice rasped in her ear. "A spare horse would have deprived me of this pleasure, my dove."

He wrapped one arm possessively about her waist, tugging her close to him.

"My thanks to you, Escabel!" he shouted to the cottage.

Jinnie held her breath. *He thinks we were chaperoned. What will he do when she doesn't answer?*

But Lancin spurred his horse away, forcing Jinnie to grab his arm for support.

With a shout from one of the men, the company headed north at a fast gallop. The landscape flew by. The sun, playing with the clouds, made the snow white and then gray.

Jinnie felt as if she were being abducted. Trapped against Lancin's body, held too tightly in his iron embrace, she fought back a strong desire to scream. The jolt of a trot broke her panic attack.

They descended into a valley. At its base, in the middle of a vast crystalline lake, stood a castle. It was cloaked in snow and ice, sparkling in the sunshine. Sculpted towers and turrets soared gracefully from walls of white stone.

"Keldonabrieve," Jinnie whispered, puzzled by the mixed impression it gave her. It was beautiful, it was home, but there was something sinister about it, too. *What?*

Her thoughts were interrupted as they reached the floor of the valley and Lancin kicked his horse to a lope. In minutes they were across the snowy terrain, slowing again as they approached a hamlet near the shore of the lake. Small cottages sat snugly close to one another as if to keep warm.

Jinnie recognized a long, rectangular structure as the stable. They rode up to it, and Lancin dismounted. He held his arms up to Jinnie. Forcing herself not to look for Griffin, Jinnie accepted her husband's help.

The stable master waddled up to them. "Welcome, my liege." He beamed at Jinnie. "Your ferry is ready, and the waters of Keldonabrieve are calm this morning."

Startled, Jinnie looked at the castle far out in the center of the lake. No bridge connected it to the main shore. They would have to reach it by boat. Why was the thought so disagreeable?

Lancin dropped his arm about her shoulders. "Come, my sweet." He led her around the corner of the stable and down to the wharf.

Jinnie flinched as she stepped onto the long wooden pier. She had a strange feeling of anxiety and despair. She listened to the footsteps behind her, seeking solace in Griffin's proximity. Her thoughts fell to the soldiers.

I know Ornack. He's the Captain of the Guard. He's loyal to Lancin and wary of me. Why wary? And the two brothers, Nickon and Trae—their fealty is to be trusted, but they are not.

And the last? What was his name? Jinnie frowned in concentration. She pictured him as an ally, but an ally against whom?

She frowned, and Lancin chucked her under the chin. "Cheer up, my pet. Do not scowl so. It is only a short ferry ride."

He bent down to whisper in her ear. "And if you are very good, I shall give you a rose from my garden in the spring."

Jinnie had a swift mental image of Lancin's garden, with its long rows of rose bushes in endless shades of red. They were Lancin's pride, and forbidden to all.

"In the center courtyard," she murmured.

"What did you say, my sweet?"

Jinnie hadn't realized she'd spoken aloud. "I said, thank you."

They stopped. Three wooden steps offered passage to the deck of the ferry. Jinnie took a step back, bumping against Lancin.

There was something about the ferry ride she knew she would hate, even fear. But what? And how else could she reach the castle? A memory teased her mind, but before she could focus on it, Lancin scooped her up and carried Jinnie aboard the ferry.

Again she felt suffocated and afraid.

"If you insist on leaving your home, my dearest, you must pay the price to return." He set her down, still holding her close.

Jinnie fought the urge to break away from him, surprised at its intensity.

Lancin pulled Jinnie with him and strolled to the bow of the boat. She risked a glance back to see Griffin and the others taking seats in the stern.

The boat creaked and groaned as the sailors in the galley below turned it from its mooring. Then they were crossing the lake.

Immediately Jinnie knew what she hated about the ferry ride. The lake, so calm to behold from a distance, churned with angry waves that heaved the boat back and forth. She gasped at the nauseating motion.

Lancin bent near. "Easy, my love. It will be over soon, and you will once again be safe within the walls of Keldonabrieve."

Jinnie looked at the castle. It seemed to tilt, then straighten, then tilt again the other way. The lake swirled and rolled, lifting and dropping the boat as if it were a toy.

A small, despairing cry escaped Jinnie.

Lancin guided her back to the stern. "I apologize, my beauty. I should never have let you take that last journey. Then you would still be safe at home and not suffering this malady."

Jinnie sank gratefully onto a seat. She tried to distract herself by thinking about the boat. She knew it had six oars on each side. It was thirty feet long and eighteen wide.

She tried to admire the carving on the railing, count the long, low benches, and calculate how many people it seated.

It was no use. Her world shrank to the folds of soft fabric in Lancin's shirt as he sat next to her. She concentrated on the color, the pattern, the weave, the thread.

I am going to be sick, thought Jinnie.

There was a thump and a scraping noise. The awful motion stopped. Jinnie looked up.

She was surrounded on three sides by white walls. Across from her, a door opened high up in the wall, and a rope ladder dropped down.

Jinnie stared at Lancin in disbelief. Words failed her.

Lancin glanced down at her. There was something in his eyes, only for a moment. It was satisfaction.

"Come, my pet."

A little unsteadily, Jinnie followed him to the ladder. It stretched ten feet above her head with as much again coiled on the deck. Willing herself to be strong, Jinnie started up.

She kept her eyes focused only on the door and the round, anxious face that peered from it.

That must be Duanna, Jinnie decided. She kept climbing. *It's like a prison*, she thought.

Jinnie stopped climbing. A wave of uneasiness made her sway on the ladder. *Maybe it is a prison.*

"My liege!" Duanna called down to her.

Jinnie rallied and continued climbing. Reaching the top, she swung herself from the ladder into Duanna's relieved embrace.

"Oh, my liege. I was so worried. Thank all the gods you're safely home."

Jinnie was propelled along the corridor, the small, round woman chastising her now for having left in the first place.

"But what about … my husband?" Jinnie looked back to the doorway.

"Oh, he will know well enough that I've taken you to your room. You know how he likes you to look your best. I've already got a bath started, and we'll have to wash your hair and pick a dress and …"

Jinnie stopped listening. She was trying to keep track of where they were, but the castle was a labyrinth. They went up stairs and down, along dark passages and brightly lit ones, through small sitting rooms and past countless doors. In dismay, Jinnie knew she would never be able to find her way back to the beginning.

Not that I need to, she tried to reassure herself. *Lancin is my husband. He wouldn't keep me prisoner in my own home. It's all just security.*

But somehow she knew that wasn't true.

Finally they went through a large, red door and stopped. Jinnie looked around the room, her room, feeling lost and out of place. In spite of its pleasant appearance, she didn't like it.

The room was large, in cool colors of almond and clover, with an enormous bed and an elegant fireplace. A full-length oval mirror stood in one corner next to an armoire. Further along the wall stood a dainty vanity. The floor was creamy marble, strewn with white furs. Two sets of glass balcony doors let sunlight lift the shadows.

"And then I'll be right back." Duanna smiled, closing the door behind her.

Not having paid attention to anything prior to that statement, Jinnie had no idea where Duanna had gone. She crossed the room, dropping her purse on the bed.

Sunlight lanced the mirror, and Jinnie went to stand in front of it. As she remembered a plainer reflection, a sharp pain stung her. Jinnie spun away.

What's happening to me? she wondered. *I feel like I'm walking in a fog, sensing my way through wraiths and visions. Only Griffin feels real.*

Thinking of him, Jinnie smiled. The pain slipped away.

Five

The hallway, dim and quiet, held large portraits against its walls, demanding silence and respect.

Jinnie tiptoed down it, glancing at the paintings, not recognizing the cold faces glaring out at her. She had been lost almost from the moment she'd left her room.

Duanna had prepared a bath for her. It was a long process, involving heavy buckets of hot water hoisted on a pulley from the kitchen far below her bedroom and poured into a tub before the fire.

Then, as Jinnie sat in the tub, Duanna washed Jinnie's hair in a separate basin, gently toweled it dry, brushed it until it gleamed, and finally drew it back from Jinnie's face with a wide pink ribbon.

"Oh, you are a lovely sight for the master. Now, what will you wear?"

Jinnie felt like a doll as Duanna fussed and bustled, choosing a long, blue dress from the armoire and helping Jinnie into it.

"Now put a hand on my shoulder," Duanna instructed as she knelt to slip plain brown shoes onto Jinnie's feet.

Jinnie had frowned at the full skirt that fell to just above her ankles.

I could never climb that ladder in this, thought Jinnie.

"Your ring!" Duanna wailed.

Jinnie looked at her left hand. The ring finger was bare.

Duanna flew to the vanity and searched frantically through a large jewelry box. "Here it is," she said, relieved. She pushed the ring onto Jinnie's right forefinger.

Jinnie stared at it. It was a pale blue stone, cut like a star, set in a silver band studded with small white stones.

"You're always taking it off and forgetting it, my liege. You must be more careful. What would the master say if you ever lost it?"

Jinnie looked at the ring now. It was beautiful, but she didn't like it. Perhaps because it represented love and trust. Even devotion. All of which she had betrayed last night, and none of which she felt for the huge man who was probably getting angry as he waited for her to join him for breakfast.

I should have let Duanna escort me, Jinnie chided herself for the tenth time.

She reached the end of the hall, glad to be free of its oppressive stillness. Which way now? Stairs rose steeply to her right. To her left, then.

Jinnie started left. This corridor was bare, and sunlight beckoned to her from its end. She hurried toward it, feeling a whisper of cold air.

A marble archway halted her. She had reached the center courtyard. Cautiously Jinnie peered out.

The rose bushes, swathed in burlap to protect them from the snow, were rows of gray lumps, making the garden ugly and unhappy. Stone statues of animals looked skeletal in the sunshine, without the roses to clothe them.

Jinnie walked parallel to the courtyard, feeling as bare and vulnerable as the statues.

Someone's bound to come looking for me, she thought, trying to reassure herself. She remembered the mismatched styles of design and architecture as she'd threaded her way through the maze of passages from her room.

"But how will they ever find me?"

"I always know where you are."

Jinnie whirled. "Griffin!"

She threw her arms about him, not caring who might see them.

Griffin pulled back. "Wait."

Putting a finger to Jinnie's lips, Griffin drew her through an open panel in the wall and slid it shut after them. A cold gloom settled about Jinnie, broken only by a lantern at Griffin's feet.

He kissed her then until she remembered nothing but him—his touch, his voice, his embrace. "Run away with me," he pleaded. "End this misery for us both."

Yes! her mind screamed. Run away with him and forget this puzzle of a life. Leave it behind and never try to remember.

Jinnie shook her head. "I can't."

In the shadowy illumination of the lamp, sorrow filled Griffin's eyes.

Jinnie touched his cheek. "Not yet. I have to …" How could she explain what she didn't understand herself?

Griffin searched her face. "My *jinnie*," he whispered. "At least tell me that you will."

"I will," Jinnie said at once. "Just give me a little more time."

He nodded. Taking her hand, Griffin retrieved the lamp and led Jinnie through the darkness. The passage was narrow, free of the twists, turns, and false exits that suffocated the rest of the castle.

"How did you know about this?" Jinnie asked.

"I found it by accident. I was drunk. I leaned against a wall for support. It didn't support me."

"Are there more?"

"I've found a dozen so far. They run like major roads all through the castle."

"Why would anyone put secret passages in a house that's already a labyrinth?"

"Perhaps so they would never get lost."

In her mind, Jinnie saw an odd little man with a long beard and shiny pate. He was hunched over a table piled with sketches of the renovations her new husband wished done. Lancin was pointing at a sketch of another corridor.

"But why so many additions?" she heard herself ask. "Keldonabrieve is beautiful in its simplicity."

Lancin's eyes had been dark and unfathomable when he looked at her, but his smile was quick, his voice light. "It will keep you safe, my treasure."

"Safe from what, from whom? Lancin, please. I'll be forever lost."

But he had ignored her, determined to protect her from his imagined foes. That obsession was one of the first signs of his jealousy and possessiveness.

When Lancin had left the room for some errand, the little man had turned his thin, kind face to Jinnie. Checking the room for eavesdroppers, he motioned her to bend near.

"Have no fear, my liege. I, too, am easily lost. I promise you, there will be a way to get about. A sure and simple way. When all is done, I will show you what it is."

But he never had the opportunity. When the renovations were completed, he had taken a last tour of the castle, climbing to the top of one of the spires. Mysteriously, he had fallen to his death.

This must be what he meant, thought Jinnie. "And Lancin doesn't know about them."

Griffin glanced back at her. "Are you certain?"

Delighted with her recollection, Jinnie trusted its truth. "Yes."

"Then we can make use of them." Griffin stopped. "We're here."

"The dining room?"

"The main hall. I'll say I found you in the library upstairs." He kissed her gently. "Come. No doubt he is furious by now."

Sliding a panel back a crack, Griffin peered out. Satisfied there were no witnesses, he led Jinnie out, closing the panel behind them. They stood still a moment, breathing in the space after the claustrophobia of the hidden passages.

Jinnie walked slowly forward. She knew this room. Directly ahead of her, two tall doors promised to lead her to freedom. They had been the main gates of the castle before Lancin had destroyed the bridge that led to them.

Jinnie blinked at the memory, recalling the sight of the long span that reached across the lake being pulled, battered, broken until it crumbled into the grasping water.

Why? She frowned. Why make it so difficult for me to leave? She felt genuine anger at the remembered destruction of the bridge, the cruel derangement of her home. Why had she said nothing? Why had she allowed him to bully her?

"Where is she?" a loud voice demanded.

Jinnie clenched her fists. "I'll go alone," she said to Griffin.

Anger spurred her, and she swept past the main staircase, down a short, wide hall and into the dining room. Jinnie stopped just inside the door.

"You yelled for me, Lancin?"

He looked at her in surprise. Anger stormed across his face. Then he laughed.

"I did indeed, my sweet." Lancin smiled. "You are late. As usual."

Back stiff, Jinnie crossed to the table, sliding into the chair at its head. "Since it's usual for me to be late, I fail to understand why you're so angry."

Lancin studied her. Without responding, he rang a small bell beside him. They waited in silence.

A minute later, a young boy appeared. He carried a silver tea service much too large for him. Walking with eyes on his burden, he brought it slowly and precariously to Jinnie. She heard him sigh in relief as he slid it onto the table.

Watching the boy pour the tea, Jinnie struggled to remember his name. Yajin? Yoin? Yogin!

"Thank you, Yogin."

The boy smiled shyly.

"Go and fetch our breakfast," Lancin growled.

Yogin scampered away.

Jinnie looked at her husband, glad the table was long and formal. A minute before, she'd been ready to confront him with her anger. Now she sat silent and uncomfortable. Danger seemed to slide about Lancin like a serpent.

The thought crossed Jinnie's mind that she really didn't like her husband very much.

His voice made her jump.

"Drink your tea, my pet. It will soothe your nerves." He raised a brow. "And your tongue."

Jinnie narrowed her eyes, but couldn't match Lancin's fierce glare. She looked down.

The cup of tea in front of her had a pleasing apricot color and a beguiling aroma. She didn't remember ever liking tea, but beneath Lancin's scrutiny, Jinnie took a sip. The taste was familiar, pleasant.

She looked up. Lancin still glowered at her, but as she drank the tea, he seemed to relax.

"Much better." He smiled a little.

Jinnie finished the cup, setting it down carefully as she tried to decide what to say to Lancin.

Obviously she had lost all arguments concerning the alteration of Keldonabrieve. What purpose would it serve to bring it up now? It would only make him angry again. But then, he was always angry.

"Why are you always angry, Lancin?" she heard herself ask, reaching automatically for the tea as Yogin refilled her cup.

"What did you say?" Lancin looked up from his plate, astonished.

"Angry." Jinnie sipped her tea. "It seems to me you're always angry about something or at someone. Is it me?"

She looked down the long table. It suddenly seemed very long indeed. Almost like a tunnel.

"Lancin?" Jinnie blinked several times, trying to bring the room into focus. She felt anxious, even afraid, and tired—terribly, terribly tired.

A hand touched her shoulder. She looked up, hoping to see Griffin, but it was her husband's face that leaned over her.

"I should have let you breakfast in your room, my dove. You are overtired from your journey."

Jinnie felt her chair slide back from the table. Strong arms lifted her and carried her away.

"What's happening?" Her voice sounded small and far away.

Lips pressed to her forehead. But they didn't belong to Griffin. He had no beard, and his voice was softer. It was Lancin who spoke.

"I am taking you to your room."

"Why?" Talking became an effort.

A chuckle. "Because you are falling asleep in my arms, my sweet. You did not even finish your tea."

"I don't like tea," Jinnie murmured. Her head slumped against Lancin's shoulder, and he knew she slept. Lancin's eyes narrowed.

Strange, he thought. *It hasn't affected her like this since the first time I gave it to her.*

He kicked open the door to her room and strode to the bed, setting Tessajihn gently in its center. "Sleep well, my dearest."

Staring down at her, Lancin traced a finger down Tessajihn's throat to her breasts. "If I could have you," he groaned, "then all this would be unnecessary. If you would love me, you would do anything I asked."

He stepped away, fingers clenching and unclenching.

"When will you cease your ridiculous pursuit of peace, Tessajihn? When will you stop fighting me and accept that eradication of the Turnak is the only way to secure the realm? Eradication of the Turnak and complete subjugation of all the other scum in your precious Alliances."

He sneered at her now, violence seeping into voice and his eyes. "I hate the Alliances. And your peace. I hate it all. I hate you, Tessajihn. How you torment me."

Lancin turned away, paused as he reached the door.

"I love you."

Six

Persistent knocking brought Jinnie slowly awake. She lay still a moment, blinking her eyes until a high ceiling came into focus. Frescos held birds frozen in flight.

Where was she?

"My liege?"

Jinnie remembered; she was in Keldonabrieve. She must have been dreaming. Dreaming she was somewhere else; someone else.

"My liege!"

"Come in." Jinnie sat up and slid over to the edge of the bed.

Duanna bustled in, carrying a tray with food and wine on it. Yogin trailed behind her with the tea service.

"Set the tray on the table by the fireplace, Yogin," Duanna directed, setting her own tray on the foot of the bed. "Pour the tea, and then you may leave."

As Yogin obeyed, Duanna marched to the armoire to pick a nightgown and robe for Tessajihn.

Jinnie stood up, surprised at how groggy she felt. She grabbed for a bedpost to steady the swaying room. Duanna hurried to assist her.

"Here, let me help you off with that dress, my liege. You'll want to put your nightgown on. You've slept the whole day away."

"The whole day?" Jinnie sat back down on the bed, letting Duanna undress her as if she were a child.

"Yes, my liege. The master thought it best not to disturb you. He said you were strained from that terrible journey. Raise your arms," Duanna instructed.

Jinnie did so, and something satiny but warm slid over her head and down her body. Then Duanna helped her into a robe, tying it at the waist for her.

"There, now don't you feel better? Come and sit by the fire. I'll get it roaring for you. Then you can have your tea."

Jinnie let herself be led to a chair and seated. She stared at the flames as they yawned and stretched beneath the skillful hand of Duanna.

"That's good." Satisfied with the fire's size, Duanna turned. "You look pale, my liege. I've brought you some supper. I put it on the bed. You must be sure to eat. All this worrying about the Alliances has made you thin.

"Now, the master has left Keldonabrieve. He said he would be away for the week. He left you in my care and Griffin's. Although why you keep a Sheninn when you've got me, I'll never know."

Jinnie broke free from her stupor. "Gone away? My husband's left the castle?"

"Yes, my liege. He had some business to attend to, though I haven't the head for remembering what, if he even said. Here's your tea now."

A cup was placed in Jinnie's hands.

There must have been something in the tea this morning, she thought. *Something strong enough to make me sleep the entire day. But what and why? And is the tea drugged again? Who can I trust? Griffin.*

"Duanna?"

"Yes, my liege?"

"Send Griffin to me. I have some last-minute business to attend to before I retire."

"But my liege, it's late. And you haven't eaten."

Jinnie frowned and looked up at Duanna, testing her authority. "I need to see my Sheninn. At once, Duanna."

"Very well." Duanna left, leaving behind a faint air of disapproval.

Free of Duanna's well-intentioned fussing, Jinnie loosened the ties of her robe and looked at the tea service.

The scent of the tea tickled her nose, tempting her even now. Before she could succumb, Jinnie poured the tea from her cup back into the teapot. Whoever had drugged her mustn't suspect she'd realized it. But what should she do with the tea?

Lifting the teapot, Jinnie went to the nearest balcony doors. She fumbled with the lock and pushed the doors wide. Frigid air snatched at her; the Chill was coming.

Taking a deep breath, Jinnie stepped onto the balcony. The stone burned her feet with its cold, but she leaned over the railing and emptied the contents of the teapot into the lake far below.

The Chill swept across the lake, and Jinnie retreated, pulling the doors tightly shut and locking them again. She returned to the fireplace and set the teapot on its tray with satisfaction.

Crossing the room, Jinnie opened the bedroom door and peered out. The hallway was empty. Where was Griffin?

Not far to her left, she noticed a light coming from beneath a partially closed door. Jinnie tiptoed toward it, about to call out to Griffin, when a snide voice from inside the room brought her to a terrified halt.

"We should check on her, Trae," said Nickon. He strode back and forth in front of his brother. "She's a wily bitch. I don't trust her."

Trae chortled. "You don't trust anyone you can't kill."

Nickon swilled his brandy and leered. "I can kill her. But she'd suit another purpose better."

Again Trae laughed. "Don't let Lancin catch you even dreaming such possibilities. He'll cut more than your throat."

Nickon wisely shut his mouth. Lancin might lack a certain ability, but swift vengeance was not it.

From a chair in the corner, Noric spoke. "Leave her be. She will have drunk her tea by now. What trouble can she make when her mind is misted by the *hartha*? She'll be a frightened mouse once more, now that Lancin has her back."

Trae rose to fill his glass. "I doubt he'll let her leave again."

"Why keep her?" snarled Nickon, lust and brandy slurring his words. "She's no use to him."

"Watch your tongue, brother." Passing him, Trae gave Nickon a shove. "What Lancin lacks in bed he more than compensates for in his plans to rid Ispell of the cursed Turnak."

Outside the door, frozen with fear, Jinnie suppressed a gasp. What horrible secret had she stumbled on?

Nickon moved to a chair and dropped into it, spilling some of his liquor on the floor. He swiped it with the toe of his boot and grunted his acknowledgment.

Trae continued. "And as for her use, what better blind for Lancin's subterfuge than letting Tessajihn lull the Alliances with soft words of peace?"

But Nickon now answered with a snore. Trae rolled his eyes and looked to Noric.

"What do you think? Shall we stay longer or drag this witless brother of mine to his bed?"

As Noric rose and crossed the room, he caught sight of Jinnie. Their eyes met. Noric's face remained impassive.

"Let's dump him in his bed and go worry the cook," he suggested. "Perhaps she'll fetch us another dinner." He gave Trae a broad wink. "And a maid or two to go with it."

Trae nodded agreement, smiling. "It's my sodden brother's mistake to lust himself into a stupor over Tessajihn."

As the two guards hauled Nickon to his feet, Jinnie scurried back to her room. Her ally had a name now: Noric.

Leaving her door open a crack, she watched the two men drag the third between them, taking him down the hallway and around a corner.

Carefully Jinnie closed the door, leaning her forehead against it as she slid the bolt into place.

"Tessajihn?"

Jinnie gasped and spun about. "Griffin!" She ran to him, throwing her arms about him in relief.

He hugged her to him. "Where were you? Are you all right?"

Stepping back, Jinnie shook her head. "No, I'm not. Something's wrong, terribly wrong."

"Come and sit by the fire." Griffin drew her to the chair by the fire and sat her down. "Do you want tea?"

"No!"

Puzzled, Griffin nodded. "All right. There's a supper tray on the bed. I'll bring it to you."

Jinnie waited, trying to breathe normally.

Returning with the tray, Griffin set it on the hearth and poured a glass of wine. He offered it to Jinnie.

"I don't want it," she said. "It might be drugged."

"Tessajihn, look at me."

Jinnie looked into Griffin's eyes.

"I don't know what has upset you," he said, "but I do know I chose this wine for you myself. It is not drugged."

Jinnie accepted the glass of wine and drained it.

Griffin poured another glass. "Sip this one," he commanded.

Jinnie obeyed, finally relaxing in Griffin's presence.

He lifted the cover from a plate. "You haven't eaten."

"I wasn't hungry."

"Then eat now. Please."

Accepting the plate, Jinnie took a small bite of the food. It was some sort of meat pie, cold but not disagreeable. She'd eaten half of it when she became aware of Griffin watching her. His brow was marred with concern.

Jinnie set the plate aside. "Do you always look after me so well?"

"Always, my liege."

"Say my name."

"Tessajihn." He smiled. "Jinnie," he whispered.

Jinnie smiled back, and for a moment the world felt sane, safe, and secure.

"Why did you say the wine might be drugged?"

Griffin's question dragged Jinnie back to the unpleasant reality entrapping her. Struggling against the horror that threatened to overwhelm her, Jinnie told Griffin what she had witnessed and overheard.

Listening, Griffin lifted the empty teacup from the tray beside Jinnie. "*Hartha*," he said, smelling the dregs of tea in the cup.

"That's what Noric said. And he said I'd be frightened again. And I am. Griffin?" Jinnie leaned toward him. "What is *hartha?*"

"It's an herbal sedative, but it makes a person anxious, even depressed, if it's taken more than a few times."

Feeling angry, Griffin almost broke the cup as he set it down. "Used constantly," he continued, "it makes a person susceptible to suggestion."

"That's how Lancin's been manipulating me," Jinnie said. "He's been making me drink tea mixed with *hartha* for months now."

She stood up, walking slowly around to the back of the chair, facing the balcony doors and thinking of the Chill outside. It suddenly seemed very cold inside, too.

"It seems that in the game of politics, I have been outplayed. My husband," Jinnie said, the words bitter in her mouth, "is a traitor. I don't know—I don't remember—how it came to this, but the Turnak are in terrible danger. It's my responsibility now to help them."

Jinnie turned to face Griffin. "And I don't even remember who the Turnak are."

Griffin rose, surprised. "You don't remember the Turnak?"

"No."

"What else have you forgotten?"

"Almost everything." Jinnie waved her arm at the room. "All of this. My life here in Keldonabrieve. It's all bits and pieces. Lancin. The Turnak. The treachery and deception all around me."

"It could be from the *hartha*, Tessajihn. After drinking it for so long, it could obscure your memory as you describe."

Jinnie shook her head vehemently. "You don't understand. I don't remember my life here, in Ispell." She clutched the back of the chair. "I haven't been able to remember anything clearly except for you."

"For how long?"

"Since the Dardidak's First Tower. Something was torn from me then. I felt different, changed." Jinnie looked down at her hands. "I feel out of place unless I'm with you."

Griffin sat down by the fire and listened, not interrupting, as Jinnie told him of her strong feelings of displacement, the half-remembered life, and the pain. He was a Kabada, and his people were not unaccustomed to magic.

"Show me the items in your satchel," Griffin said, when Jinnie finished speaking.

Jinnie looked about the room, then went to the armoire. Finding the satchel on the floor, she picked it up carefully and returned with it to Griffin.

"Sit here, beside me, Tessajihn," he said. "We'll look at the items together."

Reluctant, willing only because it was Griffin who asked her, Jinnie sat down and opened her satchel. "It's called a purse," she said suddenly.

"A purse. For coins, of course." He smiled, trying to ease Jinnie's fear. "Don't be afraid." Griffin kissed Jinnie's cheek. "I'm here."

Jinnie nodded, trying to smile. She reached into her purse and pulled out the first thing her fingers touched: her compact. Jinnie held it out to Griffin.

"I don't remember what it's called," she said. "I remembered last night, for a moment."

Griffin examined the strange metal.

"Put your thumb there and push," Jinnie instructed.

Griffin released the clasp, and the compact unlocked. He pulled it open, at once startled by the small, round mirror. He had never seen such craftsmanship. Griffin rubbed a finger in the powder, not commenting.

"And what else?"

Jinnie peered into her purse and withdrew her lipstick. Without thinking, she opened it and drew a small line across the back of Griffin's hand. "You can write with it, as if it were paint, but I think it's intended for some other use."

Examining the back of his hand, Griffin looked at Jinnie. "Anything else that you didn't throw in the fire?"

"Just a hairbrush." Jinnie handed her brush to Griffin. "But even that's strange."

Griffin stroked the strange, glossy wood of the handle, the bristles that bent beneath his fingers.

"I wish now that I hadn't thrown the other things away." Jinnie sighed. "But they didn't make any sense to me. In fact, they frightened me."

She rubbed her forehead. "The way I was frightened when you first came to get me."

Jinnie closed her eyes as a sharp pain struck her like a slap. An image flashed in her mind: Griffin waiting for her, outside her window, across the street. Jinnie could smell the autumn air.

"Tessajihn?" Griffin's worried voice chased the pain away. She opened her eyes and looked into his face as she had the day before, when she'd fallen in the snow. When she'd first felt this strange duality and lost her memory of herself.

"Is the pain like last night?" He touched her cheek.

"Not as bad. But it always hurts when I try to remember whatever it is I've forgotten."

Pulling Jinnie close, Griffin kissed her. "Don't think of it anymore tonight. Think of me. Think of us. All right?"

Jinnie nodded.

Griffin released her and returned the brush, the compact, and the lipstick to Jinnie's purse. He could think of no one who understood magical things better than the witch.

"Put this away," he said. "And get into bed. Tomorrow, when Duanna comes to wake you, I want you to pretend you're ill. It must be something vague that only Escabel's tinctures can cure. When the witch comes, we'll ask for her help."

Jinnie nodded, obeying Griffin. Griffin believed her. Griffin loved her. Now everything would be all right. As she put her purse away, Jinnie straightened suddenly, afraid again.

"But what about Lancin's plot against the Turnak?"

Griffin rose and left the fire. "I don't know. First we must look after you."

Relieved not have to think for a while, Jinnie climbed onto the bed, no longer wanting to remember. She wanted only the haven of Griffin's lovemaking.

He came to stand in front of her.

"You were quick enough to undress last night," Jinnie said, draping her arms about his neck.

"I shouldn't stay. It's too dangerous."

Jinnie felt a pang of anxiety, more at the thought of being separated from Griffin than of being discovered. "I know you're right."

Pressing her body against Griffin, she kissed him, eyes open, lips parted. Jinnie paused. "But everything around me seems dangerous and frightening." Jinnie kissed him again. "Except you. You make me feel safe."

She tugged his shirt open. "I love you," Jinnie whispered, kissing him again.

Griffin slipped his arms about her waist, aroused by the erotic exchange of their breath as their tongues caressed one another in deeper and deeper kisses.

"Say you love me," Jinnie insisted.

"I love you, Tessajihn."

"Say you want me."

"I want you." Pulling the robe from her shoulders, Griffin drew Jinnie tightly against him. "I need you." He kissed her passionately.

Jinnie looked into his eyes. "Then make me feel safe."

Griffin kissed her, and they fell back on the bed together. He felt Tessajihn's hands on his body, pulling at the waistband of his breeches, opening them. He kissed her harder, one hand drawing up the skirt of her nightgown.

Jinnie tilted her hips up, and Griffin thrust inside her, hard and fast. She wrapped her legs around his waist, pulling him deeper inside her body.

"I love you," Jinnie whispered over and over like a chant in rhythm with his body, faster and faster.

Pushing himself up, arms straight, muscles taut, Griffin lunged against Jinnie with fierce, rapid thrusts, trembling at last for one breathless minute and then lowering himself into her embrace.

Seven

Jinnie stood at the balcony doors. Far across the lake, the sun pressed a gold hand to the slope of the valley, sending shards of pink and red skidding into the dawn's sky. Some of the colors touched her nightgown, making it glow. She ran her hand over them. For this brief moment, her life seemed safe and calm.

Griffin had left her an hour ago, promising to see her later in the day and reminding her to feign a vague ailment so Duanna would send for Escabel.

Jinnie wondered now what she should suffer from. Headache? That was vague but not serious. Stomach ache? No. Duanna would only insist she drink tea. Fatigue? Chills?

A knock on the door warned Jinnie that she had better decide quickly. As she hurried back to bed, her mind called up an image of herself as a little girl. She didn't want to go to school because the other children teased her. Jinnie told her mother she didn't feel well and that she wasn't hungry. Her mother always diagnosed lack of appetite as an illness.

"Virginia, you must eat."

"No, Mommy. I don't feel well."

Jinnie winced as pain snapped at her eyes. The picture of her mother faded. Why had she called her Virginia?

"Good morning, my liege." Duanna carried a tray to Jinnie. "Did you sleep well?"

Jinnie thought of how little sleep Griffin had allowed her. With effort, she managed not to smile. "No." She kept her voice faint.

Eyebrows pinched with concern, Duanna set the tray aside and put a hand to Jinnie's forehead. "You're a shade too cold, my liege."

Jinnie wasn't surprised. It had been cold watching the sunrise. "I don't feel well today, Duanna."

"Oh, dear. I knew it. I knew you would be sick if you left Keldonabrieve. You're always traipsing about in the cold with never a thought to keeping warm. I told the master to keep you at home."

"Here, now. Try a bite of breakfast. Perhaps that will help."

"I'm not hungry."

"Not hungry?" Duanna's voice rose with worry, and Jinnie again saw her mother. "Not even for a bit of toast and cheese?"

"Take it away."

"Well, then, your tea, my liege, to settle your stomach?"

"I couldn't possibly swallow it." Jinnie shook her head in what she hoped was a feeble manner. "My throat hurts."

"Oh, dear, oh, dear. What will the master say if he comes home and finds you ill? He'll never forgive me. He entrusts your good health to me, knowing how careless you are. What am I to do?"

"Escabel often has something to soothe me when I feel ill," Jinnie suggested, feeling only a little sorry for Duanna's distress.

"Oh, that dreadful witch!"

Jinnie coughed.

"Well, she's not my idea of a doctor, but you do seem to respond to her potions, foul-smelling though they are. I'll send Griffin."

"No!"

Pressing a hand to her throat, Jinnie coughed again. "No, Duanna. I think you should send Nickon and Trae."

"But the master left them here to protect you," objected Duanna.

"Noric can protect me. And Griffin."

"Very well, my liege. I'll send the two oafs. It will do them good anyway. Always thinking themselves above their station. Now you rest. Are you certain you won't eat? Perhaps if I leave the tray?"

"Take it away," Jinnie ordered. "Even the smell of food makes me feel sick."

"Oh, dear, oh, dear." Picking up the tray, Duanna hurried from the room.

Jinnie stretched, sighing, tired of being treated like a child. *I'm a liege lord*, she protested silently. *I own property in Willen, Minas, and Delawn.*

Jinnie threw back the covers and sat up abruptly. Willen. She could see it. Mountains of ice and snow. Rivers, quick and cold. Valleys, dark and wild. Her father's homeland.

He died, Jinnie remembered. He took my mother across the Plains of Ternin, and the Shardeti slaughtered them for trespassing. Trespassing!

Barbarians, that's what the Shardeti were. Yet they were among the first to agree to an official treaty. They agreed, and others followed, tired of constant battles over property, customs, and leadership. It had been a struggle, but a group of formal Alliances had finally been accepted.

Excited at the sudden rush of memory, Jinnie tried to remember the Turnak. In her mind, she saw short, dark-skinned people with white hair and amber eyes.

The Turnak had long opposed the Sunadin for the ownership of the Twilight Hills and the valley where Keldonabrieve stood guard. Only recently, when the Dardidak had broken yet another truce, had the Turnak agreed to join the Alliances.

"And Lancin intends to destroy them," Jinnie said aloud. But why? And how?

With a frustrated groan, she flopped back on the bed, her memory failing her again.

Footsteps sounded in the hallway, and Jinnie pulled the bedcovers around her. Closing her eyes, she pretended sleep.

The door of her room creaked as someone pushed it ajar. Footsteps crossed the room.

Jinnie's heart pounded so loudly she was sure it could be heard. Had Lancin returned? She tried to breathe slowly and evenly.

A shadow fell upon her face. Warm lips pressed a kiss against her mouth. Griffin.

Jinnie opened her eyes. "You frightened me," she chastised him, even as she smiled.

"Forgive me?" He smiled back, eyes shining into hers. With a glance at the door, he straightened and spoke in a loud voice.

"Nickon and Trae have been sent to fetch Escabel, my liege. I hope you will feel better soon."

"Thank you," Jinnie answered in an equally staged voice. In a whisper, she added, "I've remembered the Turnak."

Eyes on the door, Griffin leaned close again. "That's wonderful, Tessajihn."

"But I don't understand why Lancin hates them so. And what are we to do about it?"

"Hush. A little at a time. Lancin has always been greedy for land and power. The three territories you own and the five he already has make him the most powerful liege lord next to the leader of the Turnak."

"Allowyn."

"Yes."

"But …"

Griffin kissed her quickly and stood back, holding a finger to his lips. In a loud voice he announced, "I will return when Escabel arrives, my liege."

"Thank you, Griffin." Jinnie watched him leave.

Restless, her gaze drifted about the room. No more memories awakened.

She looked up at the beautiful birds in the fresco overhead. Hadn't her mother suggested them? She concentrated. She saw herself as a little girl being tucked into bed. There was a woman bending over her, and a gentle voice.

"And if you have a nightmare, Tessajihn, you can look up at the birds, and they'll help you place beautiful imaginings over the bad."

She did call me by name. Jinnie frowned. *Then what was I remembering earlier this morning?*

"Virginia, you must eat." Virginia. Virginia.

Pain sprang at her like a lion. Jinnie cried out. Desperately she tried to place beautiful images over the ones that now marched through her mind.

"You are wasting your life."

"Another drink and a psychiatrist."

"Stop pretending, Virginia."

"It's your imagination."

"It's Jinnie and her wild ideas."

The voices increased in volume, pounding, drumming, railing inside her head until she thought it would split apart.

Someone was screaming.

Hands grabbed at her, arms held her. Another voice penetrated the din in her mind.

"Tessajihn, Tessajihn," Griffin soothed. "I'm here. You're safe now."

The other voices faltered, dimmed. The pain sidled after them, with stinging tendrils and sharp claws.

Jinnie clung to Griffin. "What happened?" Her voice was as frail as a sparrow.

"I heard you scream. You screamed again and again." Griffin smoothed Jinnie's hair away from her face. "Was it the pain?"

Jinnie leaned her cheek against his shoulder and nodded weakly, no longer needing to pretend she felt ill.

"I was remembering. The pain came so suddenly and hurt so much."

"My liege?" Noric stood at the door. He made no comment on their intimate posture.

"She's all right," Griffin answered.

Noric nodded. He glanced behind him. "Duanna's coming," he warned, then left.

Gently releasing Tessajihn, Griffin moved away.

Duanna rushed into the room as quickly as her thick girth would allow. "My liege! I heard you scream, but I was so far away. What's happened?"

She laid a hand to Jinnie's forehead. "You feel feverish, my liege." Duanna cast a scowl at Griffin. "Bring me that cloth by the pitcher and put some water on it."

Jinnie let Duanna fuss around her, placing the wet cloth on her forehead, straightening the bedcovers, and checking her pulse.

"There was pain," Jinnie explained. "It's gone now."

"I'll sit with you," said Duanna.

"No. I just need to rest."

"You shouldn't be left alone, my liege."

"Griffin can stay with me."

Duanna pursed her lips. "Very well, my liege. Although I don't think it's proper. I have tried to understand the foreign ways of the Sunadin, and I know you must have a personal guard, but …"

"That's enough," said Jinnie, exasperated. "You talk too much, Duanna. Griffin is my Sheninn. There's nothing improper about it."

"Very well, my liege. I'll say no more."

Turning to Griffin, Duanna shook a stern finger at him. "Send for me at once if it happens again. Keep the fire high and hot and pull those drapes across the doors to keep the room dark. That will be more soothing. And ring for me if my liege needs anything at all."

Grumbling, Duanna left the room.

Griffin carried out his tasks, then drew a chair near the bed and sat down.

"Griffin?"

"Yes?"

"I want you to tell me about my life." Jinnie spoke only a little above a whisper, aware of the open door across the room.

He looked uncertain.

"Please," Jinnie urged. "If I feel any pain, I'll tell you stop at once. I need to have some idea of who I am. Especially before Escabel arrives."

Watching Tessajihn carefully for any sign of distress, Griffin told her about the recent past. Since the death of her parents two years ago, Jinnie had been chief negotiator for the Alliances. Her work had been difficult, sometimes dangerous. The clans had distrusted, deceived, hated, and warred for centuries. Each clan claimed superior bloodlines and Holy Rights.

But now, except for the Dardidak and the Turnak, most of the original border lines and peace agreements were being upheld. There were still skirmishes with the Turnak along the western border of the Twilight Hills, however, and Lancin blamed the Dardidak. That was why Jinnie had gone to parley with them again.

"When did I marry Lancin?" Jinnie interrupted.

"Last autumn."

"Was a political marriage so necessary?" Jinnie sat up, angry and sad. "It's you I love, Griffin. Why didn't I marry you?"

He looked surprised. "I'm not of the Sunadin, Tessajihn. Nor am I a liege lord. My clan is the Kabada."

"I know, but I don't understand."

"None of the clans have ever intermarried. Perhaps, with peace becoming a reality, old customs will be traded for new ones. It's what you hoped for Ispell. And for us."

Jinnie lay back on the pillows. "Yes. I hoped. But I can't wait for the future to catch up with me. I love you now and always. Last night you said we'd be safe in the Casserat Mountains."

"I believe we would be. They lie far north of the last land claimed by my clan. No other clans have ventured further."

"And the Kabada would give us safe passage?"

"Yes."

Griffin rose and came to stand near Jinnie. Taking her hand, he pressed a kiss into her palm.

"Tell me, my *jinnie*," he whispered, "will you leave Keldonabrieve and run away with me?"

"Yes."

* * *

"The witch is here, my liege," Duanna announced. She stumbled as she was pushed roughly aside.

Escabel strode into the room.

Six feet tall, with copper-red hair that writhed and coiled down her back, Escabel possessed a wicked beauty. Her features were strong, almost fierce, with eyes that snapped: one green, one blue. She had high, curving cheekbones and a wide, red mouth.

"My liege." She bowed imperiously.

Jinnie sat up straighter against her pillows and inclined her head in acknowledgment.

"Leave us." Escabel curled her upper lip at Duanna. "And do not disturb us. If I have a wish for you, Calon will let you know."

From beneath the folds of her wolfskin cape, Escabel brought out a small black bird. It perched on her wrist, winked a cold eye at Duanna, then flew to the fireplace and settled on the back of the chair.

Outraged, Duanna opened her mouth to protest, but Griffin grasped her upper arm and propelled her out the door. Shutting it, he turned to face Escabel.

"I am staying," he said.

Escabel stepped close. She took his chin in a long, thin hand weighted with rings and examined Griffin's eyes. "You are her love."

Griffin tensed. "I am."

"You may stay."

Escabel crossed the room in long, regal strides. She stared down at Jinnie. "You are not sick, Tessajihn of the Sunadin."

"No," Jinnie admitted. "But I do need your help."

Escabel undid her cape and tossed it on the bed as if the room belonged to her. "Come and sit by the fire," she ordered.

Glancing at Griffin, Jinnie slid from the bed. Griffin joined her.

Escabel seated herself in the chair, motioning Jinnie and Griffin to the floor in front of her. The bird jumped to his mistress's shoulder, completing the portrait of a necromancer as Escabel sat in noble splendor, her silver gown shimmering like water in the firelight.

"You spent the night at my house."

"Yes. I'm sorry, but—"

Escabel held up her hand for silence. "You were welcome."

"I felt expected."

"You were." The mismatched eyes studied Jinnie carefully.

"I had a dream," Escabel announced. "I have a gift for dreams. They show me the future. They answer questions. They divine the truth."

"Do you know the truth about me?"

"I know a part of it. The question is, why do you not know?"

Leaning forward, Escabel placed her hands on both sides of Jinnie's face, turning her head left, then right. "You are in a state of fugue, unaware of yourself."

"I've been confused," Jinnie said, uneasy. "Since the night I spent at your house, my life feels strange to me, foreign. I feel displaced, as if I once lived somewhere else. But when I try to remember where, the memories don't make sense to me. And there's pain. Terrible pain."

Escabel nodded, releasing her. "It will pass."

"You sound so certain."

"I am."

Frustrated, Jinnie's voice rose. "Well, when will it pass, and what's causing it?"

"Be still!" Escabel commanded. "Compose yourself to listen."

Taking a deep breath, Jinnie straightened her shoulders. Her hand reached unconsciously for Griffin's hand. They waited.

"When I first met you, twenty years ago," Escabel began, "I could see, in your eyes, your true nature. You were a Phantasm, Tessajihn. A creature of twilight. They exist partially in two worlds at the same time, yet they are never wholly in one world. They are one soul adrift between two bodies. But when I dreamed four nights ago and saw you caught in the Chill, I also saw you as you are now, fused, existing only in Ispell."

"Then I have lived another life somewhere." Jinnie said.

"Not another life," Escabel corrected her, "part of this one, the other half of a dual existence."

"Why is it so painful and difficult to remember it?"

"You no longer exist in that world. Perhaps the pain is grief or shock. I have never heard of a Phantasm that merged its separate lives. They usually wither and die young, unable to withstand the strain of their duality.

"But I have heard of Travelers, beings who live successive lives from one world to another. I have often speculated on their origin and the cause of their metamorphosis."

Escabel looked thoughtful. "It is possible they are Phantasms who have united their two selves. And, once united, their twofold nature begins to chafe, eventually separating, then joining again and again. A Traveler."

Jinnie felt sick to her stomach. She had wanted help and reassurance. Not this. It felt like a condemnation to madness.

"If you knew I was a Phantasm so long ago," Jinnie said, "why didn't you tell me?"

Escabel shrugged. "For what purpose? There was nothing to be done to help you then."

"And now?"

"Now I am uncertain."

"Was she a Traveler in your dream?" asked Griffin, fearful of losing Jinnie.

"I could not tell." Tilting her head to one side, Escabel narrowed her eyes as she looked at Jinnie. "Have you felt drawn to another life?" she demanded.

Jinnie shook her head. "No." She looked at Griffin. "I'm here now, and I'm going to stay."

Escabel scoffed. "If you see visions of a future life, then you are a Traveler. If not, then you are the rarest of Phantasms, and you may yet live a single life."

"You said her confusion and pain will pass," said Griffin. "When that happens, perhaps she will remember her true self."

Escabel pierced Griffin with a stare. "I have said that her mind will clear. She will remember her life here in Ispell.

"But if you are a Traveler, Tessajihn," Escabel addressed Jinnie, "you may not linger here long. You will split apart, live half a life somewhere else, then finally Travel to that life."

Jinnie tensed. "Then I must remember my other life now. Maybe that part of me knew if I am a Traveler. Right now, all I know is that I belong with Griffin."

Jinnie looked at him. "Griffin is why I'm here now. Whole at last. I love him."

Escabel studied Tessajihn a long time. The silence in the room crept upon them like a thief.

"Love is a powerful force," Escabel conceded finally. "Very well, I will help you remember."

Rising, she drew a handful of dried leaves from a pocket and threw them on the fire. It leapt to catch them, burning bright as sunlight. A fragrance like wild honey and vanilla billowed from the flames, dancing with the shadows in the room.

Turning, Escabel went to the door, flinging it open to find Duanna waiting anxiously. "Bring wine," she commanded. On her shoulder, Calon screeched.

Escabel moved slowly back to Tessajihn. "Breathe the *somin*. Look into the flames and drift."

To Griffin, she said, "Release her hand. Let only the *somin* touch her."

The strange scent wrapped itself around Jinnie, entwining her anxiety with a wonderful tranquility.

Duanna returned with the wine. Placing it beside Griffin, she cast a suspicious glare at Escabel and left.

"Pour a glass of wine and give it to her," instructed Escabel. "Be careful not to touch her."

Jinnie was vaguely aware of movement, of a glass pressed into her hand.

Leaning over her shoulder, Escabel poured a gray powder into the wine. "Drink. Drink and remember."

"Wait—" Griffin started to protest.

Escabel held up one hand. "There will be no pain while the drug lasts."

Jinnie lifted the glass to her lips and drank deeply. The wine tasted sharp, almost bitter, but the scent of the *somin* clouded it, flavored it. She drained the glass.

Escabel knelt beside her. "What do you feel?"

"Nothing." Jinnie's voice was far away.

"You can remember now."

"What do I want to remember?"

"Your shadow," Escabel's whisper was a hiss. "That part of you that haunts you now, troubles and confuses you."

Jinnie's eyes dilated; her thoughts drifted. An angry voice in her head said, "You're too old for daydreaming, Virginia."

Jinnie sighed. She remembered. All the bothersome details of getting through the days, the seasons, the years. Waiting. Waiting for Griffin to come for her.

Living inside herself, Karen had said. Karen. Her friend.

Frightened, Jinnie began to tremble. She looked wildly around her, but everything was out of focus.

"Take her hand, now," Escabel directed Griffin. "Call her by name. She has drifted too far. I will bring her back."

She threw a small flower on the fire. The *somin* started to fade. Its aroma grew fragile.

Taking Jinnie's hand tightly in his, Griffin said her name.

"Tessajihn."

"Again," snapped Escabel.

"Tessajihn."

"She is still too far." Escabel's eyes narrowed. "What else do you call her, Griffin of the Kabada?"

"I call her Jinnie."

Escabel nodded. "Then do so."

"Jinnie. My *jinnie*."

He's calling me, thought Jinnie, turning in the direction of the voice she loved. *Where was he?*

"Where are you?" Jinnie called out, feeling lost and afraid.

"I'm here, Jinnie. Beside you. Now and always. My *jinnie*."

Jinnie tried to see through the fog that enveloped her. She blinked several times. Griffin's face came into focus: solid, real, with love for her in his eyes. No dream, no madness. She reached for that face, touched it. "Griffin."

"Tessajihn of the Sunadin." Escabel's sharp tone sliced through Jinnie's relief and happiness.

"Yes?"

"When you remembered, did that part of you know what you are or what you may be?"

Jinnie shook her head, once more afraid. "No."

Escabel rose. "Rest now."

She went to the bed. Lifting her cape, she swung it about her broad shoulders, momentarily displacing Calon. As he resettled himself, Escabel faced Jinnie.

"You were a Phantasm. I do not know what you might yet become. For now, you are Tessajihn of the Sunadin, and you are Griffin's *jinnie*. Perhaps that will be enough. Fare well."

And she was gone, the door thundering shut behind her.

* * *

In the coldest hours before dawn, Jinnie lay curled on her side, Griffin's warm body against her back, his arms about her waist, his voice in her ear.

"I love you, Jinnie," he said softly. "No more talk of Travelers or what might be. The witch was only guessing. My love for you is a certainty. You need never fear losing it." He kissed her cheek. "Or me."

Jinnie nodded, wanting to believe Griffin. *I'm not a Traveler*, she told herself and shut her eyes against the possibility.

Eight

Jinnie stood in the turret facing the west shore, watching as the ferry fought its way across the lake. She raised a gloved hand to the hood of her cape and pulled the soft white fur closer about her.

Griffin had shown her the way to the tower. Here and in the secret passages, they had discussed what they would do. Griffin wanted to escape Keldonabrieve while Lancin was away; Jinnie insisted they stay until she warned the Turnak.

"We've no way to warn them, Jinnie," Griffin had argued. "And no evidence to provide of Lancin's treachery."

Jinnie defended her decision. Her memory of Ispell was returning like drops of water from a tap. "Think about this," she said. "The Sunadin want peace, yet Lancin is certain he can instigate war. Why? If he kills the leader of the Turnak openly, the rest of the Alliances, including the Sunadin, will join against him. So he must use subterfuge. He has to use a faction to harass the Turnak. A faction he can manipulate, whose movements can't be traced back to him."

"There's no such clan."

"Not a clan. The Dardidak."

"Of course. They would be the perfect soldiers. What else have you remembered?"

"Small details which had eluded me at first. The Dardidak had killed several Turnak horses, claiming it was an accident, a misunderstanding of territory rights.

"I remember those territories now," said Jinnie. "I remember how I thought it odd at the time. When I looked at them on a map, I understood. If you look at them strategically, they completely encircle the Turnak's land."

"But the Dardidak don't value land and have no system of government. They fall to fighting amongst themselves over a piece of meat, and they've no head for warfare."

"No. But Lancin does. I believe he's organizing the Dardidak to insurrection against the Turnak. And, according to the map, everywhere after that, even here in the Twilight Hills."

"Including the Sunadin? His own clan?"

"Yes. Creating total chaos. Once the populations are decimated, Lancin can conquer and subjugate, using the Dardidak to perpetuate terror and the fear of total annihilation."

"Bringing all of Ispell under his command," Griffin said.

"Yes." Jinnie had looked away. Loathing for the abomination she had married made her sick to her stomach. What had ever made her think she could manipulate such a creature? But how could she have guessed his true nature?

Lancin had been believably smitten with her, full of promises to honor, cherish and lend his clan's titles in support of the Alliances. *Until death has parted us*, Jinnie thought. *The death of the Alliances.*

"How will he control the Dardidak?" asked Griffin. "What bribe could sway them?"

"What are the Sunadin known for?" Jinnie asked.

"The finest horseflesh ..." Griffin slowed, understanding, "in all of Ispell."

Jinnie nodded. "The Dardidak have little use for the trappings of victory: wealth, stature, power. But they'll do it for the thrill of bloodshed and the promise of horseflesh to gorge upon."

"How will you warn the Turnak? A messenger won't be safe or be believed."

Jinnie had smiled. "I'm going to have a birthday party."

* * *

The ferry was nearing the castle now, and Jinnie began the long descent from the turret, composing her thoughts as the stairs wound her round and round.

She would play the part of the meek and obedient wife. Lancin must not suspect that she was capable of anything more demanding than choosing an appropriate gown for dinner.

Griffin and Noric had searched the kitchen in the middle of the night, found the *hartha*, and replaced it with real tea of a similar color. Jinnie could drink her tea as expected, pretend anxiety and confusion, yet remain clearheaded.

She reached the bottom of the turret. Griffin was waiting for her.

"Is it Lancin?" Jinnie asked. If Lancin arrived first, there would be trouble.

"No. It's Peesha and Koldin, and the ambassadors from Willen and Rhola."

"Good."

"But another ferry has started across," Griffin cautioned. "It flies Lancin's flag."

"Then we'll have to hurry. Quickly, take me to the main hall."

Griffin led her through the labyrinth to a false exit and into a secret passage. It ran straight enough, but there were successive flights of stairs to navigate.

Jinnie stumbled in her long cape and dress, glad of Griffin's hand on her arm.

As they neared the exit, she paused. Breathless, she undid her cloak and passed it to Griffin, remembering her gloves at the last minute. She smoothed her dress, and kissed Griffin. "Now," she said.

Griffin slid the panel open, and Jinnie stepped out.

Voices were approaching. Hurriedly, Jinnie crossed to the stairs, ran halfway up, and turned, descending gracefully.

"Tessajihn! How do you fare? My, but you look splendid. No one would ever guess you were going to be thirty-six." Koldin stepped forward to take her hand, turning it over to kiss her palm.

"If only I were unmarried," he sighed in mock despair.

"But you are." Peesha poked him from behind, then stepped around him. "Tessajihn, you do look wonderful. It has been too long since we've seen you."

Jinnie smiled at her friends. She knew them to be her friends; she felt warmth toward them, happiness at seeing them. Beyond that, she could recall nothing. Jinnie hoped they wouldn't want to reminisce.

"It's good to see you, too," she said, her gaze going beyond them to the four other people who entered the hall.

Two were tall and dark like Lancin; the Sunadin occupied the lands of Willen. The other two were short and fair-haired, with round, smiling faces. They were ambassadors from the Kardin clan.

Stepping from the stairs, Jinnie moved toward them. "I am honored that you chose to attend my celebration."

They both bowed, blushing and smiling.

"Thank you," one said.

"Very much," the other added.

"I am Dulan," said the first.

"And I am Dalun," said the twin.

"I am delighted to meet you both." Jinnie turned to the Sunadin. "And you are—?"

The taller one frowned. He came forward, taking her hand with familiarity. "Can you forget me so easily, my liege?"

Jinnie searched his face. "I ... I'm sorry." She cursed her vacillating memory. "I've not been well. You must be ..."

"Ashon." He bowed low over her hand. "I'm sorry to hear you've been ill. You look as beautiful as ever, my liege."

He straightened. "My brother, Triel."

Triel bowed and stepped away.

There was something more in Ashon's eyes, but he pressed her no further for recognition.

Jinnie smiled, a little uncertainly now, and motioned them into the drawing room.

"I hope your trip was ..."

"Odd," pronounced Koldin, "as ever." He seated himself on a couch, stretching his long legs across it, prohibiting Peesha from joining him.

Peesha tossed him a cross look and went to sit near the fire. "He only means, Tessajihn, that Lancin really ought to have some stairs put in. The ferry is tolerable, but that ladder has to go."

"I could not agree more," said Jinnie.

"Then tell him," Peesha protested.

Jinnie shrugged. "I have."

There was a tacit silence in the room. It seemed everyone agreed that arguing with Lancin was not only a waste of time, but also an unwise one.

Jinnie sat in a love seat, the long folds of her green gown swirling and rustling. Ashon joined her; Triel chose a chair across from Peesha. Dulan and Dalun seated themselves on either side of a small table.

Looking about the room, Jinnie realized they expected her to speak.

"I wish," she began nervously, uncomfortable with Ashon so near, "I wish for this celebration to strengthen our friendships, both personal and political." She let the sentence drift around the room.

"Of course," Dulan agreed. "We of the …"

"Kardin," his brother interrupted, "we are content with peace."

"The Sunadin of Willen have always been peaceful," Ashon put in.

Dulan harrumphed.

"Well," Ashon smiled, turning the brilliance of it to Jinnie, "almost always."

Jinnie flushed and looked away, glad to see Duanna enter the room with Yogin and another boy trailing her. Trays of wine, fruit, and sweets were set about the room.

"Tessajihn!"

Jinnie jumped. Lancin was home.

He stalked into the room, a black scowl on his face.

Ashon rose at once to greet him. "My lord." He bowed.

"I didn't send for you, Ashon. What brings you to Keldonabrieve?" Lancin looked over the group. "Indeed, what brings any of you?"

"I invited them," Jinnie answered.

Lancin turned at her sharp tone.

"I invited all my friends," Jinnie pushed on, "my own and those of the Alliances."

"What? What for?" Lancin seethed inside, but knew he couldn't afford a scene. Not now.

"For my birthday."

The surprise on Lancin's face drew a laugh from Koldin. "Oh, sir. To forget your own wife's day of celebration is a crime indeed."

Griffin entered the room, bowing his head to all.

"My liege," he addressed Jinnie, "the second group of ambassadors will arrive presently."

"Thank you, Griffin," said Jinnie, avoiding Lancin's stare.

"What, more?" Lancin strove to make it a jest, but his eyes burned cold and angry.

"This is going to be an interesting party," observed Peesha, not missing Lancin's anger or Tessajihn's quiet defiance.

Within the hour, the drawing room was crowded with friends, ambassadors, and a few clan leaders.

One of them is Allowyn of the Turnak, thought Jinnie. *Griffin will single him out for me later.*

She grew exhausted with smiling and nodding. Lancin stayed beside her every step, anger in his eyes even as he smiled. Once free of witnesses, he would have something to say. In addition, he would be dangerous.

She smiled at some inanity. Soon it would be time for the guests to go to their rooms before dinner. At last Griffin and Duanna began escorting the guests away in two and threes.

"I think we should unravel a string," Jinnie overheard Koldin suggest to Peesha.

He'd only cut it, Jinnie thought bitterly, looking to Lancin. He glared back at her. Hastily she replaced her resentment with compliance.

Allowyn was the last to leave, escorted by Griffin. Jinnie knew he would be in the guest room directly below hers, as planned.

"My sweet." Lancin loomed behind her, and Jinnie nearly dropped the tea she held. "You seem uneasy, my pet." He took the teacup from her, setting it down on a table. "I wonder why?"

Jinnie wrung her hands and bit her lip as he turned her to face him. She'd been practicing her expressions in front of the mirror that morning.

Looking up at Lancin, she smiled guilelessly, eyes wide.

"Please, Lancin." She let her voice tremble a little. "Don't be angry. I so wanted a party this year, and I knew you wouldn't agree."

Standing on tiptoe, Jinnie kissed Lancin's cheek.

"You worry too much over my health. You're always so busy with …" Jinnie paused, seeking the right tone of carelessness, "attending to your work, and yet you hate to let me out of your sight. Why," she tried a fragile laugh, "sometimes I think you don't trust me."

Lancin's eyes bored into hers until Jinnie's skull began to pound. His jaw was tight, and his brows conferred in the center of his forehead.

The Traveler

Then Lancin's features relaxed, and he gave Tessajihn a generous smile, thinking of his coming triumph. "Very well, my dove. Stop your fretting. I won't spoil your party."

Jinnie's heart, beating frantically, began to slow. She gave him a pleased smile. "Thank you, Lancin." She turned to leave, but Lancin snatched her to him. His arms wrapped about her like a snake, squeezing her painfully tight.

"But I claim all your dances this evening, my love," he leered.

Lancin kissed her roughly, and Jinnie felt sick with revulsion. When he released her, she almost lost her balance, breathless and angry.

"Of course." Jinnie looked at the door, forcing her voice to stay sweet and not betray her disgust. She wanted to wipe her mouth. Instead, she smiled up at her husband.

"Now I must go. Duanna will have a fit if I'm late for my bath, and I have no idea what dress I'll wear."

Lancin grinned, his fears soothed. She was still under his control.

Jinnie moved quickly out of his reach, out of the room, and across the hall. In the shadows at the top of the stair, Griffin was waiting for her. Jinnie wished she could risk kissing him.

"Are you all right?" he whispered, taking her hand and leading her to a passageway.

"Yes."

"Was he angry?"

"Yes, but I think I calmed him."

"Then we're almost safe. After tonight, we can escape."

They both looked up and down the hallway. No one was to be seen. Griffin pushed a panel open, ushering Jinnie inside and stepping quickly after her. The panel slid shut.

Further up the corridor, a tall figure separated itself from the shadows. It was Ashon.

NINE

Jinnie suffered through the long dinner and the endless toasts: to her health, to her beauty, to the Alliances, to peace. She watched the people talk and laugh, feeling no connection to them. Many were members of the Six Clans who occupied the Ten Territories. Some, once lethal rivals, now sought friendship.

It was a familiar scene. She recognized it from that other life in which her mother was alive and she had countless relatives. She could remember them vaguely. They seemed like someone else's family—faces without names.

This is my family now, thought Jinnie. *Or would be, if I stayed. But Griffin and I are running away to the Casserat Mountains. Tonight, if all goes well.*

"Come, my sweet." Lancin lifted her hand and drew back her chair. "We must start the dancing."

He led her across the front hall into a large room stripped bare of furnishings to allow for dancing. The rest of the crowd followed happily.

Musicians began to play a waltz, and Jinnie was whirled about the floor. She wished she was dancing with Griffin; she tried to smile. Not once did Lancin leave her long enough for someone else to beg a dance until Ashon asked to see him in the study.

Relieved to be free of Lancin's vigil, Jinnie wandered the periphery of the room. The party showed no signs of slowing, even though it was well past midnight. She felt calm. Tonight it would all be done. The warning given, her marriage disavowed, and the true beginning of a new life: a life to share with Griffin.

Pausing to look out a window, Jinnie felt someone watching her. She turned to face her observer. Across the room, a man started walking toward her. He was tall and pale, with silver blonde hair, and green eyes. Jinnie didn't know to which clan he belonged or with what party he had arrived.

Dressed in a white shirt and trousers and knee-high black boots, the man glided toward her, passing through the dancers' bodies as if they weren't there.

Jinnie took a step back. Fear pricked at her neck, sending a shiver down her spine. She wanted to run, but the fear was paralyzing. Transfixed, Jinnie waited.

The man was almost upon her, smiling, reaching for her.

Run! her mind screamed, but Jinnie stood immobile, sick, terrified.

Then the man walked through her and was gone.

The room began to spin. Jinnie groped for a chair, found one, and sank into it.

"He wasn't real," Jinnie told herself. She stared blankly, remembering Escabel's warning about visions of a future life. "Yes, he was."

* * *

"You lie!" Lancin roared.

"No, my lord." Ashon stood his ground. "I saw them together. They entered a secret passage after talking of escape."

"I know every corridor in this castle. There are no secret ones."

"Even so, my lord. I saw them."

Lancin drew a dagger from his boot. "Liar!"

Ashon remained defiant. "Think, my lord. If they are only now planning an escape, they must have betrayed you recently."

Lancin lowered his dagger, and Ashon continued. "Think, my lord. Were they alone together outside of Keldonabrieve?"

Lancin slumped against his desk. "The witch's house. They spent the night there, sheltering from the Chill. I thought Escabel was with them."

His head came up with a snap. "No one must know."

"I will be silent, my lord."

"Yes." Raising the dagger, Lancin advanced on Ashon. "You will be."

* * *

Jinnie stood up, feeling weak and unsteady. No longer trying to smile, she made her way through the revelers and reached the door of the dining room. The candles had burned so low that shadows prowled the room like ghosts.

"My liege," a voice whispered. It was Noric.

Jinnie moved into the room. "What is it?"

Noric caught her hand and hurried her across the room and down a corridor. He spoke as they went.

"I am taking you to Griffin. You must escape now."

"But I can't. I haven't warned the Turnak."

"Lancin sent for the Captain of the Guard a few minutes ago."

"The Captain of the Guard? Ornack," Jinnie said.

"Yes. And Nickon and Trae and me. We met in the study. Lancin stood over the body of Ashon."

Jinnie gasped.

"Lancin wrote messages and sent Nickon and Trae to the mainland to deliver them at once."

"Messages? At once?"

"I do not know what Lancin spoke of to Ornack. He ordered me to remove the body and then to find you."

"But why did he kill Ashon?"

"What does it matter now? Lancin is preparing for war."

"So, it's begun," Jinnie said, stunned. All she had given up, all she had sacrificed was lost. Except for Griffin.

They reached the kitchen. Griffin was waiting, and Jinnie ran to him.

"Hurry," he said, giving her only a brief embrace. "I brought you warm clothes. Put them on quickly."

"How will we get out of here? And the Chill is still burning."

"By the time we reach the shore, it will be nearly dawn, and the Chill will be fading. Now hurry!"

Jinnie grabbed the bundle he handed her and went to undress in the pantry. It was dark and cold, but she shivered more from fear.

All the planning, all the deception, Jinnie thought, ripping at the laces of her dress. *All for nothing now. Lancin will have his war.* She glared at the heavy ring on her finger and pulled it off, throwing it to the floor in rage and despair.

Jinnie paused, noticing the clothes Griffin had chosen for her: her jeans, boots, and sweater. Her fur cape and gloves. And her purse.

Jinnie dressed and hid her gown behind a barrel, She returned to the kitchen, pulling her cape close. "I'm ready."

"Good." Griffin took her hand.

Noric led them swiftly through the kitchen into a storeroom. He searched carefully.

"There!" Noric pointed at a wall piled with barrels of ale and wine. Griffin helped him clear a narrow space for them to squeeze through. A cold wind hissed at them through the crack of a small door.

"Stand fast on the lift," Noric directed. "Hold the rails tight."

"Can you manage it?" Griffin asked him.

"Yes. Once the lift is started, it operates automatically. Now go."

Griffin nodded. He clasped Noric's arm a moment in friendship. "Thank you, my friend. Fare well. Do not underestimate the depth of Lancin's treachery. As soon as you can, seize any opportunity to flee."

"I will."

Griffin stepped through the door. "Jinnie?" he called back to her.

Jinnie paused, looking at Noric. "You must come with us," she protested.

"No, my liege. I cannot be missed. After I start the lift, I will return upstairs and say I saw you going to your room. Lancin will have the guards search the entire castle before he realizes you are gone."

Jinnie reached up and touched his cheek. "Thank you, Noric. Fare well."

"And you, my liege." He bowed his head, holding the door for her so she could slip through.

A platform beneath Jinnie's feet swayed, and she grabbed Griffin's outstretched hand for support. Behind her, the door thumped shut.

"Where are we?" Jinnie whispered. Her words echoed eerily.

Griffin raised a lantern above his head. They stood on five wide planks bolted together. A rail, about three feet high, enclosed the platform. Ropes and pulleys hung overhead, suspending them in a stone shaft.

Griffin grabbed the rail, pulling Jinnie to him. "It's the old access to the siege tunnel," he said. "Something Noric knew of from your father's time."

The lift swayed. The pulleys creaked, hinges rusted from disuse. They began to descend. Jinnie squeezed Griffin's hand, frightened.

"It's all right," he whispered, though the shaft made his words louder. "It will lower us fifty feet below the surface of the lake. Then we'll be in the siege tunnel."

Siege tunnel, thought Jinnie. *I remember now.* "My father told me something of it," she said. "It was a secret to be kept always. A great strength and weakness in the power of Keldonabrieve. It runs beneath the lake to the far side, near the Twilight Hills. I was never to speak of it to anyone in case an enemy learned of its existence."

"Did you ever speak of it to Lancin?" Griffin held her steady as the lift swayed again.

Jinnie frowned. Had she ever been so foolish as to trust Lancin that much? In her *hartha*-induced haze, had she ever confided in Lancin or thought out loud and been overheard?

"I can't remember," Jinnie answered, frustrated.

"It's all right. Even if Lancin knows about the tunnel, he'll search for hours before he considers that you might have used it. He still thinks you've been drinking the *hartha*."

Griffin kissed Jinnie's forehead. "We'll be gone long before Lancin realizes you have regained your memory and escaped. We'll be safe soon, my *jinnie*."

As the lift descended, Jinnie felt the cold reach up for them. She leaned against Griffin, watching the walls blur as her life in Keldonabrieve fell apart and away from her.

* * *

"Searching the kitchen, Noric?" Ornack's bulk filled the doorway. "What an odd place to look for Tessajihn."

Ornack's use of Tessajihn's proper name made Noric cautious. "I only thought she might have come here to get her tea."

Ornack stepped aside, and two guards stepped forward.

"Search the rooms," said Ornack. He faced Noric and smiled. "Lancin wishes to speak with you."

* * *

The lift jerked to a stop, banging and scraping against the floor of the tunnel. Griffin raised the wick of the lantern. It shone a pale light on walls slick with ice. Griffin and Jinnie climbed over the railing.

"Do you think it's safe?" Jinnie asked, unable to quell her anxiety in spite of the nearness of Griffin. Jinnie imagined she could feel the enormous weight of the lake above her. Ice snapped beneath her feet, and half-frozen slime threatened to trip her. She shivered.

Griffin smiled encouragement. "It will be safe enough for us. Come on."

* * *

"Where is she?" Lancin snarled. "Where is her Sheninn?"

"I do not know, my lord," Noric answered. "I could not find her among the guests. She must have returned to her room. Griffin must have retired early."

Lancin sneered down at Noric. "Her room is empty." He circled the chair Noric sat in.

"I know Tessajihn has betrayed me with Griffin, Noric. Spare yourself a little pain. Where is my wife?"

Pounding on the door interrupted the interrogation. One of the guards who had searched the kitchen entered the room and crossed to Lancin. He offered him something in his hand and backed out of the room.

Lancin's face reddened with fury as he clenched a fist about the object. When he spoke, his voice was a low rumble. "You have helped Tessajihn flee Keldonabrieve, Noric. No doubt Griffin is with her. Did you take them to the siege tunnel?"

"I have no knowledge of a tunnel, my lord." Noric shifted his weight in his chair, remembering Griffin's warning. "I swear by all the gods, I do not know where she and Griffin may be."

"Liar!" As he spoke, Lancin thrust his dagger deep. In a thick fury, he kicked the chair out from under Noric's body.

"We can follow her," Ornack said.

Lancin curled his lip. "What for? I have no wish to see her again." He studied the ring in his hand, then tossed it into the fire.

"I have guests to attend." His eyes darkened. "Guests who can help me mourn."

Lancin kicked at Noric's body.

"Get a messenger to the Dardidak encampment in the Twilight Hills. Tell them ... Tell them two targets are coming their way for practice."

"Yes, sir." Ornack spun on his heel and left.

"Why?" Lancin raged at no one. "Why did you betray me, Tessajihn?" His face stilled, became like stone.

"No matter. I shall strike you down as you flee. You and your lover." He spat into the fire.

* * *

Jinnie stumbled. An icy wind reminded her of her first night in Ispell.

My first night as a complete person, thought Jinnie.

"A Traveler," Escabel's words haunted her. "Visions of another life."

The wind whipped her hood back, and Jinnie blinked as the wind struck her lashes and stung her cheeks. She felt sick to her stomach. Was she a Traveler? Was the stranger at the dance from her next life?

Griffin put his mouth close to Jinnie's ear and kissed it. "We're almost there. I love you."

She smiled at him.

I'm not a Traveler, she thought. *Escabel was wrong. My life is with Griffin.*

The tunnel sloped upward, and they concentrated on walking. Far ahead, a gray light promised to release them.

Jinnie stopped. Someone was calling her. A voice was in her mind: indistinct, distant. Someone was waiting for them. For her.

"What is it?" Griffin asked.

"Don't go out there," Jinnie whispered.

"Why?"

"I don't know. I'm afraid."

He tugged on her hand. "Don't be afraid, my *jinnie*. There will be horses waiting. And, more importantly, we're together."

Jinnie held tightly to Griffin's hand, wanting to believe there was nothing to fear, that everything would be fine. They were almost free of Lancin's grasp. In a few hours, they would be in the foothills of the Casserat Mountains.

"All right." Jinnie looked toward the tunnel's mouth. The gray light was shifting to hues of pink. Dawn. The Chill was dying. "All right. Let's go."

They started back up the slope. The wind had ceased, and the quiet was loud against their ears. Now snow crunched beneath their feet. A few more steps, and they were free.

"You see?" Griffin spread his arms wide. "We're safe."

A strange whistle punctured the silence. Griffin crumpled. He fell to the snow.

"No!" Jinnie flung herself beside him, turning him over gently. An arrow impaled his side.

Hideous laughter split the dawn. Dardidak! She heard them rustling in the bushes as they closed in for the kill.

"Griffin!" She tried to lift him. "Griffin, get up! We have to go back. Hurry. We have to go back in the tunnel. Griffin, please," she begged.

He moved slightly, and opened his eyes.

"Get up!" Jinnie demanded.

Griffin grasped her shoulder, and Jinnie helped him to his feet. A shout warned her that the Dardidak knew their prey was trying to flee. Bracing Griffin under his arm, Jinnie half dragged him back into the tunnel.

They staggered down the slope. Heavy footsteps thudded close behind them.

Jinnie prayed that what she remembered about the Dardidak was true.

She forced Griffin on, not knowing what she was looking for until she found it. There! A fissure in the wall of the tunnel, just big enough to hide them.

Jinnie helped Griffin into it, pressing in behind him. She heard the Dardidak gather at the top of the slope.

"I tell you, I hit one," said a sullen voice.

"You couldn't hit your eye," a deeper voice replied.

"I could hit yours," said the first.

"Quiet, both of you," a third voice said.

"Well, I'm not going in there," the sullen voice announced. "It goes under water."

"Ugh," the deeper voice confirmed his decision. "I'm not going in either."

"And who's asking you?" the third voice demanded. "We were told to wait at the end of the tunnel and kill whoever came out, right?"

Grunts of agreement from the other two.

"Then we'll wait. They came out once. They'll come out again."

More grunts. "Let's hide in those bushes," the third voice instructed, "so they won't get suspicious."

The feet stumped away.

Jinnie released her breath, afraid to check if they were gone. Griffin slumped against her. They would have to risk leaving the fissure and moving further back into the tunnel.

She peered out. Nothing but cold air and silence. For now.

Jinnie helped Griffin from the cleft. They moved quietly away until the tunnel's mouth was only a distant circle.

Pulling off her cloak, Jinnie spread it on the frozen ground, easing Griffin onto it and leaning him back against the wall.

The arrow mocked her.

"Pull it out," Griffin whispered painfully.

Jinnie reached for the arrow. She hesitated. She looked at Griffin's pale face and into his eyes, warm with trust, cold with pain.

Grasping the arrow with both hands, she counted to three and pulled. Griffin made no sound, but he grew paler, and his gaze wavered.

Jinnie set the arrow aside, wishing she had something to staunch the blood. Frustrated, she used her gloves, pressing them into the wound and holding them there.

"Griffin." She made him look at her. "Griffin, the Dardidak won't wait long. Lancin has started his apocalypse. In a few hours, they'll be gone to join the battles. We have to wait."

Griffin nodded. He pulled her fingers from the wound and held the gloves himself.

Jinnie sat on her heels, helpless and angry. Griffin drifted into unconsciousness. She checked his pulse. It seemed strong. Perhaps the arrow hadn't penetrated far.

If they could out-wait the Dardidak, if Lancin sent no one after them from Keldonabrieve, they might still have a chance.

Jinnie froze. Someone was coming from the direction of the castle.

"Lady Jinian?"

A frigid knot tightened in Jinnie's stomach.

"Lady Jinian, are you there? Damn this rain." It was a man's voice, sounding concerned and not unkind. Whoever he was, he hadn't seen her yet.

A tear flung itself down Jinnie's cheek. Shaking with grief, she turned to Griffin. His pulse was steady; the bleeding was slowing. He would live, but without her.

Jinnie couldn't bear to wake him, couldn't bear to see the pain in his eyes when she told him she had to leave. But she had to tell him somehow.

Her purse lay across her stomach were she'd strung it from her shoulder. Fumbling inside it, Jinnie withdrew the lipstick.

Quickly now, she scrawled a message on the wall of the tunnel. The lipstick gave out as she finished, and she dropped the empty tube beside him.

"I love you," Jinnie whispered in Griffin's ear.

"Lady Jinian!" An old man appeared several feet away.

Jinnie glanced at him, looking once more at Griffin.

"I'm coming."

She stood up. Not allowing herself to look back, she joined the old man.

"Come along, come along," he urged as she reached his side. They walked toward the far wall of the tunnel and disappeared.

Ice tried to obliterate Jinnie's words, but the dye in the lipstick stained the rock beneath it. When Griffin woke an hour later, he read her message. "My love, Escabel was right. I am a Traveler. You must live our life for me. I love you ... Jinnie."

Part II
Hura

One

"No!" Jinnie doubled over, clutching her stomach. For an instant, everything was dark, cold, painful.

Someone spoke to her. A hand grasped her shoulder.

"Lady Jinian? What is it?"

Jinnie didn't answer. The pain was gone, leaving a hollow sadness. Where was she? Who was she?

"Lady Jinian, answer me."

Jinnie straightened, blinking against the curtain of cold rain that fell about her. She stood on a moor, green and brown against a dark gray sky. The rain made the horizon a smudge against the land.

"I'm all right, Tuckin." Her voice sounded strange in her ears. She stepped away from his hand, her heart beating too fast. She didn't recognize where she was, but she knew she had to reassure her companion.

"There." Jinnie lifted her arms and turned about. "You see? I'm fine."

She smiled at the old man. His crinkled face showed worry, and his spectacles were fogging in the rain. He wore a long, mud-spattered coat and held some sort of canvas canopy over his head. It was circular with a short, narrow pole in its center. Tuckin gripped the pole with gnarled fingers.

It's an umbrella, thought Jinnie, recognizing the item, but not the word.

"You are not fine," Tuckin admonished, cross because he had been frightened. "You have been out of the house every day this week. This foolishness must cease, Lady Jinian." He waved his free hand at the moor. "Wandering about in the rain without even a jacket to keep you warm. I am surprised you had the sense to wear boots."

He paused in his scolding, then continued in a kinder tone. "There comes a time, Jinnie, when one must cease to mourn."

Hearing her nickname discomforted Jinnie, but she couldn't think why. She turned her thoughts instead to what the old man had said. They stood in a graveyard. Who was she mourning?

Jinnie walked over to the nearest headstone. *Melinda Ray, Beloved Wife and Mother.* Jinnie wondered if this was her mother's headstone.

Tuckin came up behind her, sheltering her with his umbrella. "Six years," he nodded. "Let her rest in peace. Your life is just beginning."

"Yes," murmured Jinnie, feeling no sense of loss, unable to bring a face to mind. Reaching out, she fingered the headstone. It was cold, slick with rain.

I remember ice, thought Jinnie. *A stone wall—no—rock, and I was writing something.*

Pain sluiced over her like the rain, and Jinnie grimaced.

"Come now." Taking her by the arm, Tuckin escorted her out of the graveyard. "Let us get back to the house before it begins to storm."

He led her away. As they walked, their feet left impressions in the long, wet grass.

The rain will wash them away, thought Jinnie. The endless rain of Breeare. It was more than one hundred years since the last bomb fell, and still it rained.

Jinnie squinted at the sky. Dark clouds churned with the turmoil of dust, pollution, and radiation. A constant reminder to the Breearians of the folly of war: the clouds and their rain.

The rain fell harder, and Tuckin quickened their pace. Jinnie stumbled after him, wondering why her boots were too big.

"Here we are," Tuckin announced.

Jinnie glanced up. A mansion braced itself against the rain, lonely against the emptiness of the moor.

Reaching it, Tuckin hurried Jinnie into the back hall, shutting the door with satisfaction. He closed the umbrella and took off his coat, shaking the rain from its folds. As he removed his boots, he looked over at Jinnie.

"You look frightful," Tuckin grumbled. "Hurry to your room and change your clothes. And dry your hair."

He shook his head in disapproval. "Imagine if your future husband were to see you now. What would he think of you?"

Husband? An image skidded along the edge of Jinnie's memory, bringing a dull headache with it.

"I don't like my husband," she said. The headache sharpened.

"You have not yet met the man." Tuckin shook his head, frustrated with his young charge. She was as stubborn as her father was. Good luck to her husband, whoever he was to be.

"We have had this discussion many times now, Lady Jinian." Tuckin folded his arms, readying for another lecture. "I have no doubt your father will make a good arrangement for you. The very best. And you will have as good a marriage as you allow. Daydreams and wishful thinking will only make you unhappy. You are not a child. You are a Lady and must act the part."

Act the part, Jinnie's mind echoed.

Sitting down on a chair, Jinnie tried to organize her disjointed thoughts. *Husband.* That's what she had been trying not to think about all day—that, and the man in her dream.

Walking in the rain, she had felt closer to him than ever before. How long had she been dreaming of him, night after night? Jinnie couldn't remember.

I don't remember much of anything. Jinnie frowned. *I feel so out of place, so fragmented. How long have I felt like this?*

She sat still, waiting for her world to make sense again.

"Lady Jinian?" Concerned by her pale silence, Tuckin stepped over and placed a hand against Jinnie's cheek. "Are you ill?"

Jinnie looked up at him. "I feel cold," she said at last.

Tuckin frowned. "I think it best for you to get directly into bed. I will bring you some hot soup in a little while. Let us hope that a night of good rest will have you feeling better tomorrow, otherwise I shall call the doctor. And you must promise me that you will not go out in the rain again before your father returns from the City. That is only two days."

"I promise."

No argument? Perhaps he should call the doctor. "Remove your boots and leave your bag," Tuckin said, worry editing the gruffness from his voice.

Jinnie pulled free of her purse and boots. At least her socks were dry. It was then she noticed how long her pants were. And the sweater she wore—its sleeves dragged damply down her wrists to her knuckles.

Again she felt displaced. Her heart beat too fast again. Something was wrong. Jinnie was certain of it. But what?

Standing, she managed a brief smile for Tuckin and headed down the back hallway.

"I will have spice soup for you within the hour," Tuckin called after her.

Jinnie raised her hand in acknowledgment and continued down the hallway. She followed its twists and turns, almost on tiptoe, as if afraid to be heard.

Who was there to listen? *No one lives here anymore except Father, Tuckin, and me.*

She paused, looked right, and chose left. *It's like a labyrinth*, thought Jinnie, *yet I know the way.*

She reached the main hall. It was dusk now, and the wide staircase before her was draped with shadows. It reminded her of somewhere. Jinnie paused.

I haven't been away from the house in months, she thought. *Certainly not anywhere as old-fashioned as our home.*

The few remaining houses outside the City were too far apart to allow frequent visits, and most of them had been renovated after the war.

Renovated. The word brought an image to Jinnie's mind: a large house, sculpted with towers. Her head ached as she recalled it. Not a house, a castle.

"H. C.," Jinnie said aloud, "augment illumination at my approach, thirty-five percent."

The House Computer increased the overhead lighting one meter in front of Jinnie and continued to do so as she crossed the hall and climbed the stairs.

The Traveler

On the landing, Jinnie hesitated then chose a door. She entered her bedroom. For a minute, Jinnie stood still. Nothing looked like she expected, yet it all had an eerie familiarity, like that of a photograph or a painting she knew. But the scene had no texture or depth, just outlines and colors.

Jinnie rubbed her arms, still feeling cold and uneasy. Thunder crashed outside.

She went to a long, narrow window. The light overhead flung her reflection into the coming night. Dark, apprehensive eyes stared back at her from too young a face. Long blonde hair lay wet against pale, fine-boned features. The figure was thin, wearing clothes that were too large.

Jinnie pressed her fingers to the glass a moment, then turned away. She felt certain something very important had occurred, and she didn't know what it was.

What's happening to me? Why do I feel so strange? I feel like I'm watching myself from far away.

She walked about the room. *What do I know?*

My name is Jinian Ray. Tuckin Dupal is—or was—my mother's servant. He's looked after me since Mother died. My father is Churgin Ray. He's gone to the City to arrange my marriage, as the law requires.

Jinnie raised her hands in exasperation. *I know all these circumstances of my life, but I don't recognize any of them.*

"I don't recognize me," she said aloud, frightened.

Her eyes widened. Could it be the Plague, that 'trophy' of war that had killed her mother six years ago? Her mother's mind had faltered as the illness drained her life away. She had forgotten everything and everyone a little at a time. Hallucinations and pain had been her companions.

If I have the Plague, thought Jinnie, *I won't have to marry.* The Plague seemed a high price to pay for freedom.

"No." She shook her head. "My last health check was fine. I've just spent too much time wishing that things could be different from the way they are. I've let the man in my dream distract me. I'm imagining castles instead of houses, a lover instead of a husband.

"Tuckin always says 'Daydreaming is ruinous to your health.' And now I'm tired and cold and I've been out too long in the ... rain."

Why did she want to say snow?

Jinnie hauled at the sodden material of her sweater, peeling free of it with effort. Her pants, made of a fabric she didn't recognize, were even more difficult to remove. Finally free of her clothes, she put on a quilted housecoat. Its warmth calmed Jinnie, and she went to dry her hair before Tuckin arrived with her soup.

* * *

Outside, it rained. Inside, Jinnie dreamt of snow. She drifted through a dark sky pricked with stars. Voices floated past her.

"I shall give you a rose from my garden in the spring."

"You shouldn't be left alone, my liege."

"You no longer exist in that world."

Jinnie turned restlessly in her sleep, brow furrowed. She was listening for one voice. One voice she loved.

"I'm here. You're safe now."

Where are you? Jinnie tried to call to him.

"I love you, Jinnie," he whispered.

She could feel his presence, the warmth of him, his scent, his touch.

"Run away with me."

"I will," Jinnie murmured.

She twisted in her sleep, wanting him to hold her closer, but he was far away now, lost to her, and all the sweetness of his love for her was fading with his voice.

"No!" Jinnie sat up, sweating, cold, gasping for breath. Her head hurt terribly. Where was he? Where was she?

Jinnie looked about her. She was in her bedroom, and it was only the dream again. This time, however, it had been different. Almost tangible. A reality all its own. The memory of her dream was supplanting the memory of her life.

Jinnie remembered warm brown eyes, reddish-gold hair, and a voice that touched her heart. She remembered he loved her, desired her, cared for her beyond everything. And he called her Jinnie. His *jinnie.*

"And now we're separated," Jinnie whispered.

She lay back into her pillows and pulled the sheets up under her chin, remembering herself safe and warm, with the man in her dream holding her close.

What was his name? She'd known it a moment before she woke up. Jinnie sighed. It would come back to her. He would come back to her. Or she would go to him.

Sleep beckoned, and Jinnie followed.

Two

In the morning, Jinnie was restless. She wandered through her home, touching a chair, a vase, a painting. Nothing held any meaning for her. Occasionally she would stop at a window and watch the rain. It pattered prettily today, like a visitor come to tea, but it offered no solace.

She searched room after room, unable to put aside the feeling that she had lost something. The intensity of emotions Jinnie felt for the man in her dream haunted her. She half expected to see him in the next room, around the next corner.

Never before had her dream felt so real. Her lover was tender and passionate, full of a love undeniable in its constancy.

Will my marriage be like that? Jinnie wondered. Or will it be brittle and dull, with nothing but duty and responsibility to keep me company?

She drifted into the parlor. An old piano stood in the corner. Aching for a distraction from the strange malaise that gripped her, she went to the piano and sat down. Lifting the lid, Jinnie gently drew a finger across the keys.

An echo of a familiar tune encouraged her. She played a few tentative notes, a chord, then a melody. As her fingers stroked the keys, images began to dance in her head: snow, a castle, a room full of people dancing.

Jinnie's brow furrowed. Where had she heard that music? And when? A trickle of pain slid behind her eyes. *It must be a part of my dream,* she thought.

Continuing to play, Jinnie looked up. A man stood across the room. He began to walk toward her. He was tall and pale, not at all like the man she dreamed of at night.

Jinnie's fingers tripped on a chord, but the music continued in her mind. Panicking, head throbbing, she pushed away from the piano, knocking the stool over and nearly falling.

The walls pulsed in time with the pain in her head. The room seemed to tilt. Staggering, arms stretched in front of her, Jinnie groped her way out of the room and into the hall. The air felt like water dragging at her limbs as she tried to hurry, not daring to check and see if the pale man was following her.

From a great distance, she saw a door and stumbled toward it. Stairs led down. That seemed right. And it was cold. That, too, was as it should be.

Like a sleepwalker now, Jinnie descended the steps. She no longer heard the music, but wind. And a voice, his voice, loved and missed.

Reaching the bottom of the stairway, she scanned the dimly lit cellar. There should be a door, and he should be waiting for her. What was his name?

Pain seared her like fire. Jinnie fainted.

* * *

Voices hovered over her, concerned, whispering.

Jinnie opened her eyes. "Where am I?"

She sat up abruptly, and the room seesawed.

"Be still," Tuckin ordered. He settled Jinnie back among the pillows. "The doctor says you will be fine, but you must rest."

"And eat," the doctor added, eyes stern. "You have neglected your health, young lady. Tuckin has told me all about your mournful behavior." Lifting a hand, he ticked off one finger per complaint.

"Long walks in the rain. Up in the night, prowling around the house. Too little sleep and too little food. I am surprised you did not faint sooner. True, you've had reason to be sorrowful. The loss of a parent is always difficult, but you must look to your future. Soon you will be leaving your home world for the planet Hura and a new life. We must keep you strong and healthy."

The doctor placed two small green tablets and a glass of water on a table by the bed.

"These will help her relax," the doctor said to Tuckin. "Give her two more at bedtime," he instructed.

Jinnie watched them leave the room; heads bowed together, voices murmuring. The door closed, and she sat up again, this time more slowly; the room stayed still.

"The planet Hura and a new life," Jinnie repeated the doctor's words.

Slipping out of bed, she went to her dressing table and sat down. A small computer terminal was on her left, and Jinnie accessed it automatically. She checked for any messages from the council, hoping for a notice of reprieve.

Without telling her father or even Tuckin, she had sent a letter to the council requesting exemption from the marriage law because she was an only child. There had been no response.

Jinnie rose and went to the window. Pushing aside the drapes, she leaned her forehead against the cold glass.

"What now?" she asked her watery reflection. "I travel to a strange world and marry a man I've never met?"

After the war, a council had been created to pursue peace and life. In agreement with Hura, it passed a law requiring one Breearian and one Huranite from each household of each new generation to intermarry. This mixing of bloodlines was to ensure that Breearians and Huranites would never again have cause to fight one another. Jinnie had known all of this since she was five. It had seemed exciting then. Now it troubled her.

"Pale words on a page," said Jinnie, her voice bitter, "with no feeling for the people who have to make them true."

She thought of the man in her dream. He beguiled her even when she was awake. He was more like a memory, not like a dream at all.

"I feel like I've lived another life somewhere else." Jinnie spoke aloud. "A life with him. The man who loves me more than anything any world has to offer."

Her head began to ache. "Stop daydreaming!" Jinnie scolded herself.

The words evoked a vague memory of her mother chastising her. *But Mother was always patient with me,* thought Jinnie. *Who am I remembering? Tuckin?*

The headache worsened.

Wondering if the doctor's pills would ease the discomfort, Jinnie went to the table beside her bed and paused.

The first stages of the Plague can be hard to diagnose, she thought. *Perhaps the consistency and intensity of my dream is a symptom. I've haven't mentioned it to Tuckin. Should I have confided in the doctor?*

And what would I tell him? Each night I dream of a man who loves me so much that the rest of my life is only bits and pieces of a world to which I feel I no longer belong. If I ever did. Now I do sound mad.

"The man in my dream is so real," Jinnie whispered. "More real than reality. Each time I see him, he becomes more substantial to me."

And the stranger I saw this morning? Jinnie questioned. *The man who looked like a ghost? I've never dreamt of him. Is he a hallucination?*

She took the pills. *The doctor would say it's stress, my imagination run amok. I'm just worried and anxious. Anyone would be.*

Tuckin would scold her for being childish, and then he would remind her of the law.

The law required everyone to walk through an Analyzer before leaving Breeare.

If I have the Plague, Jinnie remembered, *the Analyzer will detect it.*

Her thoughts wandered. What if she didn't have the Plague? What if the man in her dream was real?

Pausing at the mirror above her dresser, Jinnie confronted her reflection. "How could he be real?" she demanded. "It's the Plague."

No, she thought, *it isn't.*

Going back to her computer, Jinnie sat down. She pursed her lips. What kind of entry would be helpful? *Dreams* would be too vague. She would be inundated with speculation and theories. She must act on the premise that the man in her dream was real. She had to be specific. Her fingers started typing: *Information on Past Life Recall.*

The computer's screen flickered as it searched for data on Jinnie's request. A minute later, a list appeared on her computer screen. There was very little. A few book titles. A monthly Contact Site for sharing experiences.

"So, we're all mad." Jinnie sighed. She felt tired. The pills were working.

Turning off the computer, she climbed into bed. Tuckin would be back soon with more pills and more soup. He would certainly be cross with her if he caught her out of bed. An image flitted by of someone else in charge of her health. A woman. Not her mother. Who?

Her vision doubled, and Jinnie lay down, afraid she would faint again. She lay still. Gradually she felt better. Tired but not sleepy, she pulled a pillow from behind her head and tossed it to the floor, trying to find just the right position. The one that would allow her to relax and escape the creeping, inexplicable loneliness that threatened to engulf her. She wished for the man in her dream.

Jinnie let her thoughts drift. *Maybe he is more than a dream. Maybe he's part of my life from another time. I've read stories about such things.*

She couldn't remember when. Her childhood was a blur of faces and people to whom she no longer felt any connection.

A thin fear permeated Jinnie. Whatever ailed her was getting worse. The Plague or a chill caught from spending too much time out in the rain. Or?

A chill. Jinnie remembered hearing the word in a different context: the Chill. What did it mean? Cold. Fearsome cold.

Pain streaked across her forehead.

Jinnie forced herself to concentrate. A voice. Not his. A woman. A woman who knew about lives, past and future.

She was explaining something to me, Jinnie recalled. *Something important about my life. Something important, like what I felt yesterday.*

For a minute, the pain increased, then the doctor's pills overtook it, and Jinnie's mind relinquished its stranglehold on her memories. She fell asleep.

Again, there was snow. It blew all around her, but she felt safe because he was with her, holding her hand, holding her.

The kaleidoscope of her dream shifted, and it was summer. She lay in long grass, dry and warm. Sunlight poured over her body. And he was there. She heard his voice.

"Best-loved," he whispered. "My *jinnie*. I love you. Now and always."

His eyes were warm, dark brown. Long, reddish-gold hair framed his face. He leaned toward her, and she tilted her chin up to let him kiss her.

An hour, two hours, and Jinnie's dream of love and passion slipped away. A tear slipped free of her lashes. Wiping her cheek, she turned on her side, hugging a pillow. She felt sad and terribly lonely. He had called her that special name again. What was his?

"You're no dream," she said into the shadows of the room. "I remember you."

But no name came to her lips.

Long after Tuckin had come and gone and her soup had grown cold, Jinnie lay awake, thinking. People travel between planets, she mused, so why couldn't they travel through time?

Jinnie made a decision before she could chide herself.

The room was dark and cold, all its shapes merging into one.

"H. C.," Jinnie murmured, sitting up slowly. "Illumination, fifteen percent."

The overhead lighting warmed the room. Jinnie threw back the covers and got out of bed, pulling on her housecoat. She went to her computer.

"Time travel," she said, typing the entry.

Within seconds, a list of headings appeared. Scanning them, Jinnie picked one. "Crossing Time: The True Account of My Other Life," Jinnie read aloud.

She pushed the print key. Taking sixty pages of text, Jinnie returned to bed. She scanned several pages, then read.

"At first I thought it was *mettubah*, that uncomfortable feeling we all have that we have been somewhere before, done or seen something previously. Gradually, I came to realize I was recognizing pieces from another part of my existence that had occurred at a different point in time."

Jinnie skipped ahead.

"When I slept, my body, being relaxed and in a dream state, allowed my mind to travel back through time. Soon it became natural for me to experience my past and present at the same time, and for many years I lived a dual existence."

"A dual existence," Jinnie whispered. She listened inward, recalling a fireplace, a dark room, a woman's voice.

The pain began again, sharp and stabbing. The words on the page blurred.

Jinnie focused on the picture in her mind instead.

"Breathe the *somin*," the woman's voice said. "Look into the flames and drift."

Closing her eyes, Jinnie gritted her teeth against the pain and breathed deeply, trying to drift, trying to remember clearly.

A white castle. A room darkened against bright sunlight. A woman speaking to her through a mist, a fog. The woman was asking her questions, and she knew only one answer—she belonged with Griffin.

Pain lurched up from her stomach, making Jinnie gasp. The pages scattered to the floor as she staggered to her bathroom and retched. She sat on the floor, shaking, sweat making her cold. She had never felt so lonely.

"Griffin," Jinnie whispered. "Where are you?"

Her head pounded. For a moment, Jinnie thought she would be sick again. Holding onto the sink, she managed to stand. She washed her face with cool water and returned to bed, ignoring the papers on the floor. She'd had enough for one night.

Jinnie curled on her side, exhausted and anxious, afraid the pain would return. All she wanted now was to be with Griffin, and if sleep and dreams could take her to him, she would sleep and dream.

Jinnie tried to get comfortable; the pain and nausea abated. She twisted and turned, kicking at the sheets and blankets, finally sitting up.

Two pills were on the table by her bed. Jinnie took them both.

"H. C.," said Jinnie, "discontinue lighting and turn off personal computer terminal, this room."

She lay back in the darkness. *Wait,* she told herself. *Let the pills work so it won't hurt to remember.*

Jinnie turned on her side again, sliding one arm under her pillow. *I wonder why it hurts. Maybe it is the Plague. I don't know. I can't think. I'll read more tomorrow. Maybe I can contact the author of the article.*

Her eyes closed. Traveling through time. She might be traveling through time.

Don't think about it now. Not tonight. Think about last night's dream. That doesn't hurt. His face, his beautiful eyes, the feel of his arms about me.

Jinnie, my jinnie. His voice blew into her mind like snow.

Griffin. Jinnie smiled.

Three

As the air car sped across the moor, Jinnie watched the rain pummel the saturated earth. After the last two days, it was easy to imagine snow instead of rain. Gentle flakes or biting sleet with wind, it didn't matter because she was with Griffin.

When Jinnie tried to contact the author of the article she'd read, her computer had printed: deceased. She briefly scanned the other listings on time travel, accessing unhelpful information from studies, articles, and research that only frustrated her.

All the people who had been interviewed believed they had been part of Breeare's history, part of Breeare's past—usually as someone of importance, but always on Breeare. Not one person had experienced a life, a memory or even a dream of life on a different world, another planet. And no one mentioned pain of any kind.

For the people who had participated in the research, recalling time travel was tranquil and hypnotic. It was a reassurance of their immortality instead of a puzzling unhappiness and discontent. Feeling thwarted, Jinnie gave up.

Time travel might be an explanation for what she was experiencing: the voices in her mind, the sense of living another life somewhere, the repeated feelings of *mettubah*, but it didn't explain the pain.

The pain had lessened only enough to let her say his name, to let her believe in him, but not enough to discount the possibility that she had the Plague. Unwilling to speak to Tuckin about it, Jinnie sought comfort in the time she shared with Griffin.

Whenever she was with him, wherever he was, Jinnie felt safe and loved.

She went to bed early and slept late, forcing herself to eat only to quell Tuckin's concern. She smiled and pretended to listen, hardly aware of the activity around her: her father's return with the confirmation of her marriage, Tuckin's excitement, the packing, the travel details.

Good-bye hugs left her unmoved. Kind words to take care went unheard. Nothing touched her but Griffin and his love for her.

I love him, too, she thought. *If this is insanity from the Plague, then I am a willing victim.*

The ghostly apparition had not returned, and Jinnie had pushed it from her thoughts, telling herself it had been stress-induced. She didn't want to think about it.

A white tower pierced the clouds as they approached the City. A memory tickled Jinnie's mind, and her head began to ache. She had never been to the City, but the tower reminded her of something or somewhere. She looked at the City instead.

Other towers took shape. Narrow buildings stood between them like stark sentries with glass eyes and metal bodies rising sixty, ninety, one hundred and twenty feet into the air. Beige umbrellas hovered and moved like furtive animals. People, swathed in capes and long coats, hurried between the buildings, hunched beneath the rain, heads bowed as if grieving.

Air cars lifted off from the ground and the tops of towers, taking Nadinger Patrols to the moors. They took food and supplies to the few outlying communities and brought Plague victims back to the City's hospitals to die.

Most Breearians lived in their cities, afraid of the isolation which had contributed to their world's downfall. Driven apart by petty prejudices, they had been slow to unite against Hura. They had diverged again during peace talks until it was almost too late. Now their common foe lived among them: the Plague.

One hundred thousand Breearians remained from a population once one billion strong. The Plague killed hundreds more each year. Intermarriage was becoming not only a necessity for peace, but for the life of both peoples.

The Huranites, too, had suffered severely. Two hundred and fifty-eight thousand survived from an original population of six hundred and fifty million.

Their world had always been inhospitable, but while most of the war had been fought near and on Breeare, Hura had suffered famine and drought. Even with its smaller population, resources had quickly been exhausted through the long years of battle.

Slowly, the two worlds were trying to revive themselves and each other. Neither was certain it would succeed.

The air car dipped slightly, swinging past the City to the Interplanetary Hangar. Solar power was impossible now for Breeare, and fuel was scarce. Only twice a month, one ship ferried people between Breeare and Hura.

As the air car slowed to land, Jinnie wondered at her memory. She could recall so much of the general circumstances of life on Breeare, and yet it held no meaning for her. Griffin and her life with him had become her reality.

Jinnie started when one of the patrolmen spoke to her.

"I'm sorry. What did you say?"

"Your baggage will be loaded for you, madam. May I help you down?"

"Thank you." Jinnie stepped out into the rain.

"Safe journey, madam."

"Safe journey," replied Jinnie. For a moment, the exchange seemed familiar, as if she'd said similar words before. She watched as the two Nadingers returned to their car and lifted off. Alone, Jinnie looked up at the Hangar's huge double doors.

Now I will find out for certain, she thought. *I will walk through the Analyzer, and an alarm will go off. I'll be sent home for a while, and I will live out my days with Griffin.*

A Council Representative was hurrying toward her, Jinnie recognized the uniform.

"Are you Jinian Ray?" The woman's voice was as old and thin as her face, but her eyes were kind and bright.

"Yes," Jinnie nodded.

"Come with me, my dear. I have your ticket."

Smiling, the woman took Jinnie by the arm and ushered her into the building. "I have the final forms for you to sign."

"Forms?" Jinnie tried to pay attention, distracted by the whirl of people around her.

"Yes, dear. The legal documents are recorded in the City's computer files, and your marriage is registered. It all takes place here, you know. When you leave Breeare, you leave as a married woman."

The woman sat down at a desk. "Sit down, dear. It won't take long."

Jinnie sat down, staring blankly at a sheaf of papers in front of her.

"I have the name of your husband," the woman went on. "Let me see. Ah, here it is. His name is Kellen Kade. Quite a fine family, apparently. Your father made a good arrangement."

"I'm certain he did his best for me," Jinnie said. She took a deep breath, feeling nervous and uncomfortable. If her father had mentioned the details, she hadn't listened. She hadn't cared.

I still don't. Jinnie squared her shoulders. *What does it matter if a piece of paper or a computer's file says I'm married? I won't pass the Analyzer exam. I'll be sent home.*

Ignoring the sudden twinge of uncertainty, Jinnie pulled the scarf from her head and loosened her coat. Sitting across from the Council Representative, she signed the forms. There were a dozen or more. She didn't read them.

"There." The woman stood up with a smile. "That's all. Now let's get you through the Analyzer and aboard that Dusscraft."

Jinnie rose and followed the woman down a short hallway to a line of gleaming metal arches.

"Here's your ticket, dear. Hand it to the attendant at the end of the Analyzer. Oh, and this is your Certificate of Marriage. Your husband will want it to confirm identification."

Accepting the ticket and a narrow scroll, Jinnie again felt uneasy.

"Go on, dear," urged Jinnie's guide. "Just walk under the arches. Don't touch them. Once you've passed through, you'll be considered a citizen of Hura. Safe journey."

Jinnie nodded. She stepped nervously under the first arch. It hummed and glowed, but no alarm sounded.

There will be an alarm, thought Jinnie. *There has to be an alarm.*

Like an automaton, Jinnie moved down the length of arches toward the attendant waiting for her at the end.

"Ticket, please."

"Pardon?"

"Your ticket, madam."

Snapping out of her daze, Jinnie whirled about. At the other end of the tunnel of arches, the Council Representative waved at her and walked away.

"But ..." Jinnie turned back to the attendant. "Aren't I sick?"

"No, madam. The Analyzer would have sent up an alarm if you even had a fever. May I have your ticket, please?"

Jinnie handed over her ticket.

"Thank you. Welcome to Hura. Proceed down the corridor to the ramp. The Dusscraft is ready to launch. You'll just make it. Safe journey."

Jinnie did as she was instructed. Dismay and trepidation made her sick to her stomach.

Reaching the ship, Jinnie walked up the ramp and stepped aboard. She didn't look back.

Inside the ship it was warm, the lighting dim. Even as she reached an empty seat, Jinnie could feel the slight vibration as the engines started.

Within minutes, the Hangar doors opened, and the cumbersome Dusscraft became an agile thing of beauty as it took slowly to the air.

Looking out the window, Jinnie saw the City fall away on her right. Now she could see the moors, now a vast expanse of horizon, now nothing but clouds pushing up against the pane.

For an instant, the ship seemed to stall, suspended between clouds and the stratosphere as it fought the gravitational pull of Breeare. Then it broke free, soaring into space, and Jinnie saw the sun, the moons, the stars.

She studied the dark outside the Dusscraft's window, seeking her new home. Finding it. Hura. It was beautiful; a crimson jewel on a satin cape. A hundred years before, all of Breeare had been able to see Hura. Dancing in the night sky, first mysterious, then welcome, then threatening. And now forever masked by clouds.

Jinnie looked down at her hands, clasped together in her lap. The knuckles were white. Her mind roared with questions.

Is this really happening? What about my life with Griffin? If it's not the Plague, what is it? What do I do now? Who can I turn to for help?

Having convinced herself she had the Plague, Jinnie was completely unprepared to be sent away from her home and given as a token of peace to a man she'd never met and didn't love.

She'd expected to have time with Griffin. Would he be with her still? Was she traveling through time, or was Griffin and their life together nothing more than an escape from a reality Jinnie didn't want to accept? A beautiful, temporary insanity?

Jinnie took a deep breath. *I have to accept my situation*, she lectured herself. *I don't have the Plague; the Analyzer proved that. I can't continue to believe something extraordinary is happening to me. I'm about to be a wife, and eventually I'll be a mother. I have to be strong.*

I don't know if I'll be loved. If I am, I know it won't be like Griffin's love for me.

Stop it! He isn't real. He can't be. Because that would mean I've lost the only love I ever wanted.

Jinnie looked out the window at the red planet, now below her. "That's what's real," she said aloud. "That's what I must accept and what I must believe in."

She tensed as the Dusscraft entered Hura's atmosphere. The ship seemed to float gracefully toward the surface before it docked, then it was awkward and ungainly once more.

Feeling unable to move, Jinnie watched as the other passengers disembarked. When the last person had gone, she stood up and left the ship.

Her heart beat crazily as she walked down a short corridor toward a creamy light. For a wild moment, she thought of snow.

No! Jinnie raged at herself. *No more! Leave it all behind now. No more daydreams or wishful thinking. No more time travel—if that was what it was. It's in the past. He's in the past. And I'm here, on Hura.*

At the doorway, she paused. The platform outside was crowded with people. She remembered what Tuckin had told her: "You are a Lady and must act the part."

Act the part, thought Jinnie, stepping forward.

Sunlight stroked her hair like warm, familiar fingers, and she tilted her head toward it, blinking. The sun shone through a brown haze high above.

Jinnie stood still and let the light soak through her.

The castle towers will be sparkling, she thought. The white towers of Keldonabrieve.

"Madam Jinian Ray?" The language was Breearian.

Keldonabrieve? thought Jinnie. Reluctant to release the memory, Jinnie turned toward the voice. She blinked several times, bringing the man who addressed her into focus.

He was much taller than she, with black hair and a neatly trimmed beard. His eyes were dark, his skin deeply tanned. He wore a loose white shirt under a sleeveless jacket of purple and red. Brown trousers were tucked neatly into short brown boots.

He reminded Jinnie of someone. Someone older, someone … unpleasant.

"Yes. I'm Jinian," she answered.

"I'm Kellen Kade." He smiled.

Receiving no response, Kellen stepped closer. "I'm your husband," he added.

Automatically, Jinnie extended her hand. Kellen hesitated, then solemnly took her hand, lifted it to his lips, and pressed a kiss against her fingers.

"None of that until tonight," a nasal voice reprimanded.

Jinnie looked down. A small man with a round belly and long curling hair glared up at her. He nodded curtly.

"I'm Prispos Pern, Master Kade's Duecan. If you will show me your Marriage Papers, Madam, we will be on our way to the reception."

Jinnie handed him the scroll of papers, astonished to see someone so small, but trying not to show it.

The little man unfurled the script gravely, subjecting it to a thorough scrutiny.

"Yes. Hmmm. Yes. All in good order. There are one or two minor documents to be signed by both of you, but that will be later. For now," he said as he bowed stiffly to Jinnie, "welcome to Hura, Madam Kade."

Four

No wind accompanied the sunset, and the stillness of the lifeless plain was oppressive. Jinnie stood at the window of her room, watching until the night swallowed the sun.

She felt disconnected from the world around her, just as she had on Breeare. Jinnie thought of Griffin. She missed him. As soon as she'd renounced her other life, she missed it. She missed it all.

"I'll start to feel love for Kellen," Jinnie told the night. "I'll get to know him and like him, and then these ideas of living another life somewhere will fade away."

Looking at the endless plain, she doubted what she said. She wanted to see snow, not grass. She wanted to feel a fire's warmth, not processed air. And she wanted to hear a certain voice whisper her special name.

Frowning, Jinnie turned away from the window. She hugged herself, rubbing her arms, cold in spite of the heat. Her floor-length dress of red chiffon was meant to keep her cool, but Jinnie's forehead was damp with anxiety.

She paced the room. It was all stark grays and harsh whites, without regard for comfort or beauty. Within its confines, Jinnie felt the loneliness of the hundred miles of nothing but brown grass and red earth outside.

The Huranites no longer lived in cities as the Breearians now did. Now the citizens of Hura lived far apart, in family groups, with each group assigned an area of land for regeneration.

"You will not be expected to participate in any of the Family's duties, of course," Prispos Pern had announced on the ride from the Station.

"The seeding, farming, and restoration of the land is the responsibility of the Family Kade. Your responsibility is to bear and raise children for the future of Hura."

"And Breeare," Jinnie had added.

"Yes, yes," Prispos had said dismissively. "Of course, you will produce a son first."

Startled, Jinnie could only nod.

That was the total conversation until they arrived at the Kade Station. Kellen had said nothing at all.

At the front door of the house, Prispos ordered Bella, the housekeeper, to escort the new Madam Kade to her room. Jinnie was to rest and then dress for the reception. Red, Jinnie had been instructed, was the appropriate color for such an official occasion. Red, the color of Hura.

The door to her room slid open, and Jinnie turned to face the stranger who was her husband. He, too, wore red, highlighted with a sleeveless jacket of white.

"You look beautiful, Jinian," said Kellen. He proffered his hand. "The reception has begun. I've come to escort you."

"Thank you."

Feeling as stiff as the conversation, Jinnie crossed the room and accepted his hand. It was cold, and his fingers curled about hers like a vise.

Looking up into Kellen's eyes, Jinnie again thought she saw something familiar. She had a strong feeling that she'd known someone like him before. Someone she disliked.

Kellen brushed a finger against her cheek. "Do they call you Jinnie?"

This time her nickname brought a flash of memory to Jinnie's mind and a sharp pain behind her eyes.

"A *jinnie* is the Kabada word for someone who is best-loved." The voice in her head was Griffin's.

"No," Jinnie lied. "No, I'm called by my proper name. Always."

"Very well. Jinian." Kellen's tone made her name an insult. "We're late."

He turned and led her quickly down a corridor toward the banquet hall. Jinnie almost had to run to keep up with his long strides.

She wished she could be free of Kellen's painful grip, but for the next hour, she was his prisoner, introduced to and inspected by dozens of people.

"Let her sit down, Kellen," a kind voice said. "She's pale."

Kellen hesitated a barely perceptible moment. Then, brushing Jinnie's hand with a kiss, he released her. "I'll send Prispos for you when it's time to sign the papers."

"Yes. Thank you," Jinnie stammered, tense and anxious. The feeling that she didn't like him persisted. Unconsciously, she rubbed her hand.

As Kellen moved off into the crowd, Jinnie turned to face her rescuer. A short, plump woman in a brown and green suit stood with her hands clasped behind her back. Graying curls haloed blue eyes and a round face. Then the woman smiled: a beauteous smile that seemed to surge up from her soul to welcome Jinnie.

"Come sit down," the woman suggested, leading Jinnie to a window seat. "I'm Susatch."

"I'm very pleased to meet you."

"That's because you haven't heard of me," Susatch teased her. "If you had, you'd be avoiding me."

"Why?"

"Well, first because I'm the doctor in these parts. Always poking my nose into other people's business."

"And second?"

"Second, because I'm the nearest thing to an anarchist you'll meet anywhere on Hura; if you listen to some."

"And if I listen to you?" Jinnie asked, liking Susatch's easy manner.

"If you listen to me, I'll bore you with my theories: the power of the subconscious mind, past lives,"–Susatch leaned forward with an air of conspiracy–"even traveling through time."

Jinnie sat very still. Had the doctor really said time travel?

Susatch laughed. "All very unprofessional theories and extremely tiresome and annoying to my patients, but they're stuck with me." Susatch chortled. "And now you are too."

"I don't think I'll find you or your theories tiresome."

"Well, now, honesty is something I find too little of." Susatch patted Jinnie's hand. "I'm in charge of the health of the Family Kade," she continued, "and three other stations in this area. That's my job. But, if you have any troubles, questions or just need to talk, call me. That's my friendship."

Jinnie felt the first genuine warmth from a person since she'd left Breeare. "Thank you, Susatch."

Susatch studied the young woman sitting next to her. Thin and pale, no doubt frightened, and yet there seemed to be something else about her: an eerie quality that didn't belong amongst the crowd of insincere well-wishers and well-spoken gossips.

"You're nervous," observed Susatch. "I bet you feel like you don't belong."

Jinnie nodded. "Yes. I'm sorry."

"No need to apologize. It's a natural response to a new situation. All these people, a new home, a new world, and a husband. Of course you're nervous. But the world is reviving, the home is in order, and the people aren't so bad, most of them. Some take themselves too seriously. They forget that a wedding is an occasion for happiness, not just a consummation of peace agreements."

Susatch nodded at the room of people. "They've been looking you over like a piece of livestock. I confess, I've been watching you, too."

"And what is your diagnosis, doctor?" Jinnie teased.

"I like you."

Jinnie smiled. Just having Susatch near made her feel better. Perhaps here was someone she could trust, even confide in. But what would she confide?

I don't like my husband? He reminds me of someone I think I once knew? Oh, and by the way, I recently thought I might have traveled through time?

"Ah, there you are." Prispos Pern marched up to them, managing to look fierce in spite of his diminutive stature.

"Master Kade is waiting for you, Madam. It is time to sign the final papers and then begin the feast. Come along."

Jinnie rose reluctantly. She had felt safe near Susatch.

"Will I see you later?" Jinnie asked her.

"Soon enough, soon enough." Susatch waved her on. "I'm always about or underfoot or looking over someone's shoulder."

Prispos had taken firm hold of Jinnie's skirt and was dragging her through the crowd.

Jinnie looked about, searching wave upon wave of strange faces. Where was he? Then a voice claimed her.

"Ah, Jinnie." Kellen smiled.

What's wrong with his smile? Jinnie wondered. It's like a mask. She had a sudden impulse to run away. She stood still, wishing he hadn't called her by her special name, but she could say nothing in front of all the people. She had to act the part, to play the lady and now the wife.

Kellen snatched her hand up. "I hope Susatch didn't bore you."

"No. Not at all."

"Good. Come then. Let's get the business done with and start the feast. And the night."

His dark eyes showed only her reflection; no warmth illuminated them or his words.

Pushing aside her trepidation, Jinnie nodded. "Of course," she answered, Kellen's prisoner once again.

* * *

Waiting for Kellen, Jinnie felt sick with anxiety. She pulled the bedcovers close. Too much wine had failed to dull her uneasiness.

Not once throughout the long feast had she felt comfortable with Kellen. He had spoken little and laughed not at all.

The bedroom door opened, splitting the dark with light. Kellen entered, the door shut, and silence was their chaperone. Moonlight slipped inside a window, allowing Jinnie to watch her husband remove his robe before he slid into the narrow bed beside her.

Jinnie lay still, heart pounding.

At last, Kellen spoke. "Your behavior this evening was perfect, Jinian. I'm certain no one suspected your dislike of me."

Jinnie inhaled sharply, not knowing what to say.

Kellen turned to her. He raised himself up on one elbow and pulled back the covers.

Jinnie flinched. She forced herself to look into Kellen's cold eyes. "I don't know what you mean. I don't dislike you," she lied.

"No matter," he said. He touched her hair. "As long as you please me."

Leaning over her, Kellen kissed Jinnie's lips possessively, hurting her. She managed to twist her head away as he pulled her hips against his.

"Be still," he whispered, moving on top of her and thrusting inside her body.

Jinnie pushed against his shoulders, but Kellen ignored her. His breath rasped in Jinnie's ear, and the motion of his hips lifted her from the bed.

The small of Jinnie's back began to ache. Screaming in her mind, she held onto Kellen and waited for it to be over. His breathing quickened, and the painful motion increased. Finally Kellen shuddered and lay still. "Jinnie," he said.

Jinnie hated the sound of his voice, the weight of his body, and the smell of his skin. She tried to move, and Kellen rolled away. After a moment, he got out of bed.

Pulling on his robe, he turned back to face her, eyes studying her still form. "I'm pleased," he said, his voice clinical and detached. "Sleep well." He paused. "Jinnie."

The slight snap of the closing door was like the breaking of a bone. Jinnie pushed herself up from where she lay, too shaken to be angry.

"Computer," she said, "soft lights."

Jinnie waited, trying to slow her breathing. Kellen did not return. Swinging her legs over the side of the bed, Jinnie stood up. Naked, she crossed to the bathroom and washed her face, letting the tepid water drip down her throat and between her breasts.

She looked in the mirror. Her body was sore, and her neck was red from Kellen's beard, but her only injury was her mind.

Returning to the bed, Jinnie noticed the bottle of wine on the table beside it. She also noticed how her hands shook as she poured herself a glass. After drinking it, she poured another. After a third, Jinnie piled the pillows against the headboard, straightened the bed, and climbed into its cool comfort.

Pulling her knees to her chest, she reached for her glass. She drank slowly this time, encouraging exhaustion to replace shock and dismay.

I'm not strong enough to endure this kind of life, Jinnie despaired. *I need Griffin. I need to feel his love for me.*

Jinnie sipped her wine. *Was it only this morning I told myself he was an escape? After listening to Susatch, maybe my first ideas were right. Maybe something extraordinary is happening to me.*

The Analyzer proved only that Griffin wasn't a Plague-induced hallucination. It didn't prove he didn't exist somewhere. And Kellen had proved to be the worst of her fears. She would be unloved. She was only a necessary part of a larger package: peace.

But what happens to me? How do I live like this? Jinnie set her glass down.

"Computer," said Jinnie, "lights off."

The room darkened to shadows defined by strands of moonlight. Sliding beneath the covers, Jinnie turned on her side.

Come to me, Griffin, she thought. *No other life, real or imagined, can be more insane than this reality.*

The wine permeated Jinnie's muscles, coaxing her to relax. She slept.

And he was there. She saw him running. Running with her. Running through snow. Then she saw a fire. The two of them together on a bed of furs.

"I have never stopped loving you. Jinnie. My *jinnie*."

As he spoke, his face became clear, and Jinnie reached to touch him.

"I remember you," she whispered.

Pain swept down on her, sharp and bitter, making Jinnie frown and twist in her sleep.

"I love you," he said. His voice was rich velvet to her ears. "Now and always."

"I love you," Jinnie murmured in her sleep. In her other life, she kissed him and wrapped her arms tightly around him. "I love you, Griffin."

The wine won the battle against the pain, and Jinnie sank into a deeper sleep. A slight smile lifted one corner of her mouth.

Five

Jinnie resisted getting out of bed, wanting only to sleep and, by sleeping, stay with Griffin. She had lost track of the length of her internment. It could have been two weeks or two months.

When she tried to contact Susatch, Jinnie was informed that the doctor was attending a conference on the other side of Hura. Left with the unpleasant reality of her new life, Jinnie stopped trying to understand her other life. Instead she retreated into it.

She still felt pain when she concentrated on details or asked herself questions. Sometimes she felt disoriented and dizzy, but Jinnie didn't care. Griffin was worth it. She embraced her other life as tightly as Griffin embraced her.

Days dragged by in silent stillness; and the nights, punctuated by Kellen's unwelcome trysts, were long and restless. Only in the predawn coolness could Jinnie find sleep and the reality of her other life with Griffin. He was always there; his love was her anchor.

Once, when Kellen had pulled her roughly beneath him, Jinnie tried to pretend he was Griffin. But Griffin would never hold her too tightly or leave her too soon, empty and wanting.

"Madam Kade!"

Jinnie sat up quickly. She pulled up the strap of her nightgown as Bella yanked the curtains apart and allowed sunlight to rape the room.

"The doctor is here. You can breakfast with her in the atrium."

"Susatch?" Jinnie heard hope in her voice.

"Yes, yes. She's returned from her business. Get washed. Get dressed." Bella marched from the room to apply order to the rest of her day.

Eager to talk with Susatch, Jinnie dressed quickly, pausing only at her dressing table. Her long, blonde hair defied haste. Scowling, Jinnie picked up her brush.

A movement behind her caught her eye. Thinking it was Kellen, Jinnie turned. She dropped the brush.

A tall man with silver-blonde hair stood next to the bed. He was the same ghostly man she had seen on Breeare. The outline of his body shimmered, but his green eyes pierced Jinnie with an unnerving steadiness.

Jinnie backed up against the dressing table.

The man advanced. The outline of his body wavered, but his stride remained purposeful. She could see the pallor of his skin, the thin line of his nose.

He spoke, but Jinnie heard no words. Then he walked through her as if she were the one who did not exist.

Shaking, sweating with fear, Jinnie sat down, gripping the edge of the dressing table. Anxiety muddled her thinking: she should brush her hair, she should scream, she should run away. She should do something, tell someone.

"Susatch," Jinnie said aloud, holding the thought like a lifeline.

* * *

In the atrium Susatch waited patiently, enjoying the flowers and the respite from the heat. The tinted glass of the roof provided shade for the many imported plants, and artificial humidity had coaxed a few of them to blossom. Greenhouses were a necessity on Hura; a private one was an expensive luxury.

"It's missing something," Susatch mused aloud.

"A fountain," said Jinnie, coming to stand beside her. "Breearians always place fountains amongst flowers as a symbol of hope."

"That's it." Susatch nodded. "I've been to Breeare once, and I remember a beautiful fountain in the city solarium. It fell in tiers, and at night each tier was lit with lights of different colors."

"That sounds like the fountain in Eridana."

"Yes. Eridana."

"Yes. That is a pretty one."

Susatch's eyes scanned the young woman beside her. *Definitely unhappy*, she thought. "How are you, Jinian?"

"Please, call me Jinnie."

"Thank you. I will. Now tell me, Jinnie, how are you?"

Jinnie opened her mouth, but Susatch held up a hand to stop her. "Don't bother to say you're fine. Bella has already told me you sleep too much and eat too little."

Jinnie nodded. "All right. I'm not fine. In fact, I think I might be going mad."

"Really?" Taking Jinnie by the arm, Susatch guided her to a small table where Bella had set out breakfast.

"I thought I was going mad once. It turned out to be sunstroke. Of course"— Susatch pointed at the chair opposite her– "you don't go out of the house. Also, people who are going mad don't generally think about their mental health. So, what's really happening?"

Sitting down, Jinnie pushed back her hair from her face and confronted Susatch's kind eyes.

"The night we met," Jinnie began, uncertain how to start, "you mentioned your interest in time travel."

"Yes."

"Well, I think I might be experiencing time travel," Jinnie said in a rush.

"Oh?" Susatch drank some juice. "Why do you think that?"

Grateful not to be ridiculed, Jinnie continued. "I feel like part of me is living another life somewhere, and that life is where I'm meant to be."

"How long have you been feeling this way?"

Jinnie looked up at the domed ceiling. "For a very long time now. At first I thought I was dreaming, but more and more, it started to feel like I was remembering."

"What do you remember?"

Jinnie hesitated. "A place." She looked down at her plate. "A man."

"Who?"

"I don't know. I mean, I know him, I know he loves me, but I can't remember clearly the circumstances that brought us together. I know his voice, his face, his touch." Jinnie looked away.

"And I remember other things: snow, a castle, people dancing." Jinnie winced as the pain, too, began to dance.

"I remember a beautiful summer afternoon." Jinnie tried to ignore the pain. "I ... I remember." She faltered, losing her focus. "I know it sounds insane, but I feel like I belong there, with him."

Susatch tilted her head thoughtfully. "Go on."

"I used to think it was a dream, and it is clearer when I'm asleep, but it all feels too real to be a dream." Jinnie looked directly at Susatch. "And then there's what happened this morning."

"What happened this morning?"

"I saw a man, more like a ghost. I saw him once before, on Breeare. I don't know who he is. He's not been part of anything I remember. He seemed to be trying to say something to me, and then he just disappeared."

"Now that is disconcerting," said Susatch. She thought a moment.

"What about the other fellow, the one who loves you?"

"Griffin," Jinnie said.

"Griffin. Do you see him when you're awake?"

"No. I remember him."

"This is a puzzle."

Jinnie rubbed her temples.

"Headache?" Susatch reached for Jinnie's wrist and took her pulse.

"Yes. Whenever I remember. And sometimes I feel sick."

"Any dizziness? Fainting?"

Jinnie thought back to Breeare: down the stairs to the cellar, icy cold, burning pain then nothingness. "Yes."

Leaning back, Susatch pointed at Jinnie's breakfast. "Eat, and then I'll do a Medical Scan."

Jinnie ate her breakfast as if it were medicine.

"Let's consider the possible medical and emotional causes first," said Susatch. "Poor diet, lack of exercise. That can have all sorts of mental repercussions."

"You think I'm having a breakdown?" Jinnie shook her head. "I thought you, of all people, would believe me."

"As a friend, I believe you. As your doctor, however, I have to consider all possibilities. For instance, I have to ask how your marriage is. Just part of the whole doctor protocol."

Susatch studied Jinnie's young face. "So, how's your marriage?"

Jinnie fingered her glass of juice. "Unhappy," she conceded.

"Yes. I worried it might be. Kellen is not an easy man to get along with. He's always struck me as a bit paranoid. The death of his first wife must have been a terrible blow."

Jinnie looked up. "I didn't know Kellen had been married before."

"I'm not surprised. That sort of thing is always hushed up. I didn't know either until I received his Health Records. It happened before my assignment to this region. His first wife fell down the stairs and broke her neck."

"What stairs? This house has only one floor."

"The stairs to a cellar."

Memories crashed against one another like waves. Jinnie stood up abruptly. "The cellar. I have to see it."

"What?" Susatch frowned. "Why?"

"I'm not sure. I remember something about a cellar leading to a place of safety. In the life I remember with Griffin."

Jinnie steadied herself. "Susatch, please." She reached for the doctor's hand. "Please help me. Show me where the cellar is."

"I haven't even examined you yet," complained Susatch.

"After the cellar. I promise. I'll do whatever you prescribe."

Faced with so much urgency and passion, Susatch relented. "All right. But finish your breakfast first. I'm not poking around an old cellar on an empty stomach."

* * *

"Why does Kellen have a fireplace in his room?" asked Jinnie, glancing over her shoulder in case Bella should appear.

Examining the mantelpiece for the release key, Susatch said, "It was part of the original house. The one destroyed in the war. The house"— she looked at Jinnie and winked,—"with the cellar."

Jinnie nodded. Before the war, Hura's winters had been very cold.

"Aha! Here it is." Susatch twisted a piece of molding, and the entire fireplace slid aside, revealing hollow blackness.

"Bring a light." Susatch pointed to her left.

Lifting a travel light from the wall, Jinnie joined Susatch by the entrance she had uncovered.

"After you." Susatch waved a hand.

Grimacing, Jinnie ducked her head and stepped into the unwelcoming pitch beyond. She stumbled as Susatch bumped into her from behind.

"Sorry." Susatch's voice bounced off the walls as she peered around. "It's a closet."

"No," Jinnie almost whispered, "it's a—" She was interrupted by the hiss of the entrance sliding shut. The small room shuddered, creaked, and descended.

"It's an elevator," said Susatch.

"Yes." An uncomfortable, familiar anxiety accompanied Jinnie as they traveled downward. "But where are the stairs?"

"I don't know. Maybe this thing is taking us to them. It's in pretty good condition for something that hasn't been in use for a hundred years," observed Susatch.

The elevator jerked to a stop; a door opposite the two women slid open. Again, blackness, now shrouded with the heavy smell of earth and decay.

"A crypt?" Susatch suggested.

Holding the travel light high, Jinnie stepped forward. Her shadow was flung unevenly against the walls of a long, crumbling corridor.

"Come on." Jinnie felt a tremor of excitement. She knew she was close to remembering something important.

Susatch was right behind her. The floor was broken in places, and the walls seemed to bleed with the red clay of Hura pressing in on them.

They crept along the corridor for several minutes. Susatch was about to suggest they give up when Jinnie stopped.

"Look!" Jinnie pointed to their right. "Stairs."

A thin railing followed narrow steps that dropped into darkness.

Jinnie started forward, but Susatch grasped her upper arm, holding her back. "I don't think they're safe, Jinnie. We've found the stairs; we know they lead to a cellar. Let's go back."

"The elevator worked," Jinnie argued. "The stairs will be safe enough."

Susatch looked skeptical.

"We have to go down them," Jinnie insisted. "I have to. Please, Susatch."

Susatch released her, admitting her curiosity only to herself. "All right. But I'll go with you. Some doctor I'd be if I let you go alone."

Jinnie smiled, relieved and grateful. "I wonder what Kellen's first wife was doing down here?"

"I wonder what his second wife is doing down here."

"Don't you see?" Jinnie turned haunted eyes to Susatch. "I'm remembering. You think I could be imagining Griffin and this other life because I'm unhappy or not eating enough or not getting enough sleep. You're even doubting your own belief in time travel now that I'm confronting you with it. I told you, Susatch. I told you I wouldn't find you or your theories tiresome or annoying."

Susatch sighed. "I know. You told me. But I reserve my right to skepticism until I have medical proof that what you're talking about is real."

"It's real," said Jinnie, her voice soft with happiness. "Somehow it's real. I know that now. Griffin's real. My other life is real. I'm not ill, and it's not my imagination."

Jinnie faced the staircase. "I'm remembering."

"Maybe," Susatch conceded. "But which man are you remembering?"

"The one who loves me."

"Uh-huh. That's who you want it to be, but suppose it's the other man? The one from this morning? Maybe he loves you, too."

Jinnie straightened her shoulders. "Either way, I have to remember."

Susatch capitulated. "Let's go then. But carefully."

Jinnie nodded. She reached for the railing, and they started down the stairs, pausing frequently to shine the light ahead of them. The stairs were steep, and a misplaced step would easily send a person tumbling to the bottom.

Cold air clutched at them. Their footsteps echoed, and their breath drifted like ghosts in the dim light. Their descent continued; it seemed endless.

"Nobody has a cellar this deep," Susatch remarked.

Jinnie tripped as the last stair met concrete, smooth and hard.

"What is this place?" asked Jinnie. Determination gave way to apprehension as she shone the travel light back and forth. Its brightness was quickly swallowed by the vast space before them.

"I've no idea," Susatch stepped around Jinnie. "It's awfully big for a cellar. It's more like a cavern of some sort."

"A cavern." Jinnie shivered as a rush of pain made her back up. A cavern. Snow. Danger. She put her hand against the rock wall to steady herself. Words on a wall. Words she had written. Griffin.

"Jinnie? Jinnie!" Susatch was gripping Jinnie's shoulders, shaking her.

"It's okay." Jinnie took a deep breath. "I'm all right."

"No, you're not. I think we'd better go back."

"Not yet. Please." Jinnie moved forward, trying to ignore the slivers of pain at the back of her neck. She had almost remembered. Any moment now, her mind would clear. She would remember again, and everything would make sense.

Jinnie lifted the light high. "Griffin?"

Beside her, Susatch gasped. An obelisk, perhaps forty feet high and twenty feet around, loomed before them.

"What is it?" asked Jinnie.

Susatch shook her head in dismay. "It's a missile, Jinnie. A bomb. It's an interplanetary bomb."

* * *

In his air car, Kellen entered the password into the private line of his computer.

"Send this to Elena, Station 55," he said.

The computer whirred. A red light blinked, indicating it was ready to encrypt.

Kellen turned the wheel of the air car a little, studying the arid landscape. "K to E. Two more are secured. Launch will begin as scheduled. Code name for launch sequence: purity."

Sunlight stabbed through the brown haze of pollution, and Kellen narrowed his eyes. He reached for his visor, thinking of Jinnie. He would have to kill her soon. It was a shame, really. She was a pretty pleasure.

Too bad she's a Breearian. His thoughts returned to Elena, his mistress. They'd be together soon now.

When all of Breeare is dead. Kellen smiled. *Including my dear wife.*

Six

Jinnie watched from her bedroom window as Susatch's car sped away from the house and disappeared over the bleak horizon.

The scenario with Susatch minutes earlier had pushed a memory of a similar situation into her mind: a memory of deception and a need to escape. Whatever she had gone through before with Griffin, Jinnie felt she was reliving it now.

"Stay in bed as much as possible," Susatch had instructed. "You're supposed to be sick. I'll have Bella bring your meals to your room."

"What do I have?"

"I'll think of something."

"What about Kellen?" Jinnie worried.

Susatch held up her hand. "I'll handle him. You're not to be disturbed. Doctor's orders. I'll return in two days. If I don't continue my rounds, there will be questions, and we have enough of our own."

Jinnie had nodded, trying to hold on to the brief happiness she had felt before they discovered the bomb.

"Okay." Susatch had given Jinnie a gentle hug. "Be strong for me, Jinnie. I'll find out what I can about what's in the cellar."

"All right."

"As for you and what you're experiencing …" Susatch snapped open her Medical Scanner, ran it quickly up and down in front of Jinnie, and snapped it shut again.

"I'll process this information at my personal lab. I won't send it to the general one. It might diagnose some physical reason for your memory disturbances. Meanwhile, if you do remember anything again, or if you have any more ghostly encounters, write it down. Don't use the computer. It's too easily accessed."

"Thank you, Susatch."

"For what?"

"For being a friend. My friend."

"Thank me later. When we've lived through what's to come."

Jinnie had tried to smile and failed. Since the discovery of the bomb, she'd been afraid. Alone now, she felt sick to her stomach at the thought of Kellen's treachery.

Treachery. The word made more memories surface. Jinnie saw a room lit by firelight. She and Griffin were talking about someone. Her husband.

"Lancin," whispered Jinnie, wincing as her head began to pound. "No." She inhaled deeply. "I've got to be strong for Susatch and Griffin."

Jinnie forced the current reality into focus: Kellen and his bomb.

Who else is involved? Jinnie pondered. What's their plan? Are there other bombs? Other bombs waiting to be deployed, waiting to annihilate Breeare?

Turning away from the nauseating speculations, Jinnie moved slowly through the heat, drifting about her room. Feigning illness, Kellen's betrayal, the possibility of war, all these separate elements were unpleasantly familiar and too much to bear without Griffin. Her head ached, and Jinnie lay down on her bed. She wished for rain. No, for snow.

Instead, a picture began to form in her mind. Jinnie saw a world of green moss and silver rivers. Granite spires rose from the earth, hundreds of feet high, their narrow columns carved with curious sculptures and symbols. Strange houses, crowned with flowers and wreathed with mist, graced the towers' pinnacles.

The sky was orange and white, streaked with soft clouds the color of amethyst. The valley below it was waiting, expectant.

Jinnie sat up. "Write it down," she said aloud.

Unnerved, Jinnie rose and crossed the room unsteadily, the vision of the unknown world still clear in her mind.

She reached the computer table. A short, determined search of its drawers revealed a thin, clothbound book. All the pages were blank. Sitting down, Jinnie wrote quickly of what she had just seen and felt. It didn't cause her pain to think of it.

Susatch will help me understand, thought Jinnie. *Maybe she can even help me find a way to get back to Griffin.*

She tapped her lips with the pen, then wrote again, more carefully. Snow. A castle called Keldonabrieve. The color of Griffin's eyes. The pain flowed and ebbed as Jinnie described her other life. She clenched her teeth and continued writing.

My hair was dark brown and my eyes ... blue. And I was taller. Older, too. Maybe 35 or 36?

Some time later, muscles aching, she closed the book. The pain lessened to another headache. Jinnie fingered the book's spine. She knew she had to hide it. The details were too intimate. If Kellen found it, he'd be furious.

Looking about her bedroom, Jinnie chose underneath her pillow as her diary's temporary hiding place. When Susatch returned, she would place it in her care.

Jinnie was certain what she'd written was from memory, all except her ghost and the strange landscape she'd just seen. They were pieces of the puzzle she couldn't fathom.

She stretched against the heat, grateful as the headache diminished. Lifting her hair from the back of her neck, Jinnie wound it into a bun. She needed a comb to hold it in place.

Jinnie looked at her dresser, at its mirror. Cautiously she crossed the room. No apparition followed her reflection, and only her anxious eyes gazed back at her. Relieved, she pushed a comb into her hair, stripped off her damp gown, and went to the closet for a light robe. As she pulled it on, the room swayed, tilted, and Jinnie grabbed the edge of the doorway.

From a great distance, she could see her bed. It stayed still while the room around it seemed to pulse like waves on a beach.

Intense pain snaked through Jinnie's body, making her gasp. She stretched out an arm and staggered forward. Reaching her sanctuary, Jinnie crawled onto the bed. The room spun crazily about her, and wind roared in her ears. She fainted.

She didn't stir when Bella brought her noon meal. At dinner time, she had only turned over onto her back. Bella drew a light sheet over Jinnie and left her alone.

Night crept into Jinnie's room and embraced her with soothing coolness. Sleep chased away the frown of pain between her brows, and a small smile lifted the corners of her mouth.

"Griffin," Jinnie whispered.

* * *

In a dark corner of the city planning offices, Susatch bent her head over a computer, quietly scanning the private details of the personal resources of the Family Kade. Her privileges as a doctor had given her access, but she had to circumvent several tags and warnings to retrieve what she wanted: land holdings and architectural plans.

It was late, and the cold of the building was no longer welcome. Susatch was about to give up when she noticed something.

"Freeze frame," she ordered.

She studied the diagram. She had found what she was looking for. Checking around the almost empty room, Susatch carefully lifted her small personal scanner and began to download the information.

* * *

Jinnie suffered through the two-day wait for Susatch. Writing in her diary offered a small reprieve from her anxiety. She drifted in and out of remembered words and the images they brought with them. Keldonabrieve, her home. Nightfall, her favorite horse. Happy memories that stirred no pain. And Griffin. Always Griffin.

She wrote down every detail she recalled, returning her diary to its place beneath her pillow before she lay down to rest, coaxing sleep to release her from her bedroom prison.

Kellen did not challenge her quarantine, and Jinnie avoided Bella by pretending to be asleep at mealtimes. She had little appetite as she waited for her friend's return. What would they do then? They had to escape. The word reminded Jinnie of elevators and tunnels, hidden passages, and whispered promises.

"Run away with me."

"I will."

Jinnie got into bed. Tomorrow Susatch should return. Tonight she would be with Griffin. She closed her eyes, remembering how safe he made her feel. Safe and warm, loved and happy. Jinnie sighed, slipping into sleep. She was flying through snow, then stretching out by a fire. He was there, bold and beautiful, warm. Lifting her out of herself, out of her life. How could she ever have left him?

"I'll come back to you," promised Jinnie.

"Come back to whom?" a harsh voice demanded.

Jinnie blinked against the sharp light. Was it morning so soon? "Griffin?"

Kellen's angry face glared down at her. "And who is Griffin?" He waved her diary before Jinnie. "Your lover?"

Sliding off the other side of the bed, Jinnie pulled on her robe and faced Kellen. "I don't know what you're talking about. I was dreaming."

"But not about me." Kellen moved slowly around the foot of the bed.

"Words on a page." Jinnie held out her hand. "And a diary is private."

"Even from your husband?"

Jinnie struggled to maintain a calm demeanor. "I don't know what you mean, Kellen. I've been ill."

"So I was told. Susatch is here to see you. I think I'll stay for the prognosis."

He came to stand before her, tall and menacing. "My nights have become tiresome without our entertainment." Kellen sneered. "Have yours?"

"Entertainment?" Jinnie lashed out, trembling but angry. "Is that what you call the casual rape of your wife?"

Kellen seized her wrist with one hand and struck Jinnie across the face with the other. "Who have you been with?"

Jinnie shook her head violently. "No one!"

"Liar!" Kellen struck her again, releasing her so that Jinnie fell hard to the floor.

She didn't hear Kellen curse her. Wind roared in her ears instead. The room tilted. She lay on the floor, more afraid of what she felt than of Kellen's jealous rage.

Jinnie looked up and saw the ghost. He strode purposefully toward her, through Kellen, then through her, and she felt a pull as if he were dragging her after him.

Jinnie screamed, closing her eyes and kicking her legs at Kellen, trying to crawl away from him as he tried to straddle her.

His weight fell from her, and Jinnie opened her eyes. Kellen lay on the floor beside her. A woman was offering her hand.

"Susatch?"

Susatch set down the chair she had hit Kellen with and helped Jinnie to her feet.

"Can you stand?"

"Yes." Standing up, Jinnie swayed. "No."

"Okay, sit on the bed. I want to make sure I didn't kill him."

Kneeling beside Kellen, Susatch checked him with her Medical Scanner. "He'll live, but you won't if we don't get you out of here."

"What do you mean?"

Susatch took Jinnie by the arm and steered her toward the closet. "Not here. Get dressed."

Still shaky, Jinnie dressed. "My diary. Where is it?"

Susatch glanced around the room and located the book by Kellen's prone form. As she picked it up, Kellen stirred, then groaned. "Come on. He's regaining consciousness."

Jinnie snatched up her purse and shoved the diary inside. "Okay."

"Follow me." Susatch waved Jinnie toward her, and they moved quietly down the long hallway. Voices came from the kitchen ahead.

"This way." Susatch stepped quickly through the servants' interior door, then through a smaller door almost obscured in the design of the wall. "Come on. This should take us to the back of the house. We can grab an air car there."

Jinnie followed Susatch through the narrow door and along a dark corridor. "What's wrong with your car? And how do you know about this hallway?"

"My car's in front of the house. They'll be watching it," Susatch said over her shoulder. "As for this emergency exit, I've been digging through blueprints and historical records. It seems your husband's family purchased over a dozen properties after the war. All of them with cellars."

"What are you saying?"

"I'm saying that a powerful family with enough resources in their control could construct interplanetary bombs on their own and eventually deploy them."

Jinnie halted, sickened, but Susatch grabbed her hand and hurried her to the end of the corridor.

"This door opens manually," Susatch said. "Step back."

Jinnie pressed back against the wall as Susatch carefully pulled the door open. They were in the car port. An air car floated only a few feet away.

Moments later the two women sped across the early morning plain, heading toward the mountains.

Susatch checked the controls and scanners, set the auto drive, and then leaned back. "I'm too old for this," she muttered. She glanced over at Jinnie. "So. How have you been?"

Vacillating between hysterical tears and laughter, Jinnie took a deep breath, releasing it slowly. She nodded. "Fine."

"Right." Susatch double-checked the perimeter alert. There was nothing on the screen. Satisfied, she turned her full attention to Jinnie. "What's in the diary?"

Jinnie looked down at her purse. "Everything I could remember. Some of it doesn't make any sense. Maybe none of it does, except for Griffin. I don't know."

"Mind if I have a look?"

"No. Not at all." Opening her purse, Jinnie pulled out her diary. "I was going to give it to you anyway for safekeeping, but Kellen found it first."

She handed the book to Susatch.

Taking it, Susatch pointed at a bottle on the side of the passenger door. "Drink that while I read," she instructed.

"What is it?"

"Juice. I don't want to risk giving you any medications until we get to my laboratory. Now drink up. Doctor's orders."

"Okay." Relief at escaping Kellen made Jinnie lightheaded. Drinking the juice, she let her gaze swerve from Susatch to the plain behind them. Nothing moved. No one was pursuing them. Jinnie sighed. It was over.

Without looking up from the page she was reading, Susatch asked, "Are you still getting headaches?"

"Sometimes. They're not as bad as they were. The pain's usually at its worst when I'm forcing myself to remember or when I'm remembering something unhappy."

Susatch closed the diary. "This is pretty amazing stuff."

"Is that the medical term?"

"Hah!" Susatch laughed. "It will be if I ever get up the nerve to document it. We'll have to do a lot of tests." She started speaking almost to herself. "First we'll have to find a safe place for you to stay. Then we'll need to come up with a reason for you to dissolve your marriage to Kellen. That might be fairly easy, actually. We could cite neglect, abuse …"

"Wait, wait." Jinnie turned to Susatch. "What are you talking about? We have to find a way to get me back to where I belong."

Susatch started. "What? Where you belong? You mean Breeare?"

"No." Taking the diary from Susatch's lap, Jinnie returned it to her purse. "I mean with Griffin. That's where I belong."

Susatch pursed her lips. "Jinnie, I'll be the first to say I'm an amateur on time travel theories and research. Nevertheless, I very much doubt that what you're suggesting is possible."

Jinnie looked at the mountains. They, too, reminded her of her other life. They had a name there. What was it? Her head began to ache, as if someone were pinching her temples.

"Jinnie?"

Jinnie continued looking straight ahead. "It must be possible, Susatch."

"Uh-huh. Well, we don't even know if time travel is the problem or the answer. Anyway, I'm not about to try building a time machine. First we test, then we talk, and then we think. I need to figure out where you're going before I can think about how to get you there. Or if you can get there. Or whatever. Now I'm getting a headache."

Jinnie stayed silent, clinging to the hope of finding a way to return to Griffin.

* * *

Kellen pushed himself up from the floor. He touched the back of his head, then checked his fingers. No blood.

But there will be, he thought, anger smearing reason and twisting it into vengeance. True, the bitch was only a Breearian, but she was his, and no one else was going to touch her.

And the next time I touch her will be the last.

Seven

Susatch parked the air car and led Jinnie toward the side of a mountain. She pressed her hand against what appeared to be nothing more than a rock wall. A door slid open.

"What is this place?" asked Jinnie. Her voice bounced back from high ceilings as she followed Susatch into an enormous, rectangular room.

"I told you." Moving down a long row of machines and computers, Susatch began flipping switches and pressing buttons. "It's my laboratory."

"I'm no scientist, Susatch, but this—" Jinnie swept an arm at the tumble of technology now humming, blinking, and whirring around her, "this is not a laboratory. This looks like some kind of research center."

Jinnie looked at Susatch. "What is it?"

Susatch folded her arms and leaned against a counter. "It's a very special kind of Analyzer, designed by me and built by a friend of mine. He shared my interests."

"I'd like to meet him."

"He died of the Plague not long ago."

"I'm sorry." Jinnie looked away. "Susatch, do I have the Plague?"

"You don't have the Plague, Jinnie. But I do need more information before I can tell you much else."

"You've read my diary."

"I need more medical information. For all my curiosity about the unknown, however improbable, I'm still a doctor. The readings from your Medical Scan were almost off the scale. It's as if you're having an allergic reaction."

"To what?"

"I'd say to your environment. To Hura."

"I'm allergic to an entire planet?"

Susatch turned back to her computers and punched in several codes. "I've never heard of it, but if what you're experiencing is time travel, anything must be considered. I haven't discounted illness yet, you know. An allergy would explain your feelings of disorientation. It could even be the cause of your mental confusion."

"I'm not confused," Jinnie objected.

"That's what we're going to find out."

Susatch pointed to a narrow table with a black, shiny surface. "Lie down."

Climbing up on it, Jinnie flinched as she lay down; the table was ice cold.

Susatch picked up five silver discs, each an inch in diameter, and began attaching them to Jinnie. She placed one disc on either side of Jinnie's forehead, one at the base of her skull, one over her solar plexus, and one just below her breastbone.

"Breathe normally," Susatch instructed, bending over a control panel. "And don't move."

"It's freezing," Jinnie complained.

"Not to worry," said Susatch, pressing a button. "It won't take long."

The table felt colder. "What does this do?" asked Jinnie.

"Quiet." Susatch frowned as the information scrolled across the screen before her.

"This penetrates to the molecular level." Susatch scowled. "And does extensive brainwave interpretation." She adjusted a dial.

Jinnie shivered. The cold worsened. It penetrated her spine and crept up her neck. A cold so harsh it burned. *It's like the Chill,* thought Jinnie.

Images of a white castle floated in her mind. She knew it and recognized it as her home.

Snow blew across the castle's lake. It blew against her cheeks. She was with Griffin. They were running from the Chill. Running toward sanctuary. Running away.

Griffin?

Run away. *We'll run away,* she thought.

"Hold it!" Susatch looked up. "Your neurotransmitter lines spiked like you'd been electrocuted. What were you thinking just now?"

"I was thinking about Griffin, wishing we were together, and as far away from all of this madness as possible."

"Hmmm. Griffin. He's definitely a constant in your diary; a very vivid and passionate memory. Someone who elicits strong emotions from you."

"Yes. I love him."

"And what about the apparition? The ghostlike man who walked through you? Think about him."

"I don't want to, Susatch."

"I'm here with you, Jinnie. You're safe. Please try. He could be of key importance."

Jinnie closed her eyes. She thought of her ghost: the mysterious stranger seemed to be pursuing her. She felt a cold wind blow against her body, then heard water. Waves were breaking against a rocky shore.

"Griffin?"

"No," a voice answered.

From a great distance, Jinnie saw a man standing on the shoreline. "Who are you?" she called.

"The one who loves you," the voice answered.

"Griffin loves me."

"I love you more." The voice was a whisper, a chant, a spell. "Come to me."

"No!"

Jinnie jerked awake, hands gripping the sides of a smooth surface.

"It's all right, Jinnie," Susatch said. "We're in my lab. You're safe. I'm here."

Jinnie turned her head. "Susatch?"

"Yes, it's me, your friendly doctor. How do you feel?" Susatch began removing the discs from Jinnie.

"Scared." Jinnie pressed a hand to her forehead. "And I have a headache."

"I'm not surprised. Can you sit up?"
"Yes. Yes. I'm fine now."
"Hardly that, but let's talk over tea."
"I don't like tea," Jinnie murmured, the words eerily familiar.
"Even better. Let's have a drink."

* * *

The two women sat in a small room adjoining the lab. "Well?" Jinnie set down her glass of liquor. It tasted like something she'd had once before. Brandy?

Susatch swirled the liquid in her glass, gathering her thoughts together. "Well, something is definitely happening to you. Your entire cell structure is undergoing a measurable metamorphosis."

"Am I dying?"

"No. But you are changing. Your body is altering itself internally. You're becoming incompatible with your environment, and I don't know why."

"Do you think it's time travel?"

Susatch shrugged. "You know, it could be."

"What do we do now?"

Susatch finished her brandy. "We hypnotize you."

Standing up, she went to a cabinet, returning with a vial and a needle.

"Hypnotize me?" Jinnie looked skeptical. "Right now? Will that work?"

"It'll work. And it's now or not at all, because Kellen will be trying to find us."

Fear padded through Jinnie's stomach. She had forgotten Kellen. "All right. What do you want me to do?"

"Just sit there. I'm going to give you a shot of Thimapoline."

"What's that? Ouch!" Jinnie rubbed at her left arm. "What is that?"

"It's a fast-acting sedative. It will let you relax into a REM state of mind, but you won't fall asleep." Susatch sat down opposite Jinnie. "Close your eyes."

"What about pain?" Jinnie briefly resisted the sudden lull of sleepiness she felt.

"I think I can help with that. Now sit back. Relax. It's like being awake in a dream. There's no pain. Nothing to fear. Breathe deeply. Relax. Let your mind drift."

Susatch carefully considered what she'd read in Jinnie's diary: descriptions of two completely different worlds and two completely different men. The details of her life and love with Griffin were the clearest. Susatch decided to start there.

"Can you hear me, Jinnie?"

"Yes."

"Okay." Susatch turned on a voice recorder. "I need to know something very personal about you, Jinnie. I need you to tell me something that perhaps you keep secret, or perhaps it's something that you don't understand yourself."

"You mean, that I'm a Traveler?"

Susatch paused. "Yes, Jinnie. Tell me about being a Traveler."

Jinnie's voice was troubled as she began to speak, reliving the night when she had learned about Phantasms and Travelers.

"And you did Travel, didn't you, Jinnie?" said Susatch. "To Breeare."

"Yes."

"Where are you going next?"

"I think I'm going to him." Jinnie's voice was sad.

"The man you describe as a ghost?"

"Yes," Jinnie whispered. "I don't want to go. I never wanted to leave Griffin. We were going to run away."

"From the ghost?"

"From my husband, Lancin." Bitterness tainted Jinnie's voice. "He's a traitor."

Susatch was silent, thinking. Finally, she spoke again. "Jinnie, can you see your ghost now? Can you talk to him?"

Tears broke free of Jinnie's closed eyes, and Susatch knelt beside her. She put her hand on Jinnie's arm. "It's all right. You're safe." She checked Jinnie's pulse.

Jinnie was silent.

"Try," Susatch urged. "I won't let him harm you, Jinnie. Let your mind drift to the world you described, the one with the towers and the orange sky. See it in your mind now. Feel it."

"He's calling me," said Jinnie suddenly.

As she spoke, Jinnie felt like she was there again, this time on the beach. The waves were kissing her ankles. She waded through them, deeper now, farther out into the welcoming ocean. The water was at her waist, making her sway. If she walked further, she would lose the soft press of sand beneath her feet.

"Come to me," a man's voice said. "I love you. Come to me."

Turning slowly, Jinnie looked at him. Tall and pale, his hand outstretched to her, his green eyes piercing her like the arrow that had struck Griffin.

"Come to me," he insisted. "I love you. You're my *hollany*."

Jinnie looked away. "I don't love you. I don't even know you."

"Yes, you do. Come to me." His voice was a warm wind in her ear. "Come to me."

A wave pushed her toward shore, and Jinnie stumbled forward. She walked slowly out of the ocean's embrace, then stopped.

"Who are you?" she demanded.

The waves roared behind her. No answer could be heard above the wind and the cries of ocean birds overhead.

The world went black, and Jinnie gasped for breath, for substance.

"It's all right," a familiar voice said. "You're okay. You're safe. Be still now."

"Am I dreaming?"

"No. You're remembering. And from now on, whenever you remember your past, there will be no pain. Say it and believe it."

"There will be no pain."

"Good. Now wake yourself up, Jinnie. Wake yourself up and remember everything we've talked about, remember your other life, and remember without pain. Wake up. Now."

Jinnie pushed her arms against a hard surface, a chair. A room took shape around her. She looked at Susatch, eyes focusing. "Susatch?"

"Yes, Jinnie. How do you feel?"

"Sad. Overwhelmed."

"Rest for a minute." Standing up, Susatch got a glass of water and handed it to Jinnie.

"All the research I've done implies time travel, if it is possible, is linear," said Susatch. "A person travels to a certain point in history, part of their planet's past or even its future. I've never read anything suggesting a person could time travel through space.

"Yet you said you travel from one world to another. Traveling through time and space. You called yourself a Traveler."

"A Traveler," Jinnie repeated, remembering when she had first heard the word. Escabel. Her room at Keldonabrieve. Griffin. "Maybe the author of that article I read didn't die after all. Maybe she was a Traveler, too."

"What article?" Susatch sat down. "What author?"

"When I was still on Breeare, I read an article called …" Jinnie thought a minute. "Crossing Time: The True Story …'"

"Of My Other Life," Susatch finished the title. "I've read it. The author was H. Arkiah. I had hoped to meet her someday. I didn't know she was dead."

"Maybe she isn't," said Jinnie. "Except she only talked about traveling into her past on Breeare."

"You're doing far more than that."

"Yes," Jinnie agreed. "I thought I'd feel reassured, knowing for certain that my other life was real. Instead, I feel like I'm trapped in a maze."

She looked at Susatch. "I don't know what's going to happen next."

"Does anyone?"

"You know what I mean," said Jinnie. "I don't want to be a Traveler."

Susatch nodded. "It's definitely a difficult way of life: brief stays, memory loss, pain. At least, that's what's happened so far. However this Traveling came about, it seems to start with a physical instability that literally makes you incompatible with your surroundings. And then the soul, if you will, projects itself outward, creating a dual existence, perhaps seeking a permanently compatible system. I don't know."

Susatch touched Jinnie's arm. "I do know you're rapidly destabilizing here on Hura. I would guess you haven't much time left before you Travel again."

Jinnie nodded. "I guess we won't have to build a time machine."

"Good thing, too. I'm not much of an engineer." Susatch studied her young friend. "I always thought discovering more about my 'preposterous' theories would be fun. It isn't."

"No, it isn't fun," said Jinnie. "It's frightening and confusing. All this information, and it still doesn't make sense to me."

"I think it will make more sense once you're more experienced with the process."

"I need answers now, Susatch," Jinnie protested. "Why am I here? What's the connection between Hura and Ispell?"

"What makes you think there's a connection?"

"Because I feel I'm being pulled forward, not propelled from behind. I'm certainly not Traveling voluntarily."

"Good point. So, what's similar? Bad husbands?"

"Bad husbands," Jinnie scoffed. She sat up straight. "War."

Susatch looked thoughtful. "That's interesting. You said Lancin was a traitor."

"Yes. And Kellen certainly intends to be."

"No doubt about that," Susatch agreed. "Anything else?"

"I remember I had to warn someone." Jinnie frowned. "That's odd." She put a hand to her forehead. "I remember, and I don't feel any pain."

"Good." Susatch sat down and ran a Medical Scanner up and down in front of Jinnie.

"That's because I instructed your subconscious not to feel pain when you remember. You'll remember your past without pain. Physical pain," she amended. "I can't prevent sorrow."

"I understand." Jinnie tried to smile. "Thank you, Susatch."

"I wish I could do more. Drink your water."

Jinnie took a sip. "There's something else that's similar, too."

"Oh?"

"The man who appears like a ghost. The one who loves me."

"I thought Griffin loved you."

"He does." She remembered his words and said them aloud. "Now and always."

Then another memory usurped Griffin. Jinnie fumbled to put the images she saw in her head into words.

"Dancing," she said. "There was a large room full of people in Keldonabrieve. And the other man was there. Like a ghost."

"Okay. And you've seen him here as a ghost."

"Yes. And just now while I was hypnotized. He was waiting for me. Telling me to come to him."

"Maybe he's going to war, too," suggested Susatch. "Maybe you're some kind of mediator or diplomat."

"If I am, I can't be a very good one. I never stay in one place long enough to make a difference. Not yet anyway."

She looked at the glass in her hand. "Do you think I'll ever stay anywhere?"

"Maybe. We're so far beyond my field of knowledge that any guess is a possibility."

"Perhaps if I Travel far enough, I'll come full circle, back to the beginning. Back to Griffin."

"Jinnie, look at me." Susatch's voice was stern. "Listen and remember this. Life is change and progression. You're not likely to be the exception to that rule, however different you are."

"You're telling me to give Griffin up."

"That's already happened. I'm telling you to accept it."

Jinnie looked away. "Do you think I'll ever stop Traveling?"

Susatch folded her arms, the doctor about to make a prognosis. "I think you might. I would say that a Traveler is like a split personality, several individual lives all linked together. Somehow the soul is drawn through the lives, seeking to establish itself in one life only. It's even possible that the soul creates new lives in its search."

"That's too cruel."

"The universe is a cruel place, Jinnie, but not maliciously so. Let go of the past, look to the future."

"And the present?"

"Will be well looked after," snarled a man's voice.

It was Kellen.

E I G H T

"How did you find us?" Susatch asked, as if starting a pleasant conversation.

Jinnie marveled at Susatch's poise, then noticed that her right hand rested casually near the voice recorder. It was still on.

"I have tracker beacons in all my air cars," Kellen answered, equally pleasant.

"See what I mean?" Susatch said to Jinnie. "Paranoid."

"I prefer security-conscious," Kellen said. He looked Jinnie up and down, eyes invasive and cold.

"In these difficult days," he continued, "the head of a large Station needs everything available. Especially …" Kellen paused, studying Jinnie's face … "visual recorders. I don't know how your lover managed to escape, but I will find him."

The corners of Jinnie's mouth lifted. She wanted to spit in Kellen's face. She had felt this way before, with Lancin; two men from different parts of her life, yet both horribly similar. Some legacy. "You won't find him, Kellen." Jinnie's voice was calm. "Not ever."

Kellen lifted his hand to strike her, but Susatch leaned forward. "You must have had a tag on your computer program," she said.

Lowering his arm, Kellen nodded. "Of course." He looked at Susatch. "Your inquiries into my property holdings were noted, Doctor."

Kellen pulled a small particle dispenser from his belt. "Get up, both of you."

Susatch and Jinnie exchanged glances. Jinnie rose, moving slightly in front of Susatch, giving her a brief moment to pocket the recorder.

"Into the laboratory," Kellen ordered.

The women filed out of the room, down the short hall, and into the cavernous lab.

"How do you explain having your own Analyzer, Doctor?" demanded Kellen.

"How do you explain having your own interplanetary bomb?" Susatch snapped back.

"You think there's only one? That's only one of many," Kellen bragged.

"How many?" asked Susatch, keeping the pocket with the recorder facing Kellen.

"Almost twenty. A few more, and that will be the end of Breeare."

"Is it just the Family Kade?" probed Susatch.

"There are others." Kellen's eyes narrowed. "Start the program. My wife,"–his eyes darted to Jinnie then back to Susatch–"is going to have an accident. Sadly, her doctor will die in an attempt to save her."

Jinnie watched Susatch begin the start-up program. Kellen stood next to her, particle dispenser aimed at Susatch.

Glancing around, Jinnie saw her purse next to the examination table. She took a step back, fingers reaching for it.

"And when Breeare is destroyed?" asked Susatch, working as slowly as she dared. "What then?"

"Then the extermination will begin. All the tainted blood will be eliminated from Hura's Family Lines."

"Uh-huh. It doesn't sound to me like you've thought this through, Kellen. We depend on Breeare."

"No longer. Stop stalling. You're both about to be the first casualties of war."

Snatching up her purse, Jinnie swung it as hard as she could at Kellen, knocking the particle dispenser out of his hand.

"Run!" Jinnie grabbed Susatch by the arm and propelled her forward.

"What are you doing?" Susatch shouted over her shoulder.

"Being diplomatic!"

Jinnie ducked behind a free-standing table.

"Get down!" she shouted as Kellen found his weapon and fired at them.

Putting her shoulder against the heavy table, Jinnie motioned Susatch to help her. Together they pushed the table over.

"Maybe that will slow him down." Jinnie looked around. "Where's the back door?"

"That way." Susatch pointed to the dark recesses of the cave.

"Let's go, let's go!" A thin beam of light shot over Jinnie's head. They ran.

The walls narrowed quickly. Only the dim glow of emergency lighting showed them that the path divided.

"Which way?" whispered Jinnie.

Susatch pointed to the tunnel at their right. "That tunnel will lead to a small Station. It's not far, and I know the family well. I believe they'll help us."

"And the left?"

"It leads to a ravine. It used to be an inland sea."

"Take the right, Susatch," Jinnie decided. "You've got the voice recorder. It's as good as a confession. I'll take the left tunnel. If Kellen's following us, I can distract him and give you time to get away."

"You've got to come with me, Jinnie."

"You know I can't. You said yourself I'm going to Travel soon. Maybe this is why I'm here. To help you prevent a war."

Susatch still waited, looking concerned and a little bit sad.

"Susatch." Jinnie hugged her friend briefly. "I'll remember now, thanks to you. Maybe it will help. I know I'll always remember your friendship, and your smile."

There was the sound of an explosion behind them.

The two women looked at each other; they had no more time. Instead of pursuit, Kellen had chosen to blow up the lab.

"Hurry," said Jinnie. "Before the tunnels collapse."

Susatch nodded. "Safe journey, my friend." She turned away, disappearing into the darkness.

Jinnie started down the left tunnel, one hand lightly touching the wall, the other clutching her purse. It was cold. The emergency lights became further and further apart. The only footsteps she heard were her own.

The sound of another explosion erupted far behind Jinnie, sending tremors through the wall and up her fingertips.

She began to jog, one hand still touching the wall of the tunnel as it vibrated from an aftershock. Another blast of energy sent a cannonball of flames into the tunnel a hundred yards behind her. Dirt tumbled from the ceiling. The emergency lights failed.

Jinnie flattened against the wall, trembling like the ground beneath her feet. Another explosion came, and another.

He's going to bring the entire side of the mountain down, thought Jinnie. She hoped Susatch was safe.

Coughing from the fumes and smoke, Jinnie squinted. Far ahead, a sliver of light appeared and disappeared like a lighthouse beacon. She started toward it, half running, half jogging as the floor split and crumbled under her. The light grew stronger and wider. The tunnel started collapsing.

A snap of wind gave Jinnie hope. Eyes burning, lungs hurting, she staggered out of the tunnel into a landslide. The side of the mountain caved in.

Rocks and boulders crashed around her. Jinnie slid, fell, got up again. She tumbled over an escarpment and quickly crawled under it for shelter. The world overhead grunted and thumped. Dust and dirt mixed with chemicals and pelted down like hail. Then it was silent.

Jinnie shivered, waited. She peered out from underneath her shelter. The world was gray. Wind wailed along a narrow ravine, clogged with debris from the landslide.

Stars blinked wearily over the disaster area. There was no sign of Kellen.

Jinnie crawled out from underneath her stone shield and picked her way along the ravine. The wind rose and the landscape blurred. Jinnie stood still a moment, feeling nauseated. A sharp pain knifed her forehead. She heard water, then felt water rising all around her.

Come to me, come to me.

Was the voice in her head? She took a step forward, stumbled, splashed, fell.

Jinnie struggled to her feet. Her dress floated on waves that knocked her backward and forward. The air smelled of salt. She heard birds.

Jinnie looked up. *The stars are different,* she thought.

"Come to me, come to me," he called.

Jinnie recognized the voice. It was her ghost, the stranger who had come to her before on Breeare and Hura. And before that, he had come to her on Ispell, in Keldonabrieve.

Jinnie waded through the waist-deep water. *I remember, Susatch. And, whatever happens, I'll go on remembering.*

She thought she saw someone on shore.

Jinnie struggled into the shallows, stumbling, finally sinking to the sand and letting the waves sweep against her feet. Aching all over, Jinnie tried to call out to him. Whoever he was, whatever he turned out to be, for now he was her lifeline.

She pushed herself to her feet and took a step forward into unconsciousness.

Part III
Yar

One

The world was painful, wet and cold. Jinnie opened her eyes, hoping to see the stars of Ispell. A dark shape moved beside her.

"Griffin?"

Jinnie tried to sit up. Small hands pushed her back down.

"She is waking, Dalia." The voice, too, was small.

"Who are you?" Jinnie pulled away from the hands. "Where am I?"

"Be still." A dark face came into focus and hovered over her.

"I am called Dalia. I intercepted your Traveling."

Jinnie sat up quickly, and the room spun. She braced herself with her arms. As her eyes adjusted to the dim light, she saw her rescuers. Two women, perhaps five feet in height, stood before her. They were dressed in dark-colored robes, and they wore their copper hair in single long braids that fell over one shoulder. "Do you know about Travelers?"

Dalia didn't answer.

Frustrated, Jinnie waited for the room to stop spinning and swung her legs over what she assumed to be the edge of a bed. Coarse cloth pricked her fingers, and dry sand hurt her bare feet. She stood up slowly and looked around.

She was in a dark room, lit only by a fire held within a small circle of stones. No windows offered light. No door allowed escape.

"If you can't tell me more," said Jinnie, "perhaps you can tell me if you've seen someone. A man. He was calling to me. He's tall and slim, fair-haired. His eyes are—"

Jinnie stopped speaking, noticing the faces of Dalia and the other woman. They were anxious and unhappy. Their hazel eyes showed worry, even fear.

"She is speaking of the Toranise," said Dalia's companion, shifting nervously on her small bare feet.

"Yes." Dalia nodded. "But do not fear. He will not discover us. He is obsessed, and we are careful."

Dalia faced Jinnie. "You will go soon."

"Where? Where will I go? I don't even know where I am."

"This world is called Yar. But we are far from the Towers. That is where you are going. The interception was unintentional. If it is discovered, we will be hunted and destroyed. The Daskiny are not allowed to use the power of their inner self. Only the Toranise may do that."

"Who are the Daskiny?"

"Metisa and I are Daskiny," Dalia answered, "but we are not part of the Valleys. We escaped many years ago."

"Just the two of you?"

No response.

"I don't want to cause trouble for you," said Jinnie. She circled the fire and stopped in front of a large tapestry. It fluttered forward, allowing salt air and the rushing sound of waves to enter the hut. She was still near the beach.

Jinnie glanced at the women, then pushed aside the tapestry. She stepped into sunshine. Jinnie shaded her eyes with one hand and looked up.

The sky was orange and white, streaked with clouds in shades of purple. It was exactly as she had envisioned it. She stood still, wondering where the towers were.

Dalia had left the hut and come up behind Jinnie. Dropping a backpack to the sand, she held up Jinnie's purse. "Your shoes were lost in the water."

It seemed to be an apology. "It doesn't matter," said Jinnie, taking her purse. "Thank you for rescuing me."

"I will try to help you if I can," Dalia offered, "but you must obey all my instructions, and you must be patient. It is dangerous for me to be with you."

"Why?"

"Do not speak here. Not here. We will talk in the *tethrid* so that Metisa will be safe."

Jinnie lifted her purse over her head and draped the strap from one shoulder and across her chest. "Thank you …"

"Dalia." The woman smiled, changing her somber features into beauty incarnate .

"Dalia," Jinnie repeated, returning the smile. "Shall we walk by the water?"

The mask of doom returned. "No. Come with me. There is a grove of *holiander* not far from here. There we can sit and speak safely."

Shouldering the backpack, Dalia extended her hand to Jinnie. "It is safer, when we walk, always to keep hold of one another."

Jinnie took Dalia's hand, closing her fingers gently as if she were taking the hand of a child to cross the street.

Together they headed down the slope and away from the beach. Looking back, Jinnie could barely discern the small hut. It was camouflaged by dunes. "It's like a lookout," she said aloud, without thinking.

"It is."

"Who are you watching for?"

"Friends and enemies."

Jinnie took a deep breath, striving for the patience Dalia had requested. She had shortened her longer strides. It didn't seem that Dalia was unhurried; more that she was deliberate, pausing often to look at the sky and glance at the sea behind them.

"Are the Toranise friends or enemies?"

"Both."

"Both," Jinnie repeated, puzzled. "Metisa seemed to know about the man I mentioned. Does he come to this place often?"

Dalia shook her head. "The Toranise do not care to venture far from their Towers and their mountain meadows. They visit only their valleys when they have need."

"The one I described to you is different," said Jinnie.

"I do not believe he is different, only that his desire has made him bold."

Dalia stopped and looked up at Jinnie. "What are you called?" she asked.

The non sequitur made Jinnie frown. "I don't know what my name is on this world."

"What were you called before?"

"Jinnie."

Dalia tilted her head at Jinnie's sad whisper. "Someone you love gave you that name."

"Yes."

"I will call you Traveler."

Jinnie nodded. They continued their slow march through the sand and sea grass toward a line of short trees. Making her question more specific, Jinnie asked, "Are you at war?"

"No."

They reached the trees. Jinnie had to duck her head and walk hunched over as Dalia led her into a maze of brambles and shrubs. The brambles tore at her dress, still wet from the ocean. Several times she had to pluck the garment free, but not once did Dalia release her hand.

"We are safe," Dalia finally announced. She released Jinnie's hand.

Glancing around, Jinnie sat down where she had stopped, almost in the center of a small circle of trees. The branches bore long, knife-sharp thorns instead of leaves and formed a canopy over her head.

Dalia freed herself of her pack and sat down opposite Jinnie, placing the pack between them. Opening it, she withdrew a wineskin.

"This is *telabah*." Holding the wineskin up, Dalia tilted her head and squirted liquid into her mouth. "It is a juice."

She offered the wineskin to Jinnie.

"Thank you." Jinnie managed a clumsy imitation of Dalia's expertise and finally got some of the juice in her mouth instead of down her chin. "It's very good."

Dalia nodded. Crossing her legs, she said, "You may speak now, Traveler. The thorns of a *tethrid* cannot easily be penetrated."

Looking around at the barrier of thorns, a cold idea made Jinnie afraid. "Do the Toranise have some kind of animal that attacks you?"

"Some kind of animal." Dalia repeated the phrase as if it were an answer.

"I can't keep trying to ask the right questions, Dalia," Jinnie said, exasperated. "Please tell me all you can. I promise not to betray you or your people."

Dalia looked thoughtful, but said nothing.

"At least tell me how you intercepted me. I felt I was being pulled to this world. I don't believe I Traveled here willingly. You said the Toranise I described was searching for me. Maybe I should find him."

"He will find you."

"How will he find me? How did you find me?" Jinnie rushed on before Dalia could give another cryptic response. "How did you intercept me?"

"Metisa and I were watching the sea. I first saw and then felt a disturbance in the waves. There was light dancing on their crests even as the sky darkened. I stretched out my inner self to probe the disruption, for this inland sea is usually calm and a good barrier between the Daskiny and the Toranise. I felt the presence of two beings, one strong, one fragile. I recognized the first presence as that of a Toranise, one who had ventured to the sands on the other side of the sea. That is a rare occurrence. I pulled back and inadvertently took the fragile presence with me: you."

"You mentioned you're not allowed to practice stretching your inner self. Why?"

"It generates energy that clouds the air currents, interfering with the Toranise and their pursuit of motion and their heart's desire."

Jinnie considered her next question carefully. On one level, Dalia seemed to be speaking of something magical. On the other, she was talking about generating energy and recognizing the manipulation of energy by someone else: someone like a Traveler.

It hadn't occurred to Jinnie that some could consider her existence magical.

"Dalia," Jinnie began. "What do you know about Travelers?"

"There is a legend among the Daskiny about a gifted person who travels from world to world, bringing peace. We are in need of peace."

"And you think this gifted person is me?"

Dalia scrutinized Jinnie. "I do not know. I am not the one to say. My knowledge is from stories told to children, stories intended to soothe young minds that are full of strife and fear because of an uncertain future."

"All futures are uncertain," Jinnie objected.

"Distant ones, yes. But immediate futures—like yours—are certain. The Toranise who seeks you will take you to him when he finds you. And he will find you. If you try to hide from him, you will expose the Daskiny who have sought sanctuary on this side of the sea. You will put those who are still to come here in peril. As well as those who are journeying to the north to build a life free of the doom that shadows the valleys of the Toranise."

Feeling overwhelmed, Jinnie looked at the canopy of tree branches. It was a shield of thorns to protect the Daskiny from some kind of animal, and from a friend who was also an enemy. *What was the persecution that the Daskiny were so obviously trying to escape? Maybe I'm here to help them.*

"It's too much to take in." Jinnie sighed. She returned her gaze to Dalia, drawing her thoughts together to face the present problem: the Toranise who searched for her.

"Have you any idea why a Toranise is searching for me, Dalia?" Jinnie asked. "You said his desire has made him bold."

"Yes. The Toranise are spoiled and selfish. What they want, they take. It may be that he heard of the legend. Some of the Daskiny in the valleys of the Toranise are Healers, and some Healers keep written stories of the peoples of Yar. Your Toranise may have learned of your existence from such a Daskiny and become curious."

"He's not my Toranise," Jinnie said, feeling defensive.

"He is. You said you have seen him before you came to Yar. It may be he was attracted to the motion your Traveling creates. It is disruptive and intense. It caught my attention. Or it may be ..." Dalia stopped.

"Yes?"

"It may be that he thinks he loves you. To spend so much time at the shore of the sea is unnatural for a Toranise. Toranise are idlers, easily bored and easily distracted, but never doubt that they are dangerous. They have subjugated the Daskiny for thousands of years." Dalia stood up. "Do not trust him. The Toranise are not what they seem."

Shouldering her pack, Dalia extended her small hand to Jinnie. "Now, come. We must take you to the sea's shore. That is where your Toranise is searching. I have said too much and not enough. I only hope you will keep your promise not to disclose my interception or the existence of my people on this side of the sea."

"I will keep my promise, Dalia." Taking her hand, Jinnie stood up. "I will keep your trust. As of this moment, I've never heard of you."

"Thank you, Traveler. It may be that I will never see you again. I hope the best of life for you."

It seemed like a formal good-bye. "I hope the best of life for you," Jinnie responded.

They wound their way back through the labyrinth of foliage. At its edge, Dalia stopped and pointed. "Walk slowly, pause often," she instructed.

"Through that patch of sea grass, then south along the shore. Let the waves touch your feet, but do not venture deeper. The motion of the tide and the energy from your inner self will draw the attention of your Toranise."

"What about the animals?"

"I believe your Toranise will find you first."

"And if he doesn't?"

Dalia said nothing.

Fighting fear, Jinnie started forward, stopped. "Dalia?"

"Yes, Traveler?"

"When you say 'inner self', what are you describing?"

"The core of your being, the source of your power. The endless renewing energy that makes you unique and yet is recognized by all other energies as part of a whole."

She's speaking of my soul, thought Jinnie.

"I understand," Jinnie said. "Thank you, Dalia."

Jinnie waded through the grass toward the beach, moving as Dalia had instructed. When she reached the waves, she let them slide over her feet.

She walked a long time, wondering why he didn't call her and trying not to think of attack animals. Or Griffin.

The sunlight disappeared behind a curtain of dark clouds, and the sudden darkness frightened Jinnie.

She wanted to call out to him, whoever he was, but she was afraid of drawing attention to herself. Instead, she forced herself to keep walking, waiting to hear him call to her.

A heavy fog enveloped Jinnie, swirling around her body and making her shiver. She couldn't see, but she felt the water rising around her.

I'm too deep, thought Jinnie, panicking. She stood still. Which way?

"Come to me, come to me."

Relief welled up and made Jinnie burst into tears. "Where are you?" she called out, staggering forward a few steps, exhaustion supplanting her fear.

A wave hit her in the small of her back, knocking Jinnie down. Water closed over her head. She struggled to the surface, gasping and spitting.

"Help me!" Jinnie flailed at the water, her purse weighing her down.

Strong arms swept around her, lifting her easily from her watery captor.

"Hollany," his voice said. "Beloved."

Two

Jinnie woke up slowly; soft pillows and a softer bed made her stretch. She sat up. The room was dark, its contents turned into grotesque shapes as moonlight danced with shadows. Curtains, provoked by a breeze, waved once and were still.

Rising shakily, Jinnie noticed someone had clothed her in a nightgown. She moved slowly across what felt like marble floors toward the drapes, disconcerted by the absolute stillness.

Jinnie drew one curtain aside, revealing an archway. The night sky that greeted her was happy with stars, not at all like the sky of Hura.

Or Ispell, Jinnie remembered. The stars over Keldonabrieve were few and never shone so brightly. Even on Earth …

"Oh, Karen," Jinnie whispered. "I got my chance and took it, but I don't think I'll ever get back to tell you about it."

Taking a deep breath, Jinnie stepped into the night. She stood on a wide balcony; its railing, flat and broad on top, was scattered with large white and yellow flowers.

Peering over them, Jinnie saw only impenetrable darkness, but she had the impression of tremendous height. She looked about. The wall of the building was smooth and curved, the balcony encircling it in either direction.

This must be one of the towers, Jinnie thought, trying to quell her uneasiness.

She waited a moment, hoping the crushing sense of isolation would pass and that memories of her life on Yar would tell her what to do. But there was only silence in her mind and in the night.

I know the tower is round, thought Jinnie. *I'll end up where I started. I can't get lost.*

Looking both ways, Jinnie arbitrarily chose right and began walking. She shivered. The gown was too thin for the cool air, and Jinnie wished she'd thought to look for a robe before beginning her walk.

At least my back is warm, Jinnie said to herself.

She stopped. Curious, she slipped her right arm behind her neck and pulled her hair over her shoulder. Lifting it, she examined the dark tresses in the moonlight. Brown.

Looking down her body, she pressed her hands against her breasts: fuller. Jinnie stuck her toes of her right foot out from under her nightgown as if that might reveal if she were taller now.

She touched her mouth: wider. Fingering her face like a blind man, she felt high cheekbones and arched brows.

I'm me again, she thought wildly. *Strange, when I was with Dalia, I didn't think about my appearance. I was too preoccupied with my circumstances.*

The skirt of her nightgown swirled in a breeze, chilling her legs. She started walking, remembering the Chill.

But this isn't Keldonabrieve, she told herself. *And it's not Griffin who's waiting for me.* The memory almost made her stop again. Jinnie made herself continue walking.

A flickering light on the path ahead slowed her steps. Not knowing what to expect, she approached cautiously.

Another archway, this one without curtains, interrupted the smooth curve of the wall. Jinnie edged toward it and peered into the room beyond.

Her 'ghost' sat at a narrow table, writing in a book. All too real now, his handsomeness was almost beautiful.

Jinnie thought she should know him. She should know his name and what he meant to her, but nothing.

Now that she remembered the past, her present was a mystery. And there was something else. Some sliver of apprehension, almost fear. It held her back as her ghost shut the book and rose, making Jinnie step back, acting instinctively, unable to reason with her sudden wish to go undiscovered. But she had been seen.

"Who's there?" the man called out.

Answer him, Jinnie raged at herself, but her throat was tight with anxiety.

"Whoever you are, come forward." His voice sounded tired and annoyed. "It's too late for games."

Jinnie felt an almost hysterical urge to run. Instead, she forced herself to step through the archway.

The man now stood with his arms braced against the mantel of a fireplace, staring into an empty hearth.

"Yes," he said wearily, without looking up. "What do you want?"

"I want to know your name."

The man's head jerked up. "Hollany!" He rushed toward her, making Jinnie skitter away in spite of herself.

He stopped. "You're not afraid of me, are you?" He took a step forward and Jinnie took a step back.

"There's no need to be afraid, beloved," he said. "Not now. Not ever again."

"Who are you?" Jinnie's voice was a frightened whisper.

"The one who loves you."

Jinnie waited for more.

"My name is Kye," he said. "Don't you know me, Hollany?"

"No. Not really. I remember seeing you, but I don't know you."

Kye gestured carefully, so as not to startle her. "Come into the room, Hollany. You're cold."

Jinnie moved uneasily past Kye and into the room. She went to stand in front of the fireplace, again pushing memories of Griffin away. "Why do you call me Hollany?" Jinnie asked.

Lifting a robe from the end of the bed, Kye brought it to Jinnie and draped it about her shoulders. He let his hands rest there.

"Because that's your name, beloved."

It doesn't make any sense, thought Jinnie. Her name, or a variation of it, had been a constant so far. Had so much changed this time? And if so, why?

Still standing close behind her, Kye spoke softly. "It's wonderful to see you awake, Hollany. Do you feel well? Would you like anything, beloved?"

Jinnie shook her head. Without memories of her life with Kye, she didn't know where to begin. "What color are my eyes?" she asked, without thinking.

Kye smiled. "Blue."

"And who am I?"

"My love," he answered softly. "My life."

"And my name is Hollany?"

"Yes, beloved."

Kye turned her gently around to face him. Jinnie had to tilt her head a little to look into his eyes.

"Do you know what I am?" Jinnie asked, determined to understand this new part of her existence.

"Yes. You're a Traveler. But, Hollany, that's not important." Kye lifted his hand to touch her hair. "You're here. I love you. That's all that matters."

"That's not enough. How much do you know about me? How do you know?"

"I'm a Toranise," Kye answered, leaning toward her.

Jinnie let him kiss her, expecting a wave of memories to come to her and make her want to return his kiss. She stood still, heart pounding in her ears. Kye's mouth was warm, his kiss gentle. It almost reminded her of ...

Jinnie pulled back and moved away. She couldn't look at Kye. A troubling unhappiness and anxiety shadowed her as she crossed the room to the desk. "I haven't remembered my life here. Not you, not this." She lifted the book. It was a diary.

Coming up silently behind her, Kye took the diary from Jinnie's hands. He set it back on the desk. "No more for tonight, beloved. Come to bed."

Jinnie straightened her shoulders. "I want to go back to my room now."

There was a moment's silence behind her and Jinnie half-turned to see if Kye was angry. Instead, she saw only disappointment.

"Then I'll take you back to your room, Hollany."

"I know the way."

"Will you let me come wake you in the morning?"

Jinnie pulled his robe closer about her, liking his scent on the cloth. "Yes."

She started to leave. "Kye?"

"Yes, beloved?"

"How long have I been here?"

"Four days and nights. I worried you'd never wake up."

"Is that all? Haven't I lived part of a life here with you?" Confused, Jinnie turned back to face Kye, waiting for his answer.

He looked away from her. "Yes," he said after a minute. "But because it was incomplete, you were lost to me." Kye stepped toward Jinnie. "I've been calling to you for a very long time."

"I heard you. I was in a ravine," Jinnie faltered, then tried again, wishing she could remember anything of her life with Kye.

"I stumbled. Then I was in the water." Jinnie bit her lip, recalling her promise to Dalia. "I thought I was going to drown."

Kye moved closer, lifting a hand to caress Jinnie's cheek and lift her hair from her shoulder. "Don't think of it anymore, Hollany. I've found you, beloved. Now you are here in Yar again. Only this time you are whole."

Jinnie looked up into the dark green eyes that had haunted her across worlds. "Yar," she nodded, forgetting to make it a question.

Kye didn't notice. "Yes. Do you remember, beloved? The name of your home is Yar."

Jinnie turned away, feeling tired and sad. She remembered only because Dalia had told her.

"I hope ..." Jinnie stopped. She had been about to use the formal good-bye of the Daskiny. "I hope you have a good night, Kye," Jinnie said. "I'll see you in the morning."

"Hollany?"

Jinnie stopped under the archway, waiting, anxious and afraid. She wanted to insist on being called Jinnie and yet, for some reason, she didn't want to hear Kye say the name, the word. "What is it, Kye?"

She heard him take a deep breath.

"Welcome home."

* * *

Kye watched as his *hollany* left his room. Taking the diary from his desk, he went to the fireplace mantelpiece and hid the book away. Swiftly now, Kye strode across the room to an interior door and moved quickly down the hall to Hollany's room.

His keen hearing identified the sound of her as she moved about the room. Kye waited until long after he heard the rustle of bedding, then he opened the door a little and stepped inside.

He stood at the door for a long time, watching Hollany sleep, his thoughts tumbling one after the other. Finally, he turned away, closed the door behind him, and returned to his room.

You're mine now, Hollany, Kye said to himself. *Mine at last.*

* * *

The predawn chill woke Jinnie. Restless, she pulled on Kye's robe and left her room to explore the house. She didn't want to face Kye yet, not when she had been remembering Griffin. She needed to remember her life with Kye on Yar. She had to forget the past she had tried so hard to remember. Forget it all, especially Griffin.

Stop it! Jinnie warned herself. *Let go of the past and look to the future, just like Susatch said.* She walked quickly away from her thoughts, allowing herself only to hope that Susatch had made it to the Station.

The dark outline of a railing drew her attention. Cautiously Jinnie leaned over it.

Two floors below her, a room full of writhing shadows beckoned. Looking along the railing, she saw a narrow, winding staircase. Almost on tiptoe, she descended.

At the foot of the stairs, Jinnie looked about in awe at the single, enormous room. Dozens of archways led from it, but Jinnie was drawn to a pair of tall, curved doors set into the outside wall. Two smooth silver handles tempted her. She tugged on one.

The door opened easily. Dainty threads of pink light trickled into the great hall as a gold sun rose. Six wide stone stairs led down to what could only be a wharf, long and narrow. Indeed, a single boat was tied to it, floating in the air as easily as a leaf on water.

"What is this place I've come to?" whispered Jinnie, awed.

Descending the steps, she watched the mists that rolled and curled below her. As the sky lightened, she could see other circular stone houses in the distance, some with turrets rising like mastheads with wreaths of flowers for sails. The sky brightened to a pale orange tinged with white while purple clouds began to disperse.

Jinnie knew there was a valley below and that somewhere, too far away for her to hear, was an inland sea. She let herself wonder for a minute about Dalia. Was she safe? Would she be able to join the other Daskiny who had made it to the north?

I shouldn't think about her, Jinnie told herself. *I don't know her. It never happened. I promised.*

I'm sure Kye will tell me about the Daskiny eventually. I'm sure I'll start to remember my life here soon. She looked at the changing clouds, the lightening sky, not feeling sure at all. *What if I can't remember?*

Jinnie recalled Dalia mentioning Daskiny Healers. *Maybe a Daskiny Healer could help me remember*, she thought, *or at least tell me more about Travelers. I'll ask Kye.*

"Hollany!" Kye's anxious call came from the house, startling Jinnie. She turned and hurried up the stairs.

"Hollany! Answer me!"

Jinnie pulled open the door and stood on its threshold. "I'm here, Kye."

His worried face appeared above the upstairs railing. "Hollany!" Swinging himself over the rail, Kye dropped to the floor twenty feet below.

Jinnie screamed. She rushed to him, and grabbed his shoulders as he stood up.

"Are you all right?" they asked in unison.

"Of course I am," Jinnie said. "I was just exploring the house. I thought it might help me remember."

Kye hugged her fiercely, then took her face between his hands and searched her eyes, looking for reassurance.

"What is it?" asked Jinnie.

"Nothing. Nothing, beloved." He kissed her softly, his eyes still looking into hers. Releasing her, Kye kissed both of Jinnie's hands.

"Why did you jump like that?" Jinnie demanded. "You could have been hurt, even killed."

"Not at all. I'm a Toranise. The stairs are for you, Hollany."

"I don't understand."

Kye led Jinnie up the stairs and back to her room.

"Get dressed, beloved." He kissed her cheek. "I'll answer all your questions. But not on an empty stomach."

Three

Jinnie sat in the prow of the boat, trailing a finger over the side as they passed the tip of a purple cloud. She watched Kye. He stood in the back of the boat like a gondolier, dipping a long oar into the air as if the air were water.

Studying him, Jinnie decided she liked the dark green of his eyes and the way his silver-blonde hair feathered about his face and fell to his shoulders.

He was tall and slim, dressed in high dark boots, soft gray trousers, and a loose white shirt. He looked very much as he had when she first saw him in Keldonabrieve.

Jinnie looked away, searching for a distraction. "Well, you could at least answer one question before breakfast," she said.

Kye smiled. "As you like, beloved."

"How does this boat stay aloft? It doesn't have a motor; what propels it?"

"I do. My will keeps it afloat in the air. In my mind, I see the boat sailing through the sky in whatever direction I steer, and then I create the reality with the energy of my inner self."

"Your inner self." Jinnie lowered her eyes, hoping Kye hadn't noticed that she recognized and understood the term. She continued quickly, "You mean you can create anything you imagine?"

The Traveler

Kye laughed. "That's two questions, Hollany. But no. I can only create motion."

"Oh." Jinnie lifted her shoulders in an elaborate shrug. "Only motion."

The boat came to a smooth halt next to a meadow. A single mountain peak stood in the distance. Leaping gracefully from the stern, Kye helped Jinnie from the boat. He led her across the meadow to a large pond guarded by fruit trees.

"That's Haven Mountain," said Kye. He plucked a piece of fruit from a tree. "And this," he said, placing the dark blue fruit in Jinnie's hand, "is breakfast."

After they had eaten, Kye took Jinnie's hand and led her past the fruit trees to another part of the meadow.

"This is Chatamer Fields," he said, his eyes fixed on something far away.

Jinnie looked about, wondering when some of it, any of it, would seem familiar. The long grass competed with dozens of white and yellow wildflowers. A breeze created a ripple across the tops of the blossoms.

Jinnie watched, waiting for a memory, any memory. Nothing came.

"I first saw you here," said Kye, "a year ago."

Jinnie let go of his hand and walked among the flowers. Puzzled, she turned back to face Kye. "Not by the sea?"

"No. That's where I would call to you. But here," Kye joined Jinnie and took her hand again, "here is where I first saw you."

He ran his fingers through her hair. "I thought you were a dream. A beautiful dream like none I had ever known. I came here every day for a month. Sometimes you were vibrant, almost alive. Other times you would be like a shadow."

Jinnie remembered Escabel's words: a Phantasm, living in two worlds at once.

I can remember Escabel, thought Jinnie. *Why can't I remember my life here? And what place did I occupy in this world if I was so impermanent?*

"You were quiet," Kye continued. "Not serene, but troubled. I could walk with you, talk to you. But whenever I tried to touch you, my hand would pass through you as if you were a cloud."

He looked up at the mountain's peak. "One day you weren't here. I went half-mad searching for you. I called to you. I searched everywhere.

Finally I journeyed to the valley. I found you at the base of the mountain, where a river runs to the sea. You were unconscious, but you were also tangible for the first time."

His eyes went to Jinnie. "I picked you up in my arms and took you home. You slept for days. Then, one night, you spoke in your dreams."

"What did I say?"

"You said, 'I love you.' The next day you were gone again. I thought I saw you once by the sea's shore. Then you disappeared."

Kye drew Jinnie to him, hugging her close, speaking softly against her head. "Again and again, I returned to the sea. I kept calling to you. Sometimes I thought I saw you out of the corner of my eye, in a reflection, in a dream. I didn't see you again until four days ago when you were floundering in the waves."

Jinnie leaned against his chest, seeking comfort in his embrace. Everything was so different this time. Why had the pattern of her Traveling altered? And why had she no recollection of her life on Yar?

Tilting her head back, Jinnie looked at Kye, wondering if she wanted him to kiss her.

Kye decided for her. He bent his head and kissed Jinnie gently, then passionately, looking into her eyes. His arms tightened about her, and Jinnie clung to him as the only sanity in a frightening, incomprehensible world.

Kye pulled her hips against his.

Thinking, 'not yet', Jinnie said, "Not here."

"Yes," Kye kissed her cheek, "here." He kissed her lips again. "Now."

"Not now." Jinnie pushed against him, turning away from his kisses.

But Kye wouldn't release her. He kissed Jinnie's neck, pulled at the collar of her dress, and kissed her shoulder. His lips returned to her mouth. He kissed her again.

"Hollany, Hollany," Kye whispered. He looked into Jinnie's eyes. "I have waited so long a time for you."

The words—painfully familiar—broke the spell. For a moment, Jinnie stood rigid, the past colliding with the present.

Kye loosened his embrace, and Jinnie pulled away. She looked at the mountain, trying to bring herself completely into the present. And the future?

"How long will we Travel together, Kye?" Jinnie asked, hoping to feel reassured instead of uneasy. "And when?"

Taking Jinnie's hand, Kye kissed her palm. "We'll be together for a very long time, beloved."

Jinnie felt a chill sweep over her body as Kye evaded her questions.

"And then?" She turned to face him. "Then what happens? Do we travel together, or do I follow you? What happens next, and how?"

"Hollany." Kye reached for her, but Jinnie backed away from him, finding it hard to breathe, swaying slightly as a wave of nausea slapped her.

"Answer me, Kye. You're a Traveler, too," Jinnie's voice tightened. "You must be. You came to me."

"I'm not a Traveler, Hollany," Kye said, his voice quiet. "I'm a Toranise. Each time I came to you, I was projecting my inner self. It was a simple matter of creating a reality of motion. Nothing more."

"Nothing more?" Jinnie shook her head. "Nothing more? I thought I was going insane. Now you tell me I'll lose you, too. That all this," Jinnie waved her arms wildly, "all this is just going to slip away?"

Kye went to Jinnie, wrapping his arms about her and holding her until her breathing slowed. "Look at me," he whispered.

Jinnie shook her head against his chest.

"Hollany." Kye lifted Jinnie's chin until she looked at him. "I love you, Hollany. We're together now. You won't leave me. You won't travel again for years and years. I'll be old then. You'll be glad to leave me."

Jinnie felt drained, beaten. "Take me home, Kye," she said listlessly.

All the way back to Kye's tower, Jinnie stayed silent and still. Now that she could remember her previous lives, now that she could remember Griffin, it felt like a betrayal to be with Kye.

Now that I can remember, she thought, *I don't want to. Susatch said she couldn't prevent sorrow, and sorrow is exactly what I have to endure. It seems the life of a Traveler is a puzzle of pieces that I have to force together without knowing what the picture is.*

Here, Kye loves me. Jinnie looked at Kye, watching as he steered them toward his tower. *It's more than I had on Hura and not as much as I had on Ispell. Or is it? I can't remember.*

What about the other part of my life on Yar? What about the Daskiny and the animals they fear?

Don't think of it, Jinnie told herself. *None of it matters until I remember. When I remember my life with Kye, then everything else will make sense. All the pieces of the puzzle will fit into place.*

At the wharf, Jinnie stood and looked at the beautiful world that was to be hers for a time. Unhappiness stained the skies, and Jinnie turned away.

"Come inside, Hollany." Kye stretched his hand out to her.

Taking it, Jinnie followed Kye inside the tower and up the stairs. At the top, he drew her close to him. "Hollany?" His voice held an ache, a sorrow.

Jinnie looked into his eyes. *They should be brown,* she thought, *and warm with love.* Kye's green eyes were full of desperation.

Jinnie pulled away. "I have to think," she answered, knowing she really meant, "I have to grieve."

Kye touched her hair, then stepped aside.

Without looking back, Jinnie walked to her room and closed the door.

The day slid into evening as Jinnie alternately paced and lay on the bed. Several times she went to the archway that led to the balcony. Twice she went to the door of her room. Once she heard Kye in the hall. He knocked, but when she opened the door, there was only a silver tray of bread and fruit.

Taking the tray, Jinnie shut the door. She thought of Griffin bringing the tray to her in Keldonabrieve. Her hunger faded.

Jinnie let herself think back further to when she first met Griffin. She had been riding with the hunt; the group had paused for a brief respite, not dismounting. Griffin had handed her a goblet of sweet wine and smiled.

Not just with his mouth, Jinnie remembered, but with his eyes. *I think I fell in love with him at that moment.*

It was months before Griffin confessed his love, but Jinnie knew long before his confession. She warned him that fighting for peace among the Alliances had to be more important to her than anything ... at least for then.

Griffin said, "I can wait, my *jinnie,* because I love you. Now and always. I can wait."

Jinnie smiled a little. For a long time, Griffin's love had been everything to her. It was her personal peace. Nevertheless, when Lancin proposed, Jinnie accepted. She knew a political marriage would give her a position of power that could help her aid the Alliances.

Jinnie poured a glass of water from the pitcher on the tray, remembering. She set the glass down without drinking.

"Let it go," Jinnie said aloud. "Let it all go because it has already gone."

A cold wind stormed her room, making her retreat to her bed. She huddled there, reaching for a decision, feeling displaced and isolated.

Time is my enemy, thought Jinnie. *I don't know how long I'll stay in Yar or even why I'm here. I know Dalia believed she spoke the truth, but maybe it was only the truth for her. I don't know if Kye is dangerous or untrustworthy. He says he loves me. Do I believe him or not?*

Stars became the sky's lanterns before Jinnie stepped out onto the balcony. She wore only Kye's robe. The wind had stilled, and the silence made Jinnie anxious as she walked toward Kye's room.

Earlier today, I wanted Kye to kiss me, Jinnie reminded herself. *And I will again. This is my life now. Kye loves me. Whatever the reason for my being in Yar, at least I have Kye's love.*

She paused at the archway to his room, heart pounding. Tonight, a fire burned in the fireplace. Jinnie walked toward the hearth, eyes searching the room. Kye wasn't there.

Taking a determined breath, she went to the bed and lay down, trying not to think of Griffin. She would wait for Kye. The day's stress blanketed her, and Jinnie slept.

An hour later, Kye returned to his room. When he had knocked at Hollany's door, she hadn't answered. Shoulders slumped with weariness, he moved to the mantelpiece above the fireplace and pressed a small carved figure on the edge. The figure swung to one side, revealing a narrow shelf.

Kye withdrew his diary from its hiding place, fingering the worn pages. Would he ever have his heart's desire?

"She wanted me this morning," he said. "I'm certain of it."

Jinnie murmured in her sleep, and Kye spun about. Disbelief froze him where he stood. "Hollany."

When she didn't wake, Kye set the diary on the desk and went to sit on the side of the bed. He reached to touch her hair. "Hollany?"

Jinnie turned on her side, away from Kye, still sleeping.

He rose and undressed, then slid into the bed next to her.

Jinnie stretched against the warm body at her back, dreaming. In her dream, she imagined Griffin stroking her hair, kissing her shoulder, her neck, her cheek. Gentle fingers freed Jinnie from her robe and caressed her body.

A stir of consciousness brought a name to Jinnie's lips. "Griffin," she murmured.

The fingers stopped for a moment, then continued.

"Hollany," a voice whispered in her ear, "it's Kye."

Opening her eyes, Jinnie looked over her shoulder. Kye was pressed against her, warming her cold legs with his.

"Will you let me love you now?" Kye asked, emphasizing me.

Jinnie turned onto her back, blinking back her dream, focusing on Kye's face, his mouth, his eyes. "Yes."

Kye kissed her passionately, and Jinnie waited to feel something, anything. She closed her eyes and returned his kiss.

Leaning back, Kye's gaze wandered over Jinnie's body. He caressed her breasts, her waist, her hips, familiarizing himself with the reality of his dream. "My *hollany*," Kye murmured. "You are as beautiful as I imagined."

Jinnie shivered beneath his touch, trying to relax.

"Look at me," Kye said.

Jinnie looked into his eyes. Kye pushed inside her body, moving slowly within her until she moved with him. He kissed Jinnie again, sliding his tongue inside her mouth. Kye moved one of her legs up, pulling her further beneath him, thrusting deeper.

Jinnie wrapped her arms up and under Kye's, watching him, kissing him, answering his body with hers. Kye's hips impacted harder against Jinnie. He bent his head over her shoulder, then his voice was in her ear.

"Hollany. Say you love me, Hollany," Kye insisted; his body insisted. He moved faster against her. "Say it, say it, say you love me."

Closing her eyes, Jinnie remembered another voice, a voice belonging to a man with warm brown eyes and reddish-gold hair. "I love you," she whispered.

Kye's thrusts became quick, short jerks. He groaned, lowering himself onto her body, holding onto Jinnie; his fingers pinched her shoulders.

"Beloved," Kye breathed. "My *hollany*."

* * *

An ocean of clouds billowed lavender, and then dark purple. In the distance, white towers caught the last strands of light, shining brilliantly against silhouettes of mountains.

Leaning on the balcony railing, Jinnie watched and waited, hoping to recognize a peak or turret, to remember a previous sunset, some small piece of her life in Yar.

Kye had kept her in bed all day. In the afternoon, he had left her only long enough to go downstairs, returning with a tray of food and a bottle of wine. This time, Jinnie stayed in the present, not allowing herself to think of the past.

When Kye slept, holding her close, Jinnie forced herself to lie still, trying to relax against the hard muscles of his body. When he woke and kissed her, she responded. He didn't insist again on hearing, "I love you," only that Jinnie look at him as he made love to her.

Did Kye suspect she hadn't meant the words? Could he know she had been thinking of someone else? Jinnie struggled to separate the images of her dream from the reality of Kye's lovemaking. Guilt over her duplicity made Jinnie angry with herself.

I should never have said I loved him, she thought. *Not yet. Not until I remember my life here.*

Jinnie frowned. *Maybe I do love Kye, and I just don't remember yet. Maybe Kye is the great love of my life. Of all my lives.*

No. Griffin is my great love, the only certainty in this madness. Griffin. Now and always. I was wrong to tell Kye I loved him, whatever the circumstances of my life here.

Jinnie straightened as Kye came up behind her, encircling her in his arms. She leaned back against his chest, grateful to be distracted from her angst.

"What's a Toranise?" Jinnie asked.

"We are." Kye gestured with an arm, encompassing the stone towers and their occupants. "We are creatures of motion and metamorphosis. After a life above the valley, a time comes when we transform. We are reborn as Dysans, winged beings like birds, and we realize our dreams of flying. It is a rich and powerful existence."

"Who else lives on Yar?"

There was a long silence. "What makes you think anyone else lives here?" Kye pulled her hair back from her neck and kissed Jinnie's shoulder.

Did Kye's voice sound guarded? Jinnie turned to face him. "I don't know. You said you live in the towers above a valley."

"Yes. The Toranise own the valleys beneath our towers as well as the mountains and meadows, everything. There are several Regions throughout the southern hemisphere."

"What's in the North?"

Kye stroked the side of Jinnie's neck. "Nothing, beloved, only cold and snow."

"And in the valleys? Does anyone live there?"

Jinnie watched Kye's face as he answered; he seemed impatient. "The Daskiny. They live and work in the valleys. We live above. It has always been so. We trade with them, wild herbs and flowers from our mountain meadows in return for labor, clothes, food, wine. All the comfortable things that make our lives in the sky more pleasant. The Daskiny fear the heights, and we Toranise dislike the feel of the earth. It is an equitable arrangement."

"Which am I? Daskiny or Toranise?"

"Neither, beloved." Kye kissed the top of her head. "You are a Traveler."

Jinnie pulled away from Kye and moved along the balcony, troubled. Lights began to glow in the towers as the twilight deepened.

She turned to face Kye again. "When I've Traveled before, there's always been a place for me. Not just a life to live, but a life that was part of the world around me. A life that made a difference."

"You're part of my world," said Kye. "You make a difference to me."

Jinnie shook her head. "That can't be the only reason for my being here, Kye."

"Why?" He walked toward her as he had in Keldonabrieve, on Breeare and Hura. Only this time, when he reached her, he could touch her. "Why isn't being here with me enough?"

"It is," Jinnie hurried to reassure him and herself. For a moment, she had felt that something was terribly wrong and that she was overlooking something important.

"I only meant that, before I Traveled to Yar, I was important. I was a key part of something that was happening or about to take place."

"You are important." Kye smiled, taking Jinnie by the waist and pulling her against him. "And what is about to take place is this." He kissed her.

Jinnie leaned into his kiss, but it didn't dispel her anxiety.

"Come inside, Hollany," Kye said. "It's cold out here. I'll light a fire for you."

Jinnie let Kye lead her back into his room. "How did you learn that I'm a Traveler, Kye? It's always been a mystery before, to me and to those around me."

Kneeling before the hearth, Kye arranged wood and paper, leaning forward to light the tinder, staring intently. "I went down to the valley. Some of the Daskiny journey among the Regions of the Toranise. They transport goods and messages and offer their skills in medicines. A few of them keep simple history records.

"I found one such Healer. She knew a little about Travelers. They were mentioned in one of her books. She said Travelers pass through the early stages of their lives quickly, seeking a haven where they can live an entire lifetime, whole and unbroken."

The fire blazed. Kye stood up and came to Jinnie, taking her hands and kissing each one. "Yar is your haven, beloved. You will no longer split apart or drift in and out of your life here. You are whole now, unbroken.

"You have my love, and you are important to me, more than you could ever imagine. I love you. Nothing else matters. Nothing means more to me than you. Why isn't that enough?"

Jinnie pulled away from him and moved toward the fireplace, watching the flames lick hungrily at something in their grasp. "It's just that everything is so different this time. Nothing is familiar, not even you. I remember my past, but not my present. I've been told before I would be whole, and it didn't last."

Jinnie suppressed a shiver of apprehension, and turned away from the fire.

"Would you take me to this Daskiny Healer, Kye? What she told you is different from what I've learned about Travelers so far. I'd like a chance to speak with her and ask her some questions. I'd like to know what makes her think I'll stay on Yar for a lifetime instead of Traveling quickly, as I have before."

A frown marred Kye's beautiful features for a moment as he listened.

"Don't you see, Kye?" Jinnie heard a plea in her voice. "Your life has a rhythm, a purpose. Mine has been so chaotic."

"The Daskiny Healer said it would take time for you to adjust to Yar," Kye's voice held frustration. "Be patient, beloved."

"If I could just talk to her. There's still more I need to know about being a Traveler. Perhaps she'd let me read her book."

Jinnie went to stand before Kye, looking up at him, wondering why she felt afraid and willing herself to appear calm. "Will you take me to her?"

Kye lifted a hand and caressed her cheek. "She's not there anymore, Hollany. She was intending to leave for another region when I found her."

"She might not have left yet. Or maybe someone else could help."

Kye pulled Jinnie into his arms. He stared down at her, his eyes fathomless. "She has left, Hollany. There is no one else."

Jinnie looked away. "Are you certain?"

Kye's silence made Jinnie return her gaze to his.

"Yes." Kye kissed her softly. "I'm certain."

Jinnie leaned her head against his chest, discouraged and uncomforted. "Then I'll never know why I'm here," she whispered.

"Not all explanations are complicated, Hollany," Kye said. "Not all questions have an answer."

Tilting her head back to look at him, Jinnie felt swallowed up in Kye's steady gaze.

"You're here because you belong with me," he said, his voice low and stern. "You're here because I love you, Hollany."

He kissed her again, and Jinnie traded the past for the present, slipping her arms about Kye's neck and returning his kiss.

Hours later, as Jinnie slept, Kye stirred the embers in the hearth. The last bindings of her diary sizzled and died, disappearing into the heat of the ashes. Satisfied, Kye returned to the bed and lay down, drawing Jinnie possessively close.

"My *hollany*," he whispered.

Four

"It's been weeks," Jinnie complained. She sat up, pulling a sheet with her, leaving Kye naked on the bed as she crossed his room to the balcony. She stopped under the archway and glared at the night sky.

"It's been days," said Kye, tolerating her outburst, knowing it would pass. "Four days, beloved. And what does it matter if you don't yet remember your life on Yar?"

He propped his head on one hand, lying on his side, watching her. "You told me that the pattern of your Traveling had changed. Yar is where you are meant to be. With me is where you belong."

Jinnie leaned against the cool stone of the archway. Had it really only been four days since she had tried to accept Kye and her life with him? "It's just so frustrating, not understanding why I'm here, what my purpose is."

"Even Travelers can't know everything," Kye teased.

Jinnie didn't answer. She stepped out onto the balcony. Across the waves of clouds, one of the other towers was alive with lights. On its wharf, a group of Toranise was boarding a large boat with nets hung from its sides. They were laughing and waving lanterns at one another.

"Kye?" Jinnie called over her shoulder.

"Yes, Hollany?" Rising, he put on his robe and went to his desk. Taking a piece of fruit from a plate, Kye came to stand beside Jinnie. "What is it?"

Jinnie pointed. "Where are they going?"

Kye examined the fruit in his hand. "Fishing," he said, without interest.

"Fishing? You told me the Toranise are vegetarians."

"As we near the time of metamorphosis, our metabolism alters. We require different sources of protein." He bit sharply into the fruit. "It changes our appetites."

Jinnie recalled Dalia's warning, 'They are not what they seem.' Looking at Kye, Jinnie guessed him to be about the same age as the Toranise who were getting into the fishing trawler.

"They don't look any older than you," she objected. "You said Toranise go through the metamorphosis when they're old."

Kye smiled. "Toranise do not age visibly, Hollany. Our bodies alter internally first, and we begin to age only when we pass through the final stage of metamorphosis and transform."

"Into Dysans."

"Yes, beloved." Kye reached an arm about Jinnie's waist, pulling her next to him.

"Then what happens? I haven't seen any Dysans on the boats that sail past your tower."

"Our tower," Kye corrected her.

"Our tower," Jinnie repeated impatiently. "Where are they?"

"The Dysans don't need boats to fly," answered Kye, setting his fruit on the ledge of the balcony railing. "And they do not live among the Toranise."

"Why not? Are the Dysans banished?"

"They prefer the mountain peaks." Kye lifted Jinnie's hair from her shoulders, running his fingers through its length. He kissed her neck.

"What do they become that they're so different from the Toranise? What will you become?" Jinnie shivered as Kye slid his hands to her breasts, caressing her through the thin fabric of the sheet.

"I don't know, Hollany." He turned her to face him. "We don't speak of it."

"Why? You said it was your heart's desire."

"You are my heart's desire."

Kye had left his robe open, and now he pulled the sheet away from Jinnie, drawing her inside his robe, naked against his body. "Hollany," he whispered, kissing her cheek, her throat, pressing his hips tightly against hers.

"Kye," Jinnie interrupted his seduction. "I might never remember my life on Yar. You have to tell me about everything. You have to answer me when I ask questions."

Kye silenced her with a long kiss. When Jinnie didn't respond, he stopped, but kept his arms about her. "I have told you everything, Hollany," Kye said, his patience slipping. "Everything of importance. Everything I can. What more is there to tell?"

Freeing an arm, Jinnie pointed again at the departing fishermen. "That. You didn't tell me about the process of metamorphosis. You didn't tell me the Dysans don't live among the Toranise. What else haven't you told me, Kye?"

Not answering, Kye backed Jinnie up against the balcony railing. He pushed her legs apart, stepping between her thighs as his hands slid down her back.

Bracing her free arm on the ledge, Jinnie pushed against Kye's chest, but this time he didn't relent. He kissed her again, opening her mouth with his tongue.

Giving in, Jinnie returned his kiss, and Kye quickly slipped his hands under her hips, lifting her onto the ledge of the railing.

"No," Jinnie gasped, clutching at Kye to keep her balance. Ignoring her, Kye forced his body inside hers, his thrusts short and rapid, his fingers gripping her painfully.

"Kye!" Jinnie tried not to struggle; Kye was her anchor against a pitiless fall.

He lunged forward, tilting Jinnie over the edge. Before she could scream, Kye pulled her back, pulled from her body, and lifted her in his arms.

Relief kept Jinnie silent as Kye carried her from the balcony and into their room. Without a word, he lowered her onto the bed, pushing inside her again before she could argue or escape.

"Look at me," he demanded, his voice harsh.

Not understanding Kye's tone, Jinnie looked into his eyes. They were no longer green. They were gold, the pupils white.

Frightened, Jinnie let Kye continue his mad lovemaking. He stared down at her, returning to the intense motion he had interrupted. His thrusts deepened; his body moved faster against Jinnie until she could barely breathe. Her heart pounded in her ears as she waited for him to let her go.

"Hollany, Hollany," Kye said, his voice far away even as his gold eyes continued to stare down at her. His hips suddenly slammed against hers, and Kye shuddered. He closed his eyes.

Jinnie reached up to touch his cheek. "Kye?" She spoke in a cautious whisper.

Kye's body relaxed slowly. Supporting his weight on his arms, but still keeping Jinnie pinned beneath him, he opened his eyes. They were green.

"Yes, beloved?" His tone was loving again.

Jinnie looked into Kye's green eyes, realizing he was unaware of what had just happened. She didn't know what to say. "I ..." Jinnie began.

Kye smiled at her. "More questions?"

Jinnie shook her head slowly. "No."

Kissing her lips lightly, Kye moved away from Jinnie. He pulled off his robe, tossed it to the floor, and stretched out beside her, pulling her close. "It's late, Hollany." Kye kissed Jinnie's forehead. "Go to sleep."

Jinnie lay still, knowing she wouldn't sleep. She had only slept a little in the past four days, dozing, dreamless, and tired, waiting for her world to take shape and make sense. Now it made no sense at all.

Kye's arm dropped slightly from Jinnie's shoulder. She waited a little longer, then moved slowly out of his embrace. He rolled over, sleeping soundly now.

Jinnie picked up Kye's robe from the floor. Putting on the robe, she tied it tightly at the waist and stole into the night. She followed the circle of the balcony, letting the cold air clear her mind.

What had happened to Kye? What had happened to his eyes? Was this the beginning of the metamorphosis?

Jinnie stopped walking. Her head ached, and she felt sick with anxiety. Kye had never been violent before. His passion had always held love.

Agitated, she started walking again, trying to walk away from the possibility that Kye was changing already. He had told her it would be years before he became a Dysan. She had to believe him. Perhaps the color change of his eyes was natural, one more thing that he hadn't told her about.

Of course. Jinnie clung to the possibility. He hadn't thought to mention it, she rationalized. He said the Toranise didn't speak of the Dysans.

Jinnie sighed in relief. That must be it.

She looked out into the night, remembering the fishermen. *Kye doesn't eat meat*, Jinnie thought. *He isn't becoming a Dysan. Yet.*

She took a deep breath and shivered. It was too cold on the balcony tonight, and she quickened her pace, wanting to return to Kye. To the Kye she knew. She couldn't think any more of what he was to become. That wouldn't be for years.

But Jinnie couldn't outpace the questions. What else changed with the metamorphosis of a Toranise? Was Kye telling her the truth about it?

She stopped walking and reached to touch a flower that draped from one of the vines. It was a simple but solid reality, its fragrance as beguiling as Kye's declarations of love.

"I have to believe in Kye," Jinnie said to the beautiful blossom at her fingertips. "I'm part of his world, at least for now. And he loves me."

Or he thinks he does, Jinnie added silently. Four days of passion wasn't proof of love, only desire.

I need to speak to the Daskiny in the valley, thought Jinnie. *Kye said only the Healer knew about Travelers, but what do the Daskiny know about the Toranise?*

Jinnie released the flower. "Why am I afraid?" she whispered, knowing the answer even as she spoke: she was afraid of the truth. She was afraid of her new, unremembered life.

Continuing her walk, Jinnie lifted the collar of Kye's robe against the cold.

I have to believe in Kye, Jinnie told herself. *He's all I have. I have to believe he's telling me the truth. I have to believe he loves me.*

She reached the archway leading to his room. *Our room*, Jinnie reminded herself. She entered, going first to the fireplace to warm up, not wanting to wake Kye with the coldness of her skin. Opening Kye's robe, Jinnie leaned on the mantelpiece. A carved figure gave way under her the weight of her hand.

Jinnie froze. Memories of secret doors and hidden passageways trampled her recent resolve. She glanced over her shoulder. Kye was still asleep. Jinnie looked back at the exposed shelf that had been hidden behind the carving. It was empty. She touched the interior of the nook with her fingertips. Empty, but not dusty. It had been used recently.

What had been so cleverly concealed? Jinnie pushed the question away, seeking the relief she had felt on the balcony.

It's probably nothing important, she decided. *I won't worry about it.* Jinnie struggled to calm herself. *I won't let my imagination destroy this fragile present.*

Jinnie carefully returned the carving to its place along the edge of the mantelpiece. She pulled off the robe and returned to bed.

Lying still, away from Kye, the cold made her seek the warmth of his back. She rested her cheek against his shoulder blade, letting his body heat soothe her.

Her mind slid in and out of sleep. Jinnie thought she heard a voice: warm, familiar. Jinnie turned on her side, hugging a pillow, remembering. Griffin.

* * *

Slipping into the warm water of the hot spring, Jinnie leaned back against Kye's chest. "Ten days," she announced. "It's been ten days, and I remember nothing."

"Do you remember I love you?"

"Yes." Jinnie cupped a handful of water and tossed it over her shoulder at Kye. Since the night of violence on the balcony, his eyes hadn't changed their color, and she had relaxed, believing in him.

"Then you remember everything."

She stalled his hands as they caressed her. "Will you take me to the valley soon, Kye?"

"Yes."

"When?"

"Soon."

"But you will take me, won't you?" Jinnie asked carefully, not wanting her voice to betray her true motive for the trip: the Daskiny.

"Yes." Kye ran a finger along Jinnie's thigh. "Why do you want to go, Hollany? Are you unhappy in the towers?"

Yes, thought Jinnie. "No," she said aloud. "I just want to see more of Yar."

"I've sailed you all over the mountains and their meadows. You've seen the fields and forests from above, where they are the most beautiful. I've even taken you above the river's course to the shore of the sea. Up here among the clouds, everything is fresh, clean, beautiful. In the valleys, there's only the dank smell of soil, animals grazing, and the cooking fires of the Daskiny."

"The Daskiny." Jinnie latched onto the word. "I'd still like to meet them, even though the Healer is gone. Are they much like the Toranise?" she asked, pretending not to know.

Kye laughed. "Not at all. They are short, and their skin is dark. They are crafty, untrustworthy, and suspicious. They take all day to make a simple piece of clothing, and they would rather languish from hunger in the winter than till their fields."

Jinnie listened carefully. "You don't like them very much."

Kye shrugged. "They're Daskiny. I neither like nor dislike them."

"But the Toranise depend on them for so much," Jinnie argued. "Clothing, furniture, even the parchments you write on and the musical instruments you play. What would you do without them?"

Kye didn't answer. When he did speak, annoyance and impatience made his voice sharp. "We protect and guard them from the wilderness beasts. We provide them with the best of things from our mountain meadows. We are their overseers, making certain they do not starve, and when they die, we see that their ashes are properly scattered."

Kye paused. He took a deep breath, calming himself. "I've told you all this before, Hollany. Have you forgotten?"

"No." Jinnie sat up, intending to stand, but Kye held her shoulders.

"I have something for you, beloved," he said softly, changing the subject.

Jinnie knew she would get no more answers today. For all his patience with her, when Kye didn't want to speak further, he was immovable.

"What have you got?" she asked, turning her head.

"Don't look." Kye reached for something beside the pool. "Close your eyes."

"I don't like surprises," Jinnie protested.

"A poor attitude for a Traveler," chided Kye. "Now, close your eyes."

Jinnie closed her eyes. She felt his hands above her head. Something metallic was pulled down over her hair until it rested around her neck, and Jinnie felt the cold press of an object between her breasts.

"Open your eyes, Hollany."

Jinnie looked down. A thin, white crystal hung from a silver chain about her neck. Lifting it to the sunshine, Jinnie admired the prism.

"It's beautiful, Kye." She leaned back against his chest again, relaxing as she watched the rainbow spin within the confines of the crystal. *It holds all the colors in all the worlds anywhere*, she thought.

She ran her fingers along the simple chain. She knew it had been made by a Daskiny. "When did you get it, Kye?" Jinnie asked. "You rarely leave me alone."

"Before you returned to me. I found it at the estuary of the river when I was searching for you. I kept it as a sign that I would find you." Kye flipped a handful of water at Jinnie. "The Daskiny were happy to prepare a chain for it. For you."

Jinnie tensed. "They know about me?"

Kye stroked her hair. "They know only that you are important to a Toranise. An important Toranise."

"Is there any other kind?" Jinnie teased.

"Promise never to take it off," Kye said, his voice had an urgent undertone.

"Why?"

"Because I ask it of you."

"All right. I promise never to take it off." Jinnie half-turned to face Kye, looping her arms about his neck. "Unless, of course, you take it off."

She had expected him to kiss her, perhaps laugh, definitely to insist on making love. But his eyes darkened instead, and the night on the balcony leapt to Jinnie's mind.

"Hollany," Kye's voice was low, tense. "Never take the crystal from around your neck. Never."

Jinnie nodded, trying to ignore the sudden feeling of anxiety. "I promise, Kye."

As he looked into her eyes, Kye's features relaxed. "I love you, Hollany."

Jinnie lowered her gaze to the crystal. She lifted it by the chain and spun it back and forth, not answering.

* * *

Days later, Jinnie circled the tower's balcony. Bored, she plucked a flower from the vine that ran along the railing and twirled it between her fingers.

Kye had been gone all afternoon. It was the first time he had left her alone for so long. It felt freeing.

Jinnie frowned. She hadn't thought about how dependent she was on Kye. She hadn't had time to think. He was always with her, and yet she felt lonely. He disliked questions about their life, and Jinnie only saw other people from the balcony.

Every three days, fresh foods were left in a basket on the wharf. Watching Daskiny being ferried to other towers, unloading parcels and baskets of food, Jinnie asked if the Daskiny could sail boats like the Toranise. Kye had scoffed and said no.

"They can do nothing for themselves. See how we ferry them? They need us for everything." He laughed then, and Jinnie had dropped the subject, reluctant to push for answers she feared she wouldn't like.

Kye did everything for her. He suggested what she should wear, brushed her hair, took her to the hot spring. He read to her, played music for her, and taught her a board game that reminded Jinnie of chess. He took advantage of every opportunity to kiss, touch, and caress her, to tell her he loved her and call her his beloved.

His eyes hadn't changed color again, and Jinnie pushed aside her doubts, waiting to feel the love Kye professed and to feel love for him in return.

Kye's lovemaking was passionate, but it never quite touched her.

Perhaps it never will, Jinnie worried. Late at night, while Kye slept, she still prowled the balcony, circling and seeking. She felt she was overlooking something important and that there was something wrong. Something obvious and yet obscured.

Jinnie worried, too, about the Daskiny. She felt a need to help them, rescue them from danger, but she had no idea how or from what. She said nothing of her feelings to Kye. Jinnie noticed that sometimes she was very careful not to upset him.

Do I love Kye? Jinnie asked herself. *He's made me the center of his existence, but that's not love; that's obsession. He's not Griffin.*

She darted under an archway, angry that she'd let her thoughts stray to someone she'd promised herself not to think of.

"I love Kye," Jinnie announced to the room. "He's wonderful to me, and I love him."

She threw the flower to the floor and stamped her foot. "This is my life now, and I will accept it," she insisted to no one but herself. Her sudden rage evaporated. Swinging between frustration and unhappiness, Jinnie sank into a chair and glowered at the room. It was the music room. Kye had played a beautiful piece of music for her the night before. He'd used a seven-stringed instrument that looked something like a guitar but sounded more like a piano. There it was in the corner. Jinnie didn't remember what he'd called it.

Her attention wandered. There were several shelves of books, mostly philosophy and poetry. The Toranise were not scientific; they had little need to be. Anything they wanted, the Daskiny provided.

Only that morning, Jinnie had seen a ferry of Daskiny disembarking at another tower. They were dressed in some sort of uniforms and carried nothing with them.

"Why are they here?" she asked Kye. "They're not delivering anything."

"They're delivering themselves," Kye said, uninterested. "To perform a service."

"But you said the Daskiny feared heights."

Kye sighed in annoyance. "What does that matter? They're only Daskiny."

Only Daskiny. The words hadn't sounded callous at the time. Kye had been irritated, and Jinnie had let the matter drop. They were Daskiny, and even though she wasn't a Toranise, her place was with Kye, wasn't it?

Jinnie felt she was being subsumed into a caste system, learning a prejudice she didn't agree with, but had no choice about. Again her thoughts turned to why she was on Yar. If she was some sort of mediator, as Susatch had speculated, then she needed to learn more about the Daskiny.

Kye was uncooperative. He kept promising to take her to the valley, but he never did. Whenever Jinnie mentioned it, Kye changed the subject. His unexplained obstinacy made Jinnie feel trapped. She desperately wanted to speak to a Healer or anyone else who might have information about Travelers. Why couldn't Kye understand that? It had been three weeks since she first arrived on Yar, and still she hadn't remembered her life.

I don't think I ever will, thought Jinnie.

Her gaze fell to the small table beside her. A single book occupied the space. Its cover was gold, and something about it seemed familiar. Picking it up, she leafed through the pages.

Unlike the few books she'd looked at on her own, the handwriting in this one was inconsistent. Some pages were blank, and others had been hastily scribbled upon. Dates were inconsistent, too, as if the writer had gone away for a long time and then hurried back to make a note to himself. Several pages were torn out, and the binding was weak from the abuse. Jinnie stopped flipping pages.

"I shall call her Hollany," she read aloud, "for that is what she has become."

Frowning, Jinnie turned back several pages. "I am intrigued by the possibility. No. Obsessed. If I can truly bring her here, it would be an incredible accomplishment."

The writing stopped, but Jinnie's mind ran ahead.

This was a diary. She remembered now where she'd seen it before. Kye had been writing in it the first night she'd awakened in his tower. Hastily Jinnie turned the pages forward, coming to the most recent entry.

"She has ceased to question her place here, and she has shown no signs of incompatibility with Yar."

Jinnie jumped as Kye's voice called to her from below. Snapping the diary shut, she returned it to the table and hurried from the room, racing along the balcony to Kye's bedroom.

She felt the same apprehension she'd experienced when she'd first come to Yar, the same foreboding she had felt in Keldonabrieve when she'd first seen Kye.

He called again, and Jinnie flung herself upon the bed, her heart thumping wildly. Something was terribly wrong; but what? She closed her eyes, feigning sleep.

A cold realization made her feel sick. Kye had a diary; she had a diary. And hers was rife with memories of her time spent with Griffin.

Where was her diary? Where, in fact, was her purse?

"Hollany?" Footsteps crossed the floor to the bed.

Stretching, Jinnie willed herself to appear calm, pretending to wake from a nap. She sat up.

"You were gone a long time." Her voice did not betray her turmoil of emotions. "Where were you?"

Kye bent to kiss her, placing a blue cape in her lap with a smile. "I'm sorry, beloved, but I have not returned empty-handed."

Jinnie lifted the velvety cape, spilling the dress from within its folds onto the bed. She pretended to admire it, giving herself time to focus her thoughts.

"It's lovely," she said, fingering the delicate, pale blue material of the evening gown, gathering her wits about her like an army. "What's it for?"

"For tonight's cotillion. I want to show you off." Kye sat on the bed, watching as Jinnie took the dress and walked to the mirror.

"A cotillion!" Jinnie smiled at Kye in the mirror. "Well," she hesitated, "then I'll need my compact. From my purse."

"Your purse?"

"My, uh, satchel. I'm sure I had it with me when I came to Yar." She turned to face Kye, all innocence now. "Have you seen it?"

Kye's green eyes darkened, but his gaze did not waver. "No, Hollany. It must have been lost in the waves when you arrived."

Rising, he came to stand beside Jinnie, lifting a hand to gently smooth her hair.

"I called to you, and you appeared near the shoreline. You almost drowned in the surf, remember? I rescued you and brought you home."

He kissed her cheek. "Your satchel must have slipped from your shoulder, beloved. I'm sorry. Was it important to you?"

Jinnie lowered her eyes, wanting to ask about the diary, but afraid to mention it. Anxiety made her hesitant and wary, too. Her experiences with jealous husbands were as clear and sharp as white on black.

Kye was all she had in this world; Jinnie couldn't doubt him. She was the one who had betrayed his trust by reading his diary.

"No." Jinnie lied. "No, not terribly." She turned back to her reflection. "Not at all."

* * *

Brinadar studied her reflection in the mirror. Tonight's cotillion would be particularly grand, and she must look flawless or someone might suspect. Brinadar also knew that tonight could prove too great a temptation to Kye. In fact, she was counting on it; she needed to meet the Traveler.

How could Kye resist attending? And when he did, he would bring the Traveler he had kept so closely guarded in his tower.

Is she a prisoner? Brinadar wondered. *Or did she come willingly, like me?*

Brinadar's Daskiny maid held up a comb. "Sit down, sit down," the little woman said. "I not finish your hair."

Brinadar touched the blonde bang of her hair, scrutinizing her hairline. No dark roots showed, and her skin was suitably pale, her eyes dark green.

Feeling suddenly nervous, Brinadar returned to her dressing table and allowed her maid to finish styling her hair.

"Is Seshabah here yet?" Brinadar asked.

"Not yet. Very soon," the Daskiny answered. She smiled. "All finished."

Brinadar rose and left the room. Unescorted, she went downstairs, crossed the dark main hall, and opened the front door.

Pausing, Brinadar looked back at the shadows of the tower. Elbanon was still sleeping.

Outside, someone called her name, and there were many voices and laughter.

Brinadar turned away from the silence and walked out the door to join her friends. They would journey to the cotillion together.

And I will meet the Traveler, she thought.

* * *

Wandering aimlessly, Jinnie wove an imaginary trail between spiraling columns of white stone and dark burgundy archways.

The cotillion was too noisy for her, full of eerie music, strange dances, and hundreds of Toranise. The men leered, and the women arched their eyebrows. Their disapproval was palpable. It was the women, Jinnie knew, who would decide whether or not she was acceptable. Kye had told her Toranise society was matriarchal. The women chose the men, based on physical beauty, control of their power, and prowess in tournaments.

"But I didn't choose you," Jinnie said, puzzled. "You found me."

"Yes," said Kye. "And because you're a Traveler and I am one of the strongest of the Toranise, it was agreed that I could claim you as mine."

"And I had no say in the matter?"

Kye had laughed. "What would you have said, beloved? 'Don't love me, Kye?'"

Yes, thought Jinnie. But she stayed still and silent.

Jinnie smiled sweetly now as she was formally introduced to one of the more powerful women. What was her name? Did it matter? She was tired of the charade of civility. Behind their words, rich with formal courtliness and empty praise, there lurked an aloofness that threatened to turn to ostracism. Jinnie felt uncomfortable, even with Kye's arm about her waist.

Kye, too, was welcomed with a reserved coolness, but it didn't seem to bother him. He acted triumphant. He seemed to dare the others to challenge Jinnie's presence there.

At one point in the evening, a Toranise woman who had stood unescorted through the introductions had separated Jinnie from Kye. Taking her by the arm, the woman insisted Jinnie come to the refreshment table, leading her to a dark corner instead.

"Your stone," the woman hissed. "Where did you get it?"

Jinnie's hand went to her crystal. "Kye gave it to me."

"You didn't Travel with it?"

"No."

The woman stared hard at Jinnie. "You're telling the truth," she decided.

"Of course I am," Jinnie snapped. "Why is my crystal so important to you?"

Jinnie looked at the other women in room: all blonde with green eyes, like the men. She looked again, more carefully. They wore no earrings or necklaces, only the occasional feather pinned in their hair or on their gowns. A few wore a feather on a chain about their necks, much the way Jinnie wore her crystal.

"Does it have a special meaning?" she asked her abductor.

"Yes. But since you do not know it, I won't speak of it tonight."

The Traveler

"That's hardly hospitable," said Jinnie, feeling hostile.

"You're right. I'm sorry." The woman smiled and extended her hand. "I'm Brinadar."

Jinnie looked at the offer of friendship and took it. "How do you do? I'm Jinnie. To my friends," she amended.

"Very well, Jinnie." Brinadar looked Jinnie over, nodding to herself.

"You must come to my tower some afternoon," she said, "and we'll talk. I would very much enjoy hearing all about your Traveling."

"It seems to be common knowledge to everyone but me," Jinnie commented.

"Oh? Is it new to you? Is Yar an early part of your journey?"

"Yes."

"Then take care, my dear, that it is not your last." Brinadar turned away, in a whoosh of material. Jinnie noticed she wasn't wearing a feather.

Now, moving away from the revelers, Jinnie fingered her crystal. What possible meaning could it hold other than the one Kye had told her?

Her head ached, and she felt slightly sick to her stomach. *Too much strange food and wine,* she thought.

Jinnie sat down on a bench that encircled one of the columns. A conversation was taking place on the other side. Feeling too ill to move, Jinnie listened.

"I think it's the height of bad taste," said the first voice, rather snide and nasal.

"Well," said her companion, "it is a remarkable accomplishment."

"That's not the point. He should never have brought her here. He will regret it."

"You must admit, she's very beautiful. That dark hair, those blue eyes. Quite bewitching. And, after all, Kye is likely to be champion this season. Let him have her as a trophy."

"Kye should have been stopped, I tell you. And the name! It is an offense."

"I'll admit that was in bad taste, but he's young. Even if she survives, he'll soon tire of her and return his focus to the true glory of being a Toranise."

The snide voice sniffed. "Perhaps. Though I doubt he will last long as a Dysan."

The two laughed loudly and got up.

Jinnie pressed against the column, and the gossips departed without noticing their audience.

Why is my name offensive? Jinnie wondered. *What is a* hollany? *And what did Kye accomplish?*

She stood up slowly. The room seemed slightly out of focus, and Jinnie braced herself against the column. Still feeling unsteady, she wound through the maze of dancers. Reaching the front door, she slipped outside.

Jinnie wished she could take one of the boats from the dock and sail to the valley below. There was nowhere else to run and no one else to run to. If Kye were lying to her in any way, she was lost.

"Hollany!"

Jinnie spun about. "Kye."

He closed the door behind him. "I saw you cross the room. I called to you. Didn't you hear me?"

Jinnie shook her head.

"What's wrong?" Kye took Jinnie by the shoulders, peering down into her face. "You look upset. Is it something Brinadar said?"

Jinnie looked away, wanting to trust him, but feeling anxious again. Kye was her only source of identity on Yar.

"What is it, Hollany?"

"Did you bring me to Yar?" She had meant to be brave, even confrontational, but the question came out as a whisper, full of doubt.

"What do you mean?"

Jinnie looked away. "Did you bring me to Yar?" she repeated, more assertively.

Kye took her face between his hands, turning her head gently, but firmly, until Jinnie had to look at him.

"I brought you here. To the towers. To my tower. From the inland sea. You know this. Now, where did this ridiculous question come from?"

"I overheard two women talking about me, about you. One of them said you shouldn't have brought me here. And the other one said I was quite an accomplishment."

Kye sighed, releasing her. "She meant as a mate, Hollany. You're quite an accomplishment for me as a mate. When I told my friends of you, they said we were too different to ever share a love." Frowning, Kye continued. "When will you cease these doubts about your life here on Yar? You're always questioning me, always doubting me."

"I don't doubt you," Jinnie insisted, trying to convince herself. "It's just that woman—that arrogant woman—she said my name was an offense. Why?"

"What?"

Jinnie stepped back from Kye's anger. How could she have forgotten his volatility?

"That's nonsense," he raged. "It's all nonsense, and you've attached all sorts of silly ideas to a conversation you weren't even a part of." Then Kye's mood changed.

"Hollany," he said, gentle and loving once more. He lifted a hand to touch her cheek, pausing when Jinnie flinched.

"Hollany," Kye's voice dropped to a whisper. "Forgive me. I know it's been frustrating for you, not being able to remember your life, our life. It may never happen, beloved, but at least you're here with me now."

He caressed her cheek, stepping close. "I shouldn't have brought you here tonight. It was selfish of me not to wait until you felt more comfortable. Forgive me, beloved. I should have been more patient, more understanding. I love you more than these snobbish shells of people can understand, and for that, they're envious. You overheard a pair of jealous gossips, nothing more. I'm truly sorry they upset you."

Jinnie listened to Kye's apology, desperate to believe it. Had she misunderstood? Had she jumped to conclusions? She'd read pieces of a diary and overheard part of a conversation and let her doubts about herself accuse Kye.

I'm the one hiding things from Kye, Jinnie thought. *It's my guilt that's making me suspicious of him. I'm being unfair. He loves me so much.*

And my purse? My diary? If Kye has read it, he was probably terribly hurt. Of course he wouldn't want me to know.

Jinnie let Kye pull her into his arms, leaning her head on his chest.

"I love you, Hollany," he said softly, kissing the top of her head. "I'm sorry they made me angry. Do you forgive me?"

"Yes," Jinnie tightened her arms about Kye's waist, not wanting to question him further.

"Come." Kye hugged her fiercely. "I'll take you home."

* * *

In the dark before dawn, Jinnie slid quietly away from a sleeping Kye. Instead of going to the balcony, she crept down the hall to the music room. She paused in the doorway. The diary was gone. In its place on the table sat a glass filled with water and the single blossom Jinnie had flung to the floor.

All her doubt and anxiety returned to Jinnie like a tidal wave.

Did Kye suspect she'd read his diary? Surely he would have said something to her if he had, especially after his apology tonight.

She searched the room carefully. No diary. Jinnie thought a minute, then headed for the stairs. Kye had been in his study before they'd left for the cotillion. The diary might be there.

Jinnie started down the winding staircase, feeling guilty but determined.

I'll find the diary and it will prove I'm being paranoid just because I can't remember. It will prove there's nothing mysterious about my life here, it's just different.

She stumbled and almost fell. The great hall below her spun at hideous angles, and nausea made her clutch the railing. Frightened, Jinnie sat down. She shut her eyes. After a moment, the nausea passed. She looked down. The hall had returned to normal.

Jinnie stood up and finished her descent, started across the hall, and stopped. Again the room refused to be confined to its proper dimensions. She swayed, dizzy and disoriented.

Where was she going?

She thought she heard Kye calling to her.

"Kye?" Jinnie turned toward the sound of his voice. Everything seemed misted, distant, and unreal.

Jinnie imagined Kye was walking toward her. He was walking across the ballroom in Keldonabrieve. No. No, he was running, and Keldonabrieve was just a dream.

Jinnie collapsed as Kye reached her. He caught her before she hit the floor, lifting her easily and carrying her back upstairs to his room.

Kye placed Jinnie on the bed and smoothed her hair back from her face. "Hollany?"

Jinnie opened her eyes. Kye was leaning over her, his face tense, eyes worried.

"What happened?" Jinnie lifted a hand to her forehead. "Where am I?"

Kye sighed in relief. "You fainted, Hollany. You're in our bed." His eyes darkened. "Why were you downstairs at this hour?"

Jinnie sat up. The room tipped. She sank back into the pillows. She was in their home, in their bed, and she was safe. But she didn't feel safe.

"Hollany?" Kye prodded. "Why were you downstairs? Do you remember?"

Jinnie shivered. The frightening nausea and dizziness had not been accompanied by pain, and yet they had dragged all the unhappy memories of Traveling to the surface of her mind, supplanting her doubts about Kye. For the moment, she didn't care how or why she came to be in Yar. She only cared that she stayed.

Jinnie looked at Kye, reaching for his hand. "Hold me," she whispered.

Kye kissed her hand and slid into bed next to her, wrapping his arms about Jinnie's body, warming her with his.

As he held her, Jinnie voiced her anxiety. "I felt ill. I thought I was about to Travel. Kye, you must take me to a Daskiny Healer."

Kye kissed Jinnie's cheek. "Don't say such things. You're not going to Travel, beloved. Not for a very long time. You're safe with me now. You have nothing to fear."

He kissed her forehead. "There's no need for a Healer. She said you might have minor relapses. I should have warned you. It won't last, beloved."

"But I felt so ill."

"The Healer said you might feel ill occasionally. I should have explained more precisely so you'd be prepared. You'll be fine. I promise you will."

Jinnie listened to his explanation and knew it for a lie. No flood of reassurance swept over her this time, only the increasing uneasiness that something was terribly wrong and Kye knew what it was. He knew.

"You'll feel better tomorrow," Kye said, kissing her cheek. "Now, go to sleep."

Jinnie let him hold her as she had asked, but it no longer brought her solace.

I won't feel better tomorrow, she thought. *I won't feel better until I understand.*

* * *

Brinadar tiptoed through the shadows of Elbanon's tower. She paused outside his room, thinking she heard something. Yes. He was moving. Soon he would be like a somnambulist, unaware and yet malleable. She could send one of the Daskiny to fetch Jinnie; even at this stage of the metamorphosis, Elbanon's power would be enough to propel the boat.

Brinadar moved carefully away from the door and across the hallway to her room. After undressing, she pulled on a nightgown and stepped out onto the balcony.

Now that she had met Jinnie, Brinadar knew she had to warn her. The crystal about Jinnie's neck was a marker; it was one of the signs that Kye was entering the metamorphosis. How far along he was, Brinadar couldn't guess. She did know that if Kye came to power, he would be within his rights to claim Elbanon's mate and end that bloodline.

Brinadar needed to escape before that possibility became a reality. She didn't know for certain what Jinnie's fate might be, but Brinadar hoped Jinnie would run away with her. Two would be stronger than one against an adversary like the Dysans.

As Elbanon had done with her, Brinadar suspected Kye had kept Jinnie ignorant of all the secrets of the Toranise, telling her only that he loved her.

She looked east, toward the inland sea, then north toward her home.

Mithan, she thought. *How I miss it now.*

A matriarchal society had sounded elite and stimulating when Elbanon had first described the world of the Toranise to Brinadar. The idea of handsome men competing for a woman's permission to mate with her had been exciting. The boat races and the tests of motion control were far beyond anything Brinadar had ever heard of or imagined.

The terrible secrets of the Toranise had been glossed over: the true purpose of the Daskiny, the watchful presence of the Dysans, and the metamorphosis.

"But if you come with me," Elbanon had told Brinadar, "you must pretend to be a Toranise so that you will be accepted."

That request had made sense at the time. In her daze of love, Brinadar had agreed. She left Mithan and journeyed with Elbanon to the house of an elderly Daskiny Healer. Not noticing the Healer's fear of Elbanon, Brinadar trusted the woman to prepare and implement a disguise; the Daskiny and the Mithanalen people had always been friends.

Brinadar had not thought more of it, until the day the Healer's son, Ketterick, had given her a little book that revealed all.

Ketterick was entrusted with bringing Brinadar the necessary medicines to perpetuate her camouflage. One day he pressed the book into Brinadar's hand.

"I know what it is like to live in fear," said Ketterick. "I will be your *krisen*. Keep this hidden, and when the metamorphosis begins, do not trust your Toranise to aid you."

Then he had smiled foolishly, as Elbanon joined them on the wharf of his tower.

"You like?" Brinadar's *krisen* had asked, bobbing his head and showing her his basket of fresh fruit.

"Yes, very much. Thank you." Brinadar had taken the basket, tucking the book into a pocket of her dress and smiling up at her Toranise, guileless.

That night, long after Elbanon's eyes had turned from gold to green, long after he fell asleep and Brinadar had soothed her conscience, she read the book. Horror had sickened her, and she still couldn't remember how she had found the strength not to throw herself from the tower. Instead, Brinadar had hidden the book and waited for an opportunity to escape.

Jinnie was her opportunity.

I must get her away from Kye, thought Brinadar. *I must begin arrangements for my plan tomorrow, as if Jinnie had already agreed.*

Brinadar looked at the peaks of the far-off towers. *Because Jinnie will need to escape, too.*

Five

The knock on the front doors echoed through the main hall. In the study, Jinnie froze. She had been searching for Kye's diary again. He'd left early in the morning, promising to return before the end of the day with something special for her.

Jinnie had smiled and returned Kye's good-bye kiss, feigning the love he expected and concealing her distrust. She had wanted him to leave the tower since the night of her faint. Fearful and unhappy, Jinnie had waited for another opportunity to find and read Kye's diary.

Somewhere in its pages, Jinnie felt certain she would find the answers to the questions she was afraid to ask. Instead of Kye, Jinnie now trusted the intuition she had ignored when she first came to Yar.

The knocking came again. Abandoning her search, Jinnie crossed the hall to the double doors and looked at the handles. Except for the deliveries of food, no one came to Kye's tower.

Who could it be? And why?

Again the knocking broke the silence of the hall. Curiosity exceeded caution, and Jinnie opened one of the doors. A Daskiny stood outside.

"Yes?" Jinnie asked. "What is it?"

The little man stood silent and grave. He raised a rolled piece of parchment toward Jinnie and pointed at a long black ship now tied to the wharf.

Taking the parchment, Jinnie unrolled it. It was an invitation from Brinadar. "Come at once. Come alone," Jinnie read aloud.

The Daskiny bobbed his head vigorously. "You hurry," he said. "Come now."

"Well." Jinnie thought a minute. *What would Kye do if she were gone when he returned?* "How long a journey is it?" she asked.

The Daskiny pointed to a place beyond the most distant visible tower. "Not long. Not far. Come now, please."

"Wait." Leaving the door half-closed, Jinnie returned to the study. She scribbled a brief note to Kye on the back of the parchment and set it on his desk.

Returning to the front doors, Jinnie paused again. She had never left the tower without Kye. It hadn't felt like home until now, when she was about to leave it for something unknown. Purposefully, Jinnie left the house, closing the door behind her.

The Daskiny's relieved smile made his narrow face almost comical. He ushered Jinnie to the ship and helped her in, then cast off and set sail. As he did, Jinnie realized what was odd about the scenario. The Daskiny was steering her through the air as masterfully as any Toranise she had seen, perhaps even more easily than Kye.

"How are you managing this?" she asked, feeling uneasy as she looked over the side of the ebony vessel.

The Daskiny held one finger to his lips and pointed at a small wheelhouse in the boat's prow. "The Toranise. I steer."

Jinnie looked at the cabin, windowless and black, door ajar. She saw something shift the shadows. "Is the Toranise sleeping?" She kept her voice low.

The Daskiny nodded.

"But … " Jinnie thought better of questioning the man. She would wait and ask Brinadar. She focused her thoughts on the voyage. The few other Toranise sailing boats today seemed to recognize the black ship, and hurried away from it.

Jinnie and her Daskiny captain sailed quickly past every tower she had ever noticed from Kye's balcony. The clouds rolled beneath the boat, separating only at the prow and closing immediately after their passage. Still they sailed.

Jinnie shivered. Kye had insisted on a lightweight dress today, all soft chiffon and ruffles, not at all suitable for a cold journey through the clouds.

Rubbing her bare arms, she drew the long skirt of the dress about her legs and tried to distract herself with the changing scenery. The mountains were darker, and their sides were sharp instead of sloped. Cliffs and caverns marred the sides like a jigsaw puzzle.

"Is it much further?" she asked.

The Daskiny pointed.

Jinnie turned. Grayish-white spires poked through the clouds like fingers through fabric. As they drew closer, Jinnie could see the house, sitting like a rock within the palm of the tower's hand. No flowers hung from its balconies, and its windows were dark.

The black ship ground against a narrow wharf. Jinnie waited as the Daskiny moored the craft, wondering if he would wake the sleeping Toranise. Her escort came to get her and helped her disembark.

"Very good. She waits for you." The Daskiny bobbed his head in the direction of the house. "Go inside. Inside."

"Yes. Thank you." Jinnie walked the length of the wharf to broad stairs cut into the stone. They were cracked and lined like worn marble. She looked up at the two main doors. Dark wood and gray metal made them look imposing and unwelcoming.

Jinnie pushed aside a feeling of uneasiness, straightened her shoulders, and ascended the stairs. As she reached the top, the doors opened.

"Jinnie! My dear old friend." Brinadar smiled. "Come inside, come inside." Her voice had an artificial lightness to it.

"Hello, Brinadar." Jinnie smiled back. "I came alone as you asked." She stepped into the main hall and stopped, startled.

Unlike Kye's breathtaking pavilion of light, polished wood and white archways, heavy curtains draped Brinadar's hall. They shifted in the afternoon breeze like uncomfortable footmen. The floor was red granite, and the dark brown ceiling overhead lent a funereal gloom to the area. The silence was palpable.

"Alone?" Brinadar repeated loudly. "Too bad. Elbanon will be so disappointed. But we will have a nice chat, won't we?"

"But your note said …"

"What a lovely gown," Brinadar commented, taking Jinnie's hand. She led her across the hall. "It's so frothy, like foam on waves." Brinadar's eyes darted about the hall, and she seemed to be listening for something. *Or acting for someone,* thought Jinnie.

"Are you all right?" Jinnie asked as they entered a room just off the main hall.

Brinadar shut the door and leaned against it, sighing. "I am, now that you're here, Jinnie."

"What's wrong?"

"Everything." Brinadar moved toward two chairs facing each other in front of a fireplace. A low table between the chairs held a decanter of wine and two elaborate cups, proving the invitation to visit without Kye was intentional.

"I need a drink," Brinadar said flatly, plunking herself down in one of the chairs.

Jinnie sat down on the edge of the other chair, watching the transformation of Brinadar from frivolous to serious. She waited for an explanation as Brinadar poured the wine.

"I don't know how long we'll have to talk," said Brinadar, her voice strained. She took a long drink. "Elbanon is almost a Dysan," she announced.

"That's good news, isn't it?"

"Not for me." Brinadar drank again. "And not, I think, for you."

"I don't understand."

"No." Brinadar smiled sadly. "You don't, but you need to. Elbanon's metamorphosis will be complete soon. Right now, he is in a trancelike state. That's how I got him to the ship. And your Kye will be suspicious of you when he finds that you have visited me."

Jinnie set down her cup. "Why?"

"They all become suspicious when they enter the metamorphosis," said Brinadar. Watching Jinnie carefully, she nodded. "His eyes have changed at least once, haven't they? And his moods are uneven? He probably leaves you alone more, too."

"Yes," Jinnie whispered, her anxiety about Kye returning.

"I knew it was coming." Brinadar finished her wine and poured more. "Your Kye was the only one as strong as my Elbanon. The other Toranise would wager during the tournaments on which of the two would rise to greater power first. Now Elbanon is almost a Dysan." Brinadar frowned at Jinnie. "And Kye will be soon."

"No." Jinnie shook her head, resisting what she already suspected. "You're wrong, Brinadar. Kye won't change for years. He told me ..."

"He told you just enough to make you believe life with him was right and beautiful, didn't he? No doubt he made you think the metamorphosis was beautiful, too?"

"Well, yes. He implied that."

Brinadar watched Jinnie closely as she spoke. "It is not beautiful, Jinnie. And it will be as lethal to you and me as the Toranise are to the Daskiny."

Jinnie tensed. "What are you trying to tell me, Brinadar?"

"The Toranise don't oversee the Daskiny, Jinnie, they herd them. They let the Daskiny believe the Toranise are their friends, that they protect them. When several Daskiny go missing, the survivors are told that wild animals have caught and killed the careless, those who wander too far from their homes or try to leave the valleys, especially at night. But it's not wild animals, Jinnie. It's the Toranise."

"The boats," said Jinnie, remembering the trawlers and the nets. She remembered, too, Kye's indifference, then his violence.

Brinadar grimaced. "Yes. The boats. The Toranise hunt the Daskiny for sport or to practice killing. They take the bodies to the caverns among the cliffs, where the Dysans live."

"And the Daskiny never suspect?"

"Some do. But they are hunted down by the Dysans as they try to escape. The Dysans can see from great heights, and they're attracted to movement."

Attracted to movement, thought Jinnie. She remembered Dalia. No doubt Dalia was one of the Daskiny who had realized what was happening and escaped, hoping to find a place free of the Toranise and, therefore, free of the Dysans. Somewhere in the north.

"I know this is painful," said Brinadar, "but you need to know the truth." Brinadar leaned forward. "Starting with my own." She paused. "I am not a Toranise. I'm a Mithanalen. Ages ago, my people lived in the valleys with the Daskiny when the Dysans created the first towers."

At Jinnie's look of surprise, Brinadar drank some wine and told Jinnie some of the history of Yar. The Dysans made the towers. They ripped great pieces of rock from the sides of the mountains and brought them to the valley floor, sculpting the towers like nests for the Toranise. The Mithanalen helped them; they built the infrastructure.

When the Mithanalen learned the truth behind the lies of the Toranise, they abandoned the Toranise, battling their way north until the Toranise gave up pursuit. The Toranise and the Dysans could not tolerate the cold.

"Those events happened so long ago, Jinnie," said Brinadar, "that when I met my handsome Elbanon, I had forgotten that the stories of Dysans were not stories at all, but truths cloaked. I had forgotten why the Dysans designed the towers."

"Why?"

"For the Toranise. You see, Jinnie, the Toranise are vessels for the Dysans; only a Dysan can impregnate a Toranise. Making the Dysans the true master race."

Brinadar stood up and went to a narrow archway. Drawing back the drape, she let in a line of sunlight. It split the room, the sudden brightness a sharp contrast to the darkness of the discussion.

"I forgot it all," Brinadar continued. "Or perhaps I simply refused to remember. I let myself love Elbanon and came away with him to the towers my ancestors had helped construct. I let myself be disguised as a Toranise: a little dye for my hair, a bit of powder to pale my skin. The eyes were more difficult. I have to drink a liquid herb every day to make my eyes appear to be the dark green of the Toranise. The most difficult part, of course, is my inability to create motion. I cannot sail a ship."

"That's why your ship has a wheelhouse," Jinnie said quickly. "So Elbanon can hide there and propel it."

"Yes. The energy he generates, even at rest, is formidable. It's more than enough to keep the ship aloft while someone else steers."

"But why disguise yourself? I'm not a Toranise, and I'm accepted."

"You're tolerated, Jinnie, because you're a Traveler; someone who is impermanent."

Brinadar stared out at the orange sky. "But not only does my race still exist on Yar, they know the dark secret of the Toranise."

"And the Toranise would kill you if your true identity were discovered." Jinnie spoke with uncomfortable certainty.

"Yes. Once Elbanon is a Dysan, I must be very far away. I don't go through the metamorphosis. I will never be a Dysan." Brinadar dropped the drape; the room became a tomb again.

"And you are safe only as long as Kye is powerful and unchallenged. Most of the women in power believe you will not survive Kye's metamorphosis; a few think you will journey on from Yar before your presence becomes a distraction."

"A distraction?"

"Yes. The Toranise are not monogamous, Jinnie—the most powerful women decide how many men they will favor with their bloodlines. One woman will have many mates throughout the course of a season to ensure that only the strongest and purest bloodline prevails. The women's metamorphosis is much slower than the men's," Brinadar continued. "Decades, really. It gives them time to bear and raise many children. The women's existence as Dysans is brief."

Jinnie recognized the description as the one Kye had given her. He hadn't lied; he had simply substituted one truth for another. What else was he artfully concealing?

"For all Kye's protestations of love to you—and I'm sure he means them for now—if he becomes champion, he must mate with the best bred of the Toranise."

Brinadar turned to face Jinnie. "I have no wish to hurt you, Jinnie, but to the Toranise, you are nothing more than the trophy of a successful challenge. And a trophy has little place among their desire for bloodlines that are strong and pure."

Jinnie felt sick to her stomach.

Returning to her chair, Brinadar sat down slowly, arranging the skirt of her dress, as unhappy to tell Jinnie the truth as Jinnie was to hear it. "To protect themselves and the Dysans, the Toranise will kill us," she said. She looked at Jinnie.

"Another race, uninfluenced by the Dysans, could destroy the Toranise rule over the Daskiny. You have seen how easily they are deceived. They have been isolated in their towers too long, lazy and self-satisfied."

"Did you truly love Elbanon so much, Brinadar?" Jinnie asked, stunned at the risk the woman had taken.

"Oh, yes. I truly loved him. And when Elbanon was a Toranise, he loved me. That changed with the metamorphosis."

Brinadar waved her hand at the room around her. "It all changed: from white to black, from parties and passion to isolation and fear, from Toranise to Dysan."

"What exactly are Dysans?" Jinnie asked, no longer certain she wanted to know.

"Creatures." Brinadar leaned forward and lowered her voice to a whisper. "Terrible creatures. Brutal, hungry, angry. Dangerous." She paused.

"The metamorphosis starts with the eyes and a volatile temperament. Soon it surges through them in waves of uncontrollable desire. Each emotion is intensified; all of their senses are heightened. Their appetite for everything becomes voracious. The Toranise call the metamorphosis their heart's desire. Their *hollany*."

"But that's what Kye calls me," said Jinnie.

Brinadar nodded. "Yes. The word has never been used for a name before, and your presence has aroused the very concern the Toranise pretend isn't possible. Do the Mithanalen still exist and if so, how much of a threat do they represent? It's only because Kye is powerful enough to defend you that he could claim you and mark you with that crystal."

Jinnie looked down at the crystal hanging on its chain. "Mark me? For what?"

"To identify you as his mate, to Dysans and to himself." Brinadar poured more wine for both of them. "Do you recall the women at the cotillion, the ones who wore feathers in their hair or on their gowns?"

"Yes."

"The feathers represent the individual mate of a Dysan. So that Dysan will recognize them after the completion of the metamorphosis and let them live."

"You mean, Kye won't recognize me?"

"A Toranise in the beginning of the metamorphosis is unaware of it at first. They fulfill their cravings without thinking and have no memory of it after. Kye was being cautious. He knows he is powerful. The more powerful the Toranise, the quicker the metamorphosis."

"Kye's been moody and possessive," Jinnie confided. "I thought it was because of me. Because I've been discontented, and I've mistrusted him."

"Do not trust him," Brinadar warned. "When Elbanon's metamorphosis began, he sailed to the cliffs to get a Dysan feather to protect me. He altered so quickly, however, that his clarity of thinking failed him. He returned empty-handed. When I questioned him, he said only that I wouldn't need one, that he would take me home. Soon."

"Soon. Yes, Kye likes that word as well. It's promising, but vague: soon."

"Yes. And I believed Elbanon. I had to. It wasn't safe for me alone." Brinadar looked at the tiles of the fireplace beside her. "And I loved him," she shrugged. "I love him still."

Her gaze lifted to Jinnie. "One night, before his transformation was complete, he came to me. I was terrified. I fought him. I screamed and kicked and hit him. For a short time, his mind cleared, and he warned me not to trust him. He told me to run away, fast and far, with the Daskiny." Brinadar's voice saddened. "Then his mind shifted, his face … he was once so handsome, Jinnie … and he forgot what I had been to him, all that I had meant to him, but he left me alone."

"He's been dormant for a month, in the final stage of his metamorphosis. I've been trying to formulate an escape. Meanwhile," Brinadar gestured at her pale green gown, almost as recklessly frilly as Jinnie's, "I pretend he is still a Toranise to keep myself safe and to protect the Daskiny here at the house."

Brinadar paused, looking again at the fireplace. "It's been difficult. Nightmarish, really. I can't believe this is my life."

Leaning forward, Jinnie stretched out her hand in compassion, touching Brinadar's arm. "What can I do to help?"

Brinadar looked at her with a steady gaze. "Run away with me."

Griffin's words, pushed far back into her memory, brought all the pain of his absence and all the horror of life on Yar into focus. *If only I could run to Griffin*, thought Jinnie.

Seeing her hesitation, Brinadar rose and went to the hearth. She lifted a tile from one corner and withdrew a small book. "My *krisen* gave me this to warn me. It's a Daskiny book of the Dysans. I think you should look at the picture."

Jinnie took the little book from Brinadar. It was thin and old and smelled of the dead. Afraid to open it, Jinnie asked, "What's a '*krisen?*'"

"It's a Daskiny word meaning, 'truest friend.'" Brinadar pointed at the book. "I am your *krisen*, Jinnie. Look at the picture."

Fingers trembling, Jinnie opened the book and turned the pages until she came to a page with an illustration. She stared at the creature depicted on the parchment.

It was a gargoyle of a man. The hands were curled, with talons on the fingers; huge feathered wings spread from behind muscular shoulders. A crest of feathers started near the brow and covered the head.

Feeling sick, Jinnie made herself look at the face. From either side of a long, thin beak where a nose should have been, gold eyes stared at her. She dropped the book, standing up abruptly, panicked, looking for escape.

Brinadar put her arm around Jinnie's shoulder and sat her down again. "I'm sorry, Jinnie. You had to know. If we were Toranise, the transformation would be natural for us. But we are not. And if we wish to survive, we must escape tomorrow night."

Jinnie turned blank eyes to Brinadar. "Tomorrow night?"

"Yes. There will be a Masquerade Ball. All the Toranise who have participated in the tournaments this year will attend, including the two champions, Elbanon and Kye.

"If Elbanon does not appear, the Toranise will consider Kye victorious." Brinadar sat down. "And they will know for certain that Elbanon has become a Dysan."

"And you're unmarked," said Jinnie. "You won't be safe."

"No, I won't," whispered Brinadar, her voice——held in control all afternoon–wavered. "I don't think you will be either. If it's discovered that I'm not a Toranise, the others might ignore the crystal and kill you in their paranoia."

Jinnie looked down at her hands, clenched in her lap. "How will we escape?"

Brinadar took a deep breath. "I found the key to this tower's interior. All the towers are partly hollow inside, including the Center Tower where the Masque will be held. The key will work for all. The Mithanalen made the master passkey as a precaution when they came to distrust the Dysans."

Jinnie remembered the secret compartment in Kye's mantelpiece. "Go on."

"Once we gain access to the tower's interior, we can climb down the stairs to the valley."

"What about Kye? He'll want me at his side."

"I have a casual friend among the Toranise. Seshabah. She will switch costumes with you as a jest on Kye."

"What about my hair?" Jinnie reached toward her neck, where her long, dark hair lay plastered against it with sweat.

"The Toranise wear headdresses to the Masque as part of their costumes. The gear caps the head with a veil down the back. The substitution will not be noticeable. Seshabah will keep her distance from Kye, dancing with other Toranise. Kye will be the center of attention. He won't be able to keep track of you or her until it's too late."

Brinadar stopped, exhausted at the intensity and rapidity of her speech.

Jinnie waited, hands now gripping the arms of the chair.

"My *krisen* will meet us at the base of the tower," Brinadar continued, "with shirts and trousers. We'll look like male Toranise, and no one will question our presence in the valley. My *krisen* can take us to the inland sea. He has a contact who will meet us there."

Jinnie thought of Dalia, watching for friends and enemies.

A knock on the door made both women jump.

"Enter!" commanded Brinadar. Smoothing her hair, she stood up, motioning Jinnie to do the same.

A Daskiny woman opened the door. "The ship must sail. The Toranise, Kye, returns from the valley."

"Good. My friend is ready to return to her tower."

The little woman bowed and left, leaving the door open.

Jinnie looked at Brinadar, terrified. "I can't go back to him," she whispered.

"You must," Brinadar whispered back. She began escorting Jinnie across the main hall to the front doors.

"You're a Traveler. You must have some experience with deception. Play your part. I will play mine. If all goes well, tomorrow night we will be safe."

Brinadar opened the door. "I'm so very glad you could come to visit." Her voice was loud, her smile brilliant. "Thank you for helping me decide what to wear, my dear. These events can be so complex, and one must attend to every detail."

Jinnie smiled back, rallying her strength and nerve. "Oh, you're very welcome, Brinadar. Your friendship is worth the trouble."

Jinnie left the house, walking stiffly down the steps. Calm outside, screaming inside.

She barely noticed the captain as he helped her aboard the black ship. All Jinnie could look at was the ship's wheelhouse. This time the door was closed. Trembling, she sat down.

What do I do tonight? Jinnie panicked. *How can I let Kye make love to me, knowing what he is about to become? What if he transforms? Will the crystal protect me?*

She clutched the crystal with one hand and the side of the boat with the other. Tomorrow night it will all be over, Jinnie comforted herself. *What's one more lie when I have lived through so many?*

The sun spread slivers of light across the mountaintops. Around her, the clouds were separating, thinning like an outgoing tide. Jinnie thought she could see the valley far below. The beauty gave an illusion of peacefulness beyond Jinnie's grasp.

The ship slid against the wharf of Kye's tower.

"Hollany!" Kye was just mooring his boat. Leaping gracefully to the wharf, he strode toward the black ship. Kye pushed the Daskiny aside and helped Jinnie from the boat. He held a large bundle under one arm.

"I see you've been with Brinadar," Kye said quietly. "I recognize Elbanon's ship."

Jinnie decided on an offensive tack. "You've left me alone so much lately, Kye. How could I resist Brinadar's invitation to visit her?"

Kye studied Jinnie's face. "You're right, beloved. I have left you alone too much." He kissed her quickly and waved away the Daskiny.

"Go back to your master," he ordered.

Kye led Jinnie into the tower. "I have a present for you, Hollany. And I think, when you see it, you will forgive my absences."

Jinnie crossed the hall to the stairs, willing herself to climb them, trying not to think of everything that had transpired that afternoon or the picture Brinadar had shown her.

Play your part, Jinnie, she told herself. You've done it before when you had to, with Lancin and then Kellen. You can do this. She took a deep breath.

"Did you go to the valley, Kye?" Jinnie kept her voice light.

Kye followed her up steps. "Yes. I told you I'd have something special for you."

He smiled at her as they reached the top of the stairs and, for that moment, Jinnie could believe he loved her.

She smiled back. "What is it?"

"Come and see." Kye led her to the bedroom. He set the bundle of cloth on the bed.

Jinnie went to open it, preparing to feign surprise. If she created a deception that could be discovered now, Kye would be less suspicious of her tomorrow.

A silver gown and cape spilled from the folds of the coarse cloth wrapping. A second bundle lay on the cape. It held a silver cap studded with pale pink stones. A long veil attached to the back of the cap, just as Brinadar had described. A silver mask on a wand completed the elaborate headdress.

"What's it for?" Jinnie picked up the mask and held it to her face. She looked at Kye.

"Tomorrow night there will be a ball, a masquerade. You and I will attend. I will be the sun," Kye reached for a gold mask on a chair and held it to his face, "and you will be my moon."

Jinnie pursued her plan. "Not another cotillion, Kye," she complained. "The Toranise don't like me."

"They don't have to like you," he said sharply, then he calmed himself. "Everyone of importance will be at the Masque to welcome the new champion. It's tradition. We will be going."

Jinnie noted the tone of command. Had he always spoken to her that way?

Kye paused, setting down his mask. "Brinadar will be there, too," he added. His voice held the trace of suspicion Jinnie was waiting for.

"Oh?" She put aside her mask.

"Yes." Kye went to Jinnie. He pulled her close, lifting her onto the bed and lying down beside her.

"Why did you visit Brinadar without me?" His casual tone belied his watchful eyes. "What did you talk about?"

"Oh!" Jinnie rested a hand on his chest, "you've caught me. Brinadar told me all about the masquerade. She wanted to ask my opinion about her dress. She thought, as a Traveler, I might have an interesting point of view. I think she just wanted to gossip. That's all we talked about, clothes and hairstyles."

Jinnie smiled up at Kye. "I'm sorry it spoiled your surprise."

Kye's features relaxed a little. He stroked Jinnie's hair. "It's all right, beloved."

He leaned forward, slipping one hand behind her neck and pulling Jinnie into a rough kiss.

"I missed you, Hollany," he said, his mouth against her ear, her cheek. One hand tugged at the shoulder of her dress. When the fabric didn't yield, Kye tore at it, ripping the dress down the front, as if he were eviscerating Jinnie.

She tensed, expecting an assault, but Kye's sudden violence dissipated. He braced his weight on one arm, caressing her, gently drawing the dress from her body. He kissed Jinnie again, slowly, then stood up and undressed.

Jinnie stayed absolutely still except for her frantic heartbeat.

Returning to her, Kye pulled her hips against his and kissed Jinnie again.

"Hollany," he whispered, "I love you, Hollany."

Jinnie closed her eyes.

Six

"It's too tight, Kye," Jinnie complained. "Do I have to wear it?"

"Yes." He finished cinching the embroidered corset of her costume. "It looks beautiful. You look beautiful."

Kye ran his hands over Jinnie's hips, following the skirt of the gown where it fanned out in layers of silver lace.

"I can't breathe." Jinnie scowled at her reflection. The strapless dress pinched her breasts, and the corset pushed them up too high, catching the crystal between them and making it scratch her skin.

Kye looked at her in the mirror; intent, watchful. When he spoke, his words were clipped. "I had it made especially for you."

He pulled Jinnie's hair into a ponytail and tied it with a silver ribbon. Then he took the chain and knotted it at the back of her neck, making the crystal hang just along her collar bone. "That's better."

Still watching Jinnie in the mirror, Kye toyed with the crystal a moment, then ran his fingertips across her breasts. He turned Jinnie to face him.

She looked up at Kye. His green eyes were dark. "Why do I have to wear this, Kye? It's so uncomfortable. The dress will look just as pretty without the corset."

"Enough!" He handed her the headdress. "Put this on."

Jinnie lowered her eyes. She had to be more cautious. Taking the headdress, she turned back to the mirror.

"I'm sorry, Kye." Jinnie made her voice meek. "It's not the dress. It is beautiful. I'm just nervous. The other dance you took me to was so awful for me."

Jinnie adjusted the cap, making certain the veil completely cloaked her dark hair. She waited as Kye draped her cape about her shoulders.

He handed Jinnie her mask. "The Masquerade Ball is an important conclusion to the season, not a private party."

Taking Jinnie's hand, Kye led her out of the bedroom and down the stairs. "There won't be any sneers of condescension or rude conversations. The very best of the Toranise are gathering to celebrate."

Jinnie struggled to catch her breath as Kye hurried her to the front doors. "How do you decide who's best?"

Kye helped her into his boat and cast off. "You know that throughout the season we hold tournaments: races of speed, contests of power, challenges of skill in manipulating motion. Whoever wins the most challenges is honored at the Masque."

"How many challenges did you win, Kye?"

"All of them."

Jinnie sat still, posture perfect, unable to lean forward in the corset, as much a prisoner of the costume as she was of circumstance.

They sailed around Kye's tower, heading across the clouds in a different direction from the other towers. They began a gradual descent, and Jinnie immediately felt nauseated. She swallowed hard, wishing she could take a deep breath.

"You haven't taken me in this direction before. Kye."

"No." Kye seemed preoccupied, and the ride was choppy.

"Why do we have to descend?"

"Our destination is in a valley near the inland sea."

Jinnie looked quickly away, not wanting Kye to see her surprise. Taking this route, Kye was unwittingly assisting her escape.

"Brinadar said the ball took place at a Center Tower," said Jinnie, thinking of her friend and hoping she was all right.

There was silence for a moment. "What else did Brinadar say?"

Jinnie turned to look at Kye. He was stunning in his cape of gold, set off by a lace shirt and white trousers. "Only that she looked forward to seeing me there."

Kye's eyes narrowed as he leaned against the long paddle, steering the boat left. They began ascending at an angle. "Look ahead," he ordered.

Jinnie faced the front of the boat again. They were rounding a low hill wreathed with mist. Beyond it, in the center of a deep valley, a single tower soared toward the rising moon. The house spiraled like a magic castle from the tower's support, white and shining, with lights sparkling like stars from every window.

It looks like Keldonabrieve, thought Jinnie. Disquieting memories poured over her. *A dance, a plot, lies, deception, and an escape if we're successful. Brinadar will be returning to Mithan, but where will I go?*

A ship swooped by their boat, and Jinnie jumped, startled from her brooding. The occupants aboard the other ship called greetings to Kye. He waved in response.

"See how different it is tonight, Hollany? Tonight and every night and every day after, I will be honored."

"Honored?" Jinnie pulled herself back into the present. "For your tournament wins, of course." She smiled.

"Yes." Kye's voice was rich with anticipation. "No one will challenge me now. It will be formally acknowledged that I have the superior power and ability of all the Toranise."

"I'm so happy for you, Kye," said Jinnie automatically.

For a moment, she felt Kye's full attention. There was lust in his eyes, and a flicker of suspicion. "Are you?" he demanded.

Jinnie pulled her cape tighter about her shoulders. "Of course I am."

They drew closer to the tower. Several wharfs extended from it, already lined with an assortment of boats. Kye brought their craft to a smooth halt and moored it.

"Leave your cape in the boat."

"But it's cold," Jinnie objected.

Kye swept an arm about her, pulling the cape away. Jinnie suppressed a shiver, feeling exposed and angry, but saying nothing further. Kye's tension was palpable, as if he were expecting something.

Elbanon, Jinnie realized. *Kye's worried that Elbanon will be at the Masque.* She let Kye take her hand, and they joined the press of people heading into the main hall.

"Kye! The season is yours," an angular man greeted them. He held a lion-like mask in front of his face, tilting it only for a moment to leer at Jinnie.

"It's fitting that your lady is a moon," the man went on. "A beautiful satellite in honor of this year's winner."

Kye smiled. "Don't speak too soon, Ahdin. Elbanon may yet appear."

Ahdin scoffed. "No one can match your power and ability, Kye. You have surpassed us all, including Elbanon. The honor will be yours, unchallenged." The man leered once more at Jinnie, then elbowed his way into the crowd.

Jinnie leaned toward Kye. "What did he mean, unchallenged?"

"I won the tournaments over all other challengers to Elbanon. As last year's victor, his was the skill to surpass." Kye stopped walking. "He can give way gracefully by not attending the Masque or he can attend and challenge my position."

Jinnie struggled to stand still. "Will Elbanon come?"

Kye pierced her with a cold stare. "I don't know, Hollany. Do you?"

"How would I know?"

Kye studied her face, and Jinnie smiled graciously under his scrutiny. Before Kye could question her further, the crowd jostled them forward. Kye's fingers tightened about Jinnie's hand. He stopped repeatedly to accept praise and congratulations from other Toranise.

Jinnie felt uneasy. The masks prevented her from seeing the people's expressions.

As Kye moved her slowly through the crowd, she was reminded of Kellen escorting her at their marriage reception. All the people there had worn masks, too: masks of false politeness and frozen smiles.

Tonight Jinnie's smile was equally frozen. She looked around, realizing that she hadn't asked Brinadar what her costume would be.

Everywhere Jinnie looked, elaborate masks disguised the Toranise, creating the illusion of animals, flowers, even stars. No two were alike.

Bird masks, Jinnie noted, were absent. Was it more Toranise denial or simply good manners? Jinnie tilted the wand that held her mask, scanning the crowd again, hoping to recognize Brinadar.

A woman wearing colors of cinnamon and rust approached Jinnie. She held a mask that reminded Jinnie of a fox. "You must keep your mask before your face, dear Jinnie." Brinadar's hand lifted Jinnie's wand, setting the mask in place.

"Brinadar!" Jinnie tried to pull free of Kye's grip. "Kye, Brinadar is here."

"So I see." Kye held onto Jinnie's hand. "A pleasure to see you, Brinadar." Kye looked past her as he spoke. "You've come alone?"

"I came with Seshabah." Brinadar waved at someone. "A big, lovely group of ladies. Just for fun. You must try and have fun, Kye," Brinadar reproached him. "And I must take your lovely lady to meet Seshabah."

Brinadar placed her hand on Kye's, commandeering Jinnie. "She so wants to meet her," she smiled. "And you wouldn't want to disappoint Seshabah, would you? Tonight of all nights?"

Kye's eyes narrowed. The three of them stood deadlocked in the middle of the room, the other Toranise bustling about them. Music started.

Kye bowed his head, briefly. "No," he said, annoyance tinting his voice, "I would not want to disappoint Seshabah."

Brinadar smiled sweetly. "Come along, my dear," she said, and pulled Jinnie next to her. "Let Kye enjoy the company of other ladies for a while."

"Bring her back quickly," Kye instructed.

"Yes, yes!" Brinadar waved at him, leading Jinnie through the crowd.

Kye scowled as the two women left him. He didn't trust Brinadar, and he disliked her being with his *hollany*.

Is it because of Elbanon? he asked himself. *No. There's something else about Brinadar I dislike. The pitch of her voice, the way she moves, even her scent. All subtly different from the other women but, unlike Hollany, displeasing to the senses.*

He took a step to follow the women and was interrupted by another well-wisher. Kye enjoyed the praise, but he kept his eyes on Hollany.

Brinadar smiled and laughed as she hurried Jinnie across the room.

"Who's Seshabah?" Jinnie asked, almost running to keep pace with Brinadar. "Why was Kye willing to give in to her? And where's Elbanon?"

"Not here," Brinadar whispered. She waved at another imaginary friend.

"There's a Resting Room over on the left. Stay close to me. Smile!" She waved again and Jinnie waved, too.

"In here!" Brinadar pushed Jinnie into a small room and shut the door.

In the sudden quiet, Jinnie slouched in relief. "Damn!" She straightened as the corset bit her skin. "Damn this thing."

"Damn everything," Brinadar agreed, her voice taut.

Jinnie stopped fussing with her gown and looked closely at her friend. "What is it? What's happened?"

"Elbanon," answered Brinadar. "His metamorphosis is complete." She moved slowly toward a velvet-covered bench and sat down, letting her mask drop into her lap.

Jinnie sat down beside Brinadar. "Tell me," she said gently.

Brinadar looked down. "He killed the Daskiny in the house, every one of them. I couldn't stop him. He wouldn't listen." She shook her head.

"I ran. I knew Seshabah was coming, and I ran for the door." Brinadar looked at Jinnie. "Elbanon started after me, but my *krisen* intervened." Brinadar stopped speaking.

Jinnie answered the silence. "Elbanon killed him, too, didn't he?"

Brinadar nodded, quiet tears sliding down her cheeks.

"Oh, Brinadar." Jinnie put an arm about her friend and hugged her. "I'm so sorry. I want to tell you everything will be all right, but I don't know that it will be. It's not over yet. We have to be strong. We have to play our parts, remember?"

Brinadar wiped at her face. "Yes. Yes, I remember." She took a deep breath. "I need a drink." She sat up straighter. "And so do you."

Seeing Brinadar recover, Jinnie stood up. "No, I ..."

"Yes," Brinadar rose. "We both need a drink because Seshabah is going to meet us by the punch table."

"Who is Seshabah?" asked Jinnie as she helped Brinadar straighten her headdress. "And why did Kye give in when you mentioned her? He certainly didn't want to."

A sly, foxy smile lifted Brinadar's lips. "Seshabah is a very pure-blooded and, therefore, a very important Toranise. Kye may be this year's victor, but he's only a male."

Jinnie nodded. "Of course. It's just that Kye is so powerful and so many concessions have been made for him. Like me."

Brinadar laughed, sounding like herself again. She quickly lowered her voice, looking over her shoulder to make certain they were still alone in the room. "No concessions have been made; Seshabah and the others are merely waiting to confirm that Kye has usurped Elbanon."

Jinnie's anxiety about Kye mixed with her worry about the night. The room rocked like a boat, and Jinnie stood absolutely still. The motion stopped, but this time she knew the symptom for what it was. She was going to Travel again, and soon.

Unaware of Jinnie's consternation, Brinadar finished restoring her makeup and her calm, then took the lead once more. "Now come on."

The women returned to the main room, pressing into the crowd again and forcing their way through. Head down, Jinnie followed Brinadar's bright dress.

I won't travel yet, thought Jinnie, *the symptoms aren't pronounced enough. Or maybe I'm becoming accustomed to them and I haven't noticed when they occur?*

She thought about when she had felt ill on Yar. Nausea, dizziness. At the cotillion! Then at Kye's tower and just now. *Perhaps, any time I felt sick to my stomach, I was experiencing the start of Traveling.*

I have to help Brinadar escape, Jinnie thought. *That may even be the reason why I'm here in Yar. I can't Travel now. I can't.*

Jinnie stumbled into Brinadar as she stopped abruptly.

"Seshabah!" Brinadar clapped her hands together. "You were so right to wear the floral mask. I could see your costume from across the room. What a perfect choice for tonight." Brinadar elbowed Jinnie.

"Oh, yes, yes," Jinnie stammered. "It's lovely."

"This is my friend, the Traveler," Brinadar continued. "She's been so excited about meeting you."

Brinadar turned to Jinnie. "Haven't you, Jinnie dear?"

"I have." Jinnie smiled. "Very much. It's a privilege." Not knowing the protocol, Jinnie chose a curtsy.

Seshabah laughed and lowered her mask. "What an alarmingly enchanting child," she announced. The group of women around her nodded their heads in instant agreement.

Seshabah waved them away. She raised her mask beside her face like a shield. "Tell me, Brinadar, do you still plan to test Kye's love for the Traveler? It should be quite an amusing game, watching him fret and fuss for the female he professes is his heart's desire."

She turned to Jinnie. "The young males are so hopeless in their passions, are they not?"

"Oh. Yes." Jinnie smiled nervously, glancing at Brinadar. "Terribly amusing. And, if I understand the game correctly, it's extremely kind of you to participate."

Seshabah waved her hand. "Mistaken identity, true love lost and then found, what could be better?" She leaned forward, suddenly serious. "Meet me on the east balcony after the next waltz," she whispered.

Stepping back, Seshabah laughed loudly. "Frivolity, my dears! Frivolity!" Placing her mask in front of her face again, she moved away, the crowd parting for her.

Brinadar and Jinnie exchanged a glance.

"What do we do now?" asked Jinnie, worried that Kye might be looking for her.

"We'll wait near the east balcony's archway." Brinadar decided. She stood on tiptoe, looking around. "Follow me," she said, her voice firm.

They headed back into the throng. There were fewer people as they neared the archway and the two women hung back. They listened to the music, waiting for a waltz.

"Hollany!" Kye grasped Jinnie's upper arm. "I thought I'd lost you. Come with me."

Kye looked at Brinadar but spoke to Jinnie. "I assume your visit with Seshabah is over."

"Kye!" Jinnie smiled up at him, turning her alarm into excitement. "I'm having the nicest time, just like you said I would."

Surprised at her change of attitude, Kye released his grip. Slipping an arm about Jinnie's waist, he kissed her quickly and smiled. "I'm pleased, Hollany. You've seemed unhappy lately."

He took a step back, lifting his mask to admire her. "She is beautiful, isn't she, Brinadar?"

"Naturally, dear Kye. Why wouldn't you seek the most beautiful woman anywhere to be at your side? Nevertheless," Brinadar said as she stepped up to Kye, "I must insist on sharing this dance with you. After all, you'll have Hollany forever."

Several Toranise stood close by, and Kye was caught. He had to acquiesce or display bad manners.

"Very well, Brinadar," he said politely. "But only this one dance." He looked at Jinnie. "The rest are for Hollany."

"We'll see." Brinadar was already maneuvering Kye toward the dance floor. "I do believe Seshabah thought it best if you let Hollany mingle tonight. She knows so little of our ways. And her manners, Kye!" Brinadar smiled over her shoulder at Jinnie. "Why, they're positively barbaric."

The music began, and the reluctant couple were lost among the other dancers. Relieved, Jinnie moved under the archway. The cold night air revived her. She turned and walked onto the balcony.

There's no harm in being early, she decided. *Brinadar will join me the moment she can get rid of Kye.* Jinnie paused at the thought. *How quickly my life changes. Too quickly. Not quick enough.*

"A beautiful night for the Masque, isn't it?"

Jinnie spun about. "Pardon me?" She searched the dark.

A man stepped from the shadows near the archway. He joined Jinnie by the balcony railing. "I've been watching you," he said. "You're Kye's mate, the Traveler."

"Yes," said Jinnie, wary of the stranger. He didn't hold a mask, near his face or in his hand. "Who are you?"

"No one of consequence." The man gave Jinnie a slight smile. "Are you waiting for Kye?"

"No," Jinnie blurted. She took a small step to one side. "I mean, I'm with Kye, of course, but I'm not waiting. I just wanted some fresh air. The hall is so crowded."

"Yes." The man looked her over. "Hold up your mask," he said.

Jinnie did so, taking another step toward the archway and the safety of the crowd in case the man meant her harm.

"The moon?"

Jinnie nodded.

"It suits you. A Traveler must be ever changing, like the moon."

"Who are you?"

The man shrugged. "A friend. I'm near the end of my metamorphosis and can't attend the Masque openly. So, here I am, confined to the shadows; a voyeur and an eavesdropper. I've heard of you, Traveler, from the Daskiny. I used to visit them long ago."

The man turned away from Jinnie, facing the night. "I used to do many things, but now I just watch and listen. And wait."

Calmer, Jinnie waited too.

A breeze ruffled the man's white-blond hair. He hadn't turned around, and Jinnie thought she saw feathers near the base of his neck.

The Traveler

Remembering Dalia's caution, Jinnie stood still. Movement would only attract his attention. Would her crystal protect her?

"I can hear your friend, Brinadar," he said.

"Oh?"

"Didn't Brinadar tell you? The metamorphosis heightens all the senses. I've heard your entire conversation tonight, from the moment she arrived and took you to the Resting Room."

"What are you saying?" Jinnie whispered. How much did this man know? Was he here to betray her to Kye?

"Only that the shadows are not always empty, Traveler."

"Don't be vague," insisted Jinnie, too angry now to be afraid. She had been through too much to let the escape with Brinadar fail.

"What do you think you know?" Jinnie demanded.

The man tightened one hand into a fist, then flexed the fingers. Jinnie stared. The veins pulsed, the skin wrinkled, then the change passed.

"I think I know that Elbanon isn't coming tonight. Perhaps I know that Brinadar is planning to flee the towers. I am certainly aware that Brinadar is an unmarked female," he paused, "who cannot sail a boat. Perhaps I've been watching her as well as you. I am, as you can see, in need of a mate."

He turned to face Jinnie. His eyes were gold. "I might also know, Traveler, that you are not safe with Kye. I may have seen him among the fishermen these past weeks, after he lies with you and to you. I may know that you, like Brinadar, are planning to run away from the Towers and the Toranise. And the Dysans."

Jinnie clutched at her crystal, risking a glance inside the hall. Brinadar was moving swiftly toward her from one side of the room, Seshabah from the other. She couldn't see Kye.

"What are you going to do?" Jinnie whispered.

The man blinked several times. His eyes returned to dark green. "I'm going to help you, Traveler. I told you—I'm a friend."

Brinadar and Seshabah hurried through the archway. "What's he doing here?" Brinadar complained. She confronted the man. "Who are you?"

"Why, it's Krisen," Seshabah announced. She turned to the two women, standing side by side, holding their breath. "I gave him the nickname when he was still a very young man. He was always wasting his time helping others, usually the Daskiny. Not at all a proper Toranise thing to do."

Seshabah turned to Krisen. "You should have been improving your power and practicing your abilities. Now look at you. About to alter, and still without a mate to keep you company."

Stepping up to Krisen, Seshabah took his chin in her hand. She turned his head to the right, then to the left. "Look at me," she commanded.

Krisen stared into Seshabah's eyes. "You are very close at last, my Krisen."

"Yes," Krisen's voice was low, pained.

"I have a few years more," Seshabah mused. "Perhaps I will take one more mate. One who excels at being helpful."

Reaching behind Krisen's neck, Seshabah tugged at his hair. A feather came away in her hand. "Yes," she said. "Very close."

A lazy smile lifted the corner of her mouth. "We could use someone who is inclined to be helpful. You will help, will you not? Of course you will."

"Yes." Krisen smiled at Jinnie.

"It seems we are looking for a door," said Seshabah. "A secret door. Perhaps one you might have noticed? You see so much these days. It has not escaped my attention that you have been spending as much time here, at the Center Tower, as you have spent sailing. And following Brinadar."

"What?" Brinadar glared at Krisen.

Seshabah held up her hand. "Oh, he has only been watching for a mate. You should be flattered. After all, you are still unmarked. Obviously Elbanon doesn't suit your taste."

"I know of a door," Krisen admitted. "It's locked."

"And where is it, my helpful young *krisen?*" Seshabah asked him.

"In the art room."

"Perfect!" Seshabah turned to Brinadar and Jinnie. "Ladies, we are going to the art room with Krisen."

Astonished, Jinnie and Brinadar fell in line behind Seshabah and Krisen. The four of them moved swiftly along the balcony, following the curve of the house to a wide archway filled with drapes.

"In here," Krisen whispered. Holding back a drape, he motioned them inside.

"Now." Seshabah took charge. "We have to hurry."

She began to undress. "The ceremony of honor will begin soon. It is short and very dull. Once it is finished, Kye will be looking for Hollany.

"Traveler, undress and give me your costume. My gown might be a little loose on you, but it will do, of course.

"Krisen, show Brinadar the secret door, and then stand guard. No one will be looking at portraits tonight, but a quiet room is sometimes a romantic refuge."

Seshabah looked at her charges. "Well? Not tomorrow, now!"

Krisen hurried Brinadar to a stack of canvases, pushing them aside to reveal a narrow door. She pulled a key from the bodice of her gown.

Jinnie removed her headdress as Seshabah helped her with the corset.

"This is fun," Seshabah confided.

"Isn't it?" Escaping the corset, Jinnie undressed and accepted Seshabah's bright yellow gown in return. Uncertain how much of the truth Seshabah knew, Jinnie remained taciturn.

"The key works," Brinadar announced from behind the stack of canvases. "It smells awful in there, and it's very dark. We're going to need a lantern."

"I'll get one," Krisen volunteered.

"Be careful," Seshabah warned, struggling with Jinnie's corset. "If you are noticed, you will be escorted from the Masque in disgrace."

Seshabah looked Krisen up and down. "That would certainly spoil the fun. And, naturally, my mood as well."

Krisen nodded and left the room.

Brinadar came to help Jinnie lace the corset on Seshabah.

"It's not going to fit," worried Jinnie.

"It doesn't have to fit," Brinadar said, tugging on the laces. "It just has to stay in place as Seshabah moves."

"Oh, my," said Seshabah. "Who chose this outrageous costume?"

"Kye," Jinnie and Brinadar said together.

"Naturally." Seshabah sighed. "They are always trying to control the world around them, are they not, Brinadar? Fine and foolish men, especially during the metamorphosis."

She turned to Jinnie and patted her cheek. "But do not worry, child. Kye's change will go quickly. He is powerful. He deserves tonight's honor." She fingered the crystal hanging from Jinnie's neck. "And you, you are already marked."

She stepped back from the women. "How do I look?"

"You need the headdress, Seshabah," said Brinadar. She turned to Jinnie. "See if you can tighten the corset more."

Jinnie nodded, jumping as Krisen returned. He held up a lantern.

"Excellent." Seshabah bestowed a suggestive smile on him. "If only you could escort me while I play the game. What is the game, anyway?" she asked Brinadar.

"To test Kye's faithfulness. He should be watching Hollany. You. If he does, then we know his token mark is true. If he doesn't—"

"Of course, of course. A test of true love, I remember. Always an amusing game."

Seshabah noticed the door, ajar behind the canvases. "But what do you need that for? You should be watching from here to see if Kye passes your test."

"Oh." Brinadar shrugged. "It's just in case someone comes into the room. So we can hide."

"Yes." Jinnie helped her friend. "As you said, it's a perfect place for a tryst."

"Is it not?" Seshabah laughed and took up Jinnie's mask, using it to tap Krisen lightly on the chest. "I shall see you at my tower later tonight, I think."

She held up the feather to his eyes, then tucked it between her breasts.

"Frivolity, my dears." Seshabah went to the drapes. Krisen immediately held one back for her to pass.

"Seshabah!" Brinadar hurried to her. "Remember not to talk. Just smile, all right? Otherwise the game is over."

Seshabah smiled. She lifted the moon mask to her face and disappeared.

Brinadar looked up at Krisen. He nodded in the direction of the door. "A clever exit to the valley."

Brinadar sighed. "Yes," she said, deciding to trust him. "It is."

"If you're a true friend," Jinnie spoke up, "why can't you sail us to the valley?"

Krisen faced Jinnie. "A boat going to the valley is always under surveillance by the Dysans. Tonight it would be suspect and searched. You wouldn't be safe. You're not safe now."

His eyes blinked gold then green again. "I have to leave for Seshabah's tower," Krisen said quietly. "I hope the best of life for you."

Jinnie recognized the Daskiny phrase. "And I hope the best of life for you, Krisen."

He smiled, ducked beneath the drapes, and was gone.

Seven

Kye strode across the main hall of the Center Tower. He no longer had to push his way through. The crowd parted for him, allowing him to move easily toward his goal: the art room. Kye was certain he had seen Hollany in that area.

The ceremony of honor had taken place uninterrupted. Elbanon had not appeared to challenge him, and Kye was besieged with congratulations. He had his position of power, and no one could question his decisions except Seshabah. Perhaps Hollany was with her.

Kye approached a group of women. Seshabah was not among them.

"Have you seen Hollany?" Seeing the confusion on their faces, Kye explained. "My lady, the Traveler. She's costumed as the moon. She was with Seshabah earlier this evening."

"We haven't seen Seshabah for some time, but I see a mask of the moon there," one woman said. She pointed.

Kye looked. Across the room, Hollany was dancing gracefully with someone else. Angry, Kye thanked the woman and headed back in the direction he had come.

Hollany disappeared before he reached her. Kye stood still, searching the room again. He saw Hollany by an archway. Something was different about her.

Kye focused on her movement. Her posture was relaxed. She'd loosened the corset. But there was something else.

Hollany was keeping her mask in place, not letting it tip. She glanced in his direction and smiled. Kye waited for her to come toward him.

Instead, Hollany let a male Toranise take her hand and kiss it. Jealousy clouded Kye's senses; for an instant, his eyes snapped gold.

Moving carefully, Kye stalked Hollany. He joined a group of people and pretended to listen to their talk as he watched Hollany move closer, unaware of how near he was.

Where is Brinadar? Kye wondered, moving closer to his target.

Hollany paused, leaning close to listen to someone. She smiled a little.

Kye stared at her neck. She wasn't wearing the crystal. He moved toward her, silent and determined. The scent of another woman hit his nostrils.

Stepping behind the imposter, Kye encircled her with his arms. "You've lost your crystal," he whispered into the woman's ear.

She gasped, half-turning even as Kye escorted her to a Resting Room. He shut the door and grabbed for the mask, revealing the deception. "Seshabah!"

Seshabah laughed. "My dear Kye! It took you no time at all. Why, I have played this game with many admirers, and they took hours longer than you did. Of course," she continued as she moved to a mirror to admire the embroidered corset, "you are more motivated. The Traveler is very fine indeed, and you, dear Kye—" Seshabah sashayed over to where he stood——"you are in the metamorphosis."

Kye stepped away from Seshabah, agitated. "I can't be. It will be years before I'm that old. Years I will spend with my *hollany*."

Seshabah tilted her head to one side, assessing Kye as he paced the small room. "It should be years. I think something has happened to accelerate the change."

Seshabah thought for a minute. "Perhaps the presence of your Traveler?" she suggested. We know so little of her, really. Although she is delightful, in her way. As for you, dear Kye, you have a month, perhaps two or three, and then the metamorphosis will take hold. No wonder your lady wanted to test your devotion. I shall tell her you won the game."

Kye stood still. "Where is she, Seshabah?"

"Why, in the art room. I saw you focus there. I thought you might find her before you discovered me."

Seshabah lifted the hem of the silver gown, admiring it. "I thought she might be tempted to impersonate me more openly. I suppose my costume did not fit her well enough. Ah, well. Frivolity, my dear Kye. Frivolity. We'll go and fetch her together."

Seshabah took Kye's arm as he started past her. She slowed him down and they left the room together. Seshabah kept the mask in front of her face. The sun and its satellite passed through the crowd to the far side of the main hall.

Kye opened the door to the art room. "Hollany?"

Seshabah swept past him. She peered around the room. "Brinadar?"

Going behind the stack of canvases, Seshabah pushed against the narrow door. It was locked.

"What's there?" Kye came up behind her. "Where does that door lead?"

"I have no idea," Seshabah admitted. "I hope it leads to another room, because your Traveler has my costume, and this corset—" Seshabah tugged at the stiff material—"is becoming uncomfortable"

Kye pried at the door. It was flush with the wall, without a handle. It wouldn't open.

"I have to find her," Kye insisted. "Now!"

"Calm yourself," ordered Seshabah. "We will search the rooms of the house; my friends will help us. We can make a game of it. If we do not find her, then you may take a boat home."

"She won't be there," Kye said abruptly. *She'll be in the valley*, he thought, *looking for a Daskiny Healer.*

He hit the door with the flat of his hand. "I must go!"

"You cannot leave until dawn, Kye. You know that." Taking his arm again, Seshabah led him to the balcony archway.

"Do not forget you are the guest of honor tonight." She waited for Kye to pull the drapes aside for her.

"You will be the center of attention, Kye. All the ladies will want to dance with you. They will not care that you have promised the Traveler that you will be hers."

Stiff-backed and reluctant, Kye pulled aside a drape for Seshabah. "I have to find her," he said, trying to modulate his voice from angry to reasonable.

Seshabah rolled her eyes.

"Do not fret so, Kye. It is unbecoming of a Toranise, especially one who has just been honored. You spoil the night. Your lady must be here somewhere. After all, she is a Traveler. She cannot leave without you." Seshabah smiled and stepped onto the balcony.

"Yes, she can," Kye murmured, following Seshabah.

But I can bring her back, Kye said to himself, thinking of the crystal.

* * *

"Brinadar! Slow down." Jinnie held tightly to the railing of the spiral staircase. Nauseated, she leaned against the cold column of the stairs, one hand on her stomach.

"Are you ill?" Brinadar climbed back up several steps to join Jinnie.

Jinnie shook her head. "I'm going to Travel."

"When?"

"I don't know." The nausea passed, and Jinnie sighed, relieved. "I'm better now. Let's keep going."

"All right," said Brinadar. She started the descent again. Jinnie followed.

"It must be terrible for you," Brinadar said, keeping her voice low. "Traveling without knowing when you are going. Do you ever know where?"

"No. At least, not yet." Jinnie stumbled on Seshabah's gown. It was too long for her. She yanked it up higher.

Uncomfortable with the subject, Jinnie changed it. "What will we do when we reach the bottom of the tower? I'm sorry, but your *krisen* won't be there."

Brinadar lifted the lantern, revealing bits of rubble strewn on the cracked steps. "I'm sorry, too," said Brinadar. "But our plan will stay the same. Netab, my Daskiny boatman, went to the valley while you visited with me. He made the arrangements for our clothing then. That's how my maid knew Kye was returning. Netab saw Kye in the valley, speaking with the Daskiny Healer."

Jinnie stopped. "The Daskiny Healer? Has she returned?"

"Returned? My dear, Jinnie, she never left. Kye has been keeping you isolated from everyone to protect himself. He didn't want you to learn what I told you yesterday. He definitely didn't want you speaking to the Daskiny. I don't know why."

Jinnie said nothing. She felt a pain that wasn't a symptom of Traveling: the pain of loss and betrayal. Kye's love, however transitory, had been a lifeline for her.

"Brinadar," said Jinnie, deciding as she spoke.

"Yes?"

"I have to go the Daskiny Healer. You'll have to journey on without me."

Brinadar paused. "Kye will come after you, Jinnie."

"I know, but I must see this Healer. I have to speak with her. If she has any knowledge about Travelers, it will be worth the risk." Jinnie looked into her friend's frightened face. "You'll be fine, Brinadar. You'll be disguised." Wanting to ease her friend's worry, Jinnie lifted the crystal at her neck.

"Take my crystal," she offered. "Just in case you're seen. It may help."

Brinadar shook her head. "I can't. The crystal is exclusive to you. All the Toranise know of it."

Jinnie thought a moment. "Then look for a feather."

"What?"

"A feather. You said the Dysans designed this tower. They might have used this staircase during construction. Let's look for a feather as we descend. If we find one, you can keep it in your hand, just in case your disguise fails or you are stopped by a Dysan."

"Very clever, dear old friend." Brinadar smiled a true smile of appreciation. She nodded her head. "All right, we'll look."

They continued down, searching the steps for their token. Several times, both of them stumbled, clutching each other for support as the railing wobbled. A small stone slipped inside one of Jinnie's shoes.

"Wait a minute," she said. She sat down and pulled off the shoe, shaking out bits of dust and gravel. A flutter caught her eye.

"Brinadar!"

"I see it!" Brinadar grabbed for the feather. Catching it, she held it up, triumphant. "I've got it, Jinnie. Oh, you are wonderful."

"Tuck it in your bodice." Jinnie stood up, and a wave of dizziness slapped her. She steadied herself with a deep breath.

"Are we almost there?" she asked.

"Almost," said Brinadar. "Be careful. Some of the steps are broken."

"All right." Jinnie followed Brinadar, fighting her emotions. Fear of discovery, anxiety about Traveling, and sorrow and regret at leaving Brinadar and the Daskiny.

Brinadar stopped then moved forward into the darkness of the stairwell. She turned to Jinnie. "We're here! I'm at the door."

Jinnie hurried down the last few steps, staggering a little. She joined Brinadar in the lantern's light. They both leaned near the door, listening.

"I don't hear anything," Brinadar whispered.

"I'll go first," Jinnie decided. "Stay back until I say it's safe. If I'm caught, hide here. If you're found, the feather should protect you."

Brinadar shook her head. "We'll go together." She put her hand on the latch of the door. "Come on."

The two of them pushed the door a little. Fresh air beckoned.

They looked at each other. Brinadar abandoned their lantern, and they pushed the door completely open. The night was empty. Only moonlight watched as Brinadar and Jinnie stole out of the tower's base and under the surrounding trees. They kept silent, moving cautiously through the undergrowth. Occasionally Brinadar would stop and peer at the bushes.

"What are we looking for?" Jinnie risked whispering.

"That." Brinadar pointed and pushed her way toward a thicket. Crouching, she reached into the bushes, fumbling to grasp something.

"Here it is," said Brinadar, relieved. She handed Jinnie a heavy cloth bag, dusting leaves off her dress as she stood up.

Jinnie recognized the coarse cloth. *Daskiny,* she thought.

"We can change our clothes right here and use the same thicket to hide our gowns," suggested Brinadar.

"Good idea."

Jinnie changed quickly, familiar with trousers and boots, shirts and vests. She helped Brinadar, then stood back to be a mirror for her friend.

"Tuck your hair up under the hat," Jinnie instructed. She did the same.

A rustling of branches made them duck. Half-crouched, they tried to slip away unnoticed.

"Stop, please," a small voice said.

Brinadar took Jinnie's hand. Making her voice deep, she called into the darkness. "Who are you?"

"A *krisen*," a man's voice answered. "Netab told me to watch for the Lady Brinadar. I am here to help you."

He paused. "I have instructions for the Traveler, from the Healer."

Jinnie caught her breath. A shiver made her straighten her shoulders. She stepped from behind the tree, leading Brinadar.

"I'm the Traveler," Jinnie announced, voice firm. "What are the Healer's instructions?"

The Daskiny man pointed to his left. "Follow the path to the river. The Healer will join you there."

"And my friend?"

"I am to accompany the Lady Brinadar to the inland sea. A Daskiny boat will meet us there."

"You will go with her?" asked Jinnie, wanting reassurance of Brinadar's safety.

"Yes. We will take the forest road and follow the coastline to the agreed meeting place." He whistled softly. There was an awkward rumbling noise behind him. A creature resembling a small horse appeared; it pulled a two-wheeled cart.

"A Dysan has been seen," the Daskiny said. "He is hunting."

"Elbanon," Brinadar whispered.

Jinnie squeezed her hand. "You have the feather, and you are disguised. Be strong for me."

Brinadar tried to smile. "I thought we were escaping together."

"We were," said Jinnie. "We have. You're going home now, Brinadar."

"And where are you going?"

Jinnie looked at the path the Daskiny had indicated. "I'm going on."

Brinadar hugged Jinnie fiercely. "I hope the best of life for you, Jinnie," she whispered. "Dear old friend."

Jinnie hugged her back. Then, letting go, she walked past the Daskiny and started down the path. Hearing another whistle, she turned.

Brinadar waved to her from the cart as they pulled away, and Jinnie raised her hand in acknowledgment, then entered the forest.

The night closed about her. Tree roots made a lattice of the path, and Jinnie had to pick her way through. Like an acrobat, she extended her arms for better balance.

Moonlight managed to pierce the branches of the trees, guiding Jinnie forward. Ahead of her, water gurgled. Anxious to meet the Healer, Jinnie increased her pace. She tripped and fell.

"You need to pay attention to where you are," said a woman's voice, "not just to where you are going."

Sprawled on the ground, Jinnie looked up.

An odd little woman approached Jinnie from behind the trees. Her copper hair knotted and curled tightly about a face the color of creamed tea. She wore a beige robe, and her feet were bare.

"Are you injured?" the woman asked.

Pushing herself to her feet, Jinnie brushed dirt from the back of her trousers and her hands. "No. No, I'm all right, thank you."

She looked into the woman's hazel eyes. "Are you the Healer?"

"I am. You may call me Ninehtah." She motioned Jinnie to follow her and continued along the path, Jinnie treading carefully, Ninehtah moving easily without looking down.

"We will walk by the river," Ninehtah said.

"Won't that attract Dysans?"

Ninehtah pointed overhead. The trees had thorns instead of leaves. "We will be safe enough for a little while."

They reached the river's edge. The water bubbled, sparkling as it broke against rocks, running quick and narrow.

Ninehtah led Jinnie to a trail wide enough for them to walk side by side. She paused for a moment, stepping up to Jinnie.

Placing a gentle hand on Jinnie's chin, Ninehtah looked deep into her eyes. "You are ill," she pronounced.

"Yes. The Traveling makes me ill."

"Yes. It would." Ninehtah began walking again. "I see more than illness. I see questions. Ask them."

Jinnie hesitated. "Are you the Healer who met with the Toranise, Kye?"

"Yes."

"Did you tell Kye I would stay whole once I reached Yar?"

"No. You were only an extension of your true self. I told Kye this."

"I don't understand."

"I think you do," said the Healer. "You know that Kye has been lying to you. Strong intuition is a gift of Travelers. It helps us to feel our way through our many lives."

"What do you mean, our way?" Jinnie interrupted.

"I am a Traveler, too," said Ninehtah. "But I am ahead of myself. Tell me, how many bridges have you crossed?"

"I don't know what you mean. There weren't any bridges. I just appear. Suddenly. Usually painfully. And I leave the same way."

"I see." Ninehtah looked thoughtful. "You have lost your understanding of what it means to be a Traveler."

"I never had an understanding," said Jinnie.

"Then I will help you now. First, tell me of your Travels as we walk. Everything that has happened to you until tonight. Tell me where you went, how you felt, who you met, and who you loved. Everything."

Jinnie sighed. "I looked out the window," she began. When Jinnie finished, she waited for Ninehtah to speak. The woman seemed lost in listening. They walked in silence.

"Travelers," Ninehtah said at last, "create bridges between worlds, bridges of time which we cross when our next lifetime is fully formed. As we become incompatible with one world, we split apart, then gradually become whole, as your Escabel told you.

"We lead pivotal lives. Lives that affect and shape those we meet and what we touch. Our dual existence, from world to world, gives us time to let go of one life and embrace the next. We age slowly, imperceptibly. Our life span is long, over a thousand years. This allows us to endure the emotional pain of Traveling and garner patience from experience."

"Over a thousand years?" Jinnie's voice betrayed her dismay.

"I am one thousand and three years of age," said Ninehtah. "But this life, on Yar, is my last."

"How do you know it's your last? How will I know when it's mine?"

"We cease to split apart. There are no more dual existences to endure, no bridges to cross. We begin to age at a normal pace and live our final lifetime with a sense of peacefulness I cannot describe. You will know, in the deepest part of your being, that you belong."

"And that's how you feel here?" Jinnie found it hard to picture Yar as a happy place.

"Yes."

"Does Kye know you're a Traveler? Will you be safe? He never mentioned your name. He told me only that he had spoken to a Healer who knew a little about Travelers."

Ninehtah held up her hand to stem Jinnie's burst of anxiety. "Kye does not know or even suspect I am a Traveler. I will be safe."

"He's lied so much and so easily," said Jinnie. "I rarely recognized when he spoke the truth. I think part of me wanted to believe his lies."

Jinnie looked at the river. "And I lied too. I lied to placate him, and myself. I didn't want to feel suspicious. I didn't want to be all alone here. Without Griffin."

She looked at Ninehtah. "Why are you here, Ninehtah? Is it to help the Daskiny?"

"Yes. I am helping them escape to the north, to a part of Yar far beyond the reach of the Toranise and the Dysans."

"Where the Mithanalen live," said Jinnie.

"Yes. The Daskiny and the Mithanalen coexisted peacefully once before. I think they will again. A strong leader or advisor could even unite them against the Toranise."

"That's the connection," Jinnie interrupted. "The similarities between my lives that Susatch and I tried to establish. War."

"No." Ninehtah shook her head. "Peace. To live among the Mithanalen might have been your destination, if your Traveling had been successful."

"What went wrong?" Jinnie asked.

Ninehtah looked sad. "You have been moved through your lives at an accelerated rate, crossing bridges of time that had not yet solidified. That is why your Traveling has been painful and why you could not easily remember your previous life. You were not yet completely compatible with Ispell.

"On Hura, you were so far out of sync that your physical appearance was altered. That occurs only occasionally, and we learn to manipulate it.

But on Hura, you were decades ahead of your time. You were fortunate to survive.

"Now, on Yar, you do not yet even exist as either Daskiny or Toranise." Ninehtah looked up at Jinnie. "Or Mithanalen."

Before Jinnie could speak, Ninehtah continued. "Your physical appearance, therefore, is the one with which you are most familiar. You are almost one hundred years ahead of your time. You have been Traveling out of sync with your place in Time and Space. That is what has been making you ill."

"But I can't be out of sync. Kye said he saw me here several times. Or was that a lie, too?"

"No. But you were insubstantial, a mere shadow of what you would eventually become. I do not know why he met you when he did, but it was not meant to be. I told him this. I warned him to let you alone. I explained how your presence would fade in and out of Yar for many years until a strong dual identity had developed between yourself as Jinian and whoever you were meant to be here. I also warned him that if you were to arrive in Yar too early, there could be repercussions. Your presence could disturb the energy around you."

"Repercussions? Do you mean Kye's early metamorphosis?"

"And Elbanon's."

Jinnie lifted her arms and dropped them to her sides. "Then why am I here if it's causing so much trouble? I don't want to be here. If I had to Travel at all, it was only Ispell and Griffin that I wanted."

"Kye," said Ninehtah.

"Kye?" Jinnie felt a cold apprehension.

"Kye is responsible for your crossing bridges before you were ready. He is a Toranise. He can create motion. He has done so. He has brought you to him, through your lives, to this one."

Appalled, Jinnie stopped walking. She stretched an arm out to a tree trunk, leaning on it for support as her world turned upside down and inside out. Turning away from Ninehtah, Jinnie sank to her knees and retched.

Ninehtah stooped by the river. Producing a cloth from her robe, she wet it and returned to Jinnie. Kneeling beside her, Ninehtah wiped Jinnie's face. Ninehtah's eyes were kind and understanding.

"It is always difficult, the first few times we Travel," she said gently. "Your Traveling has been particularly harsh. Faced with so much confusion and pain, you are remarkable in your strength."

Jinnie clutched one hand to her stomach, forcing out the next question. "If Kye hadn't pulled me through my lives, would I still be with Griffin?"

"You would not yet be with him, but you would have been in time."

"And the war?" Jinnie stared at Ninehtah. "Could I have stopped the war?"

Ninehtah stood up. "I doubt there would have been a war if you had been allowed to cross your bridge to Ispell when you were ready. As I said, Traveling prematurely has disturbed the energy that surrounds you."

"What energy?"

"All Travelers produce an energy," Ninehtah explained. "It is like a magnetic field. The Daskiny and the Toranise would call it the inner self."

"What do we call it?"

"Call it whatever you like: your heart, your soul, your magic. The name will change, but the energy will remain constant. It alters the pace of events in time that are malleable. It lies deep within us, entirely subconscious. The energy provides us with our intuition. Unfocused as yours has been, it has upset the natural balance of your environment, evoking consequences that otherwise would not have been."

Jinnie thought the pain she felt would stop her heart. She wished it would.

Over a thousand years of pain and sorrow? Jinnie looked at Ninehtah's peaceful countenance. *Will I ever attain that?*

She climbed to her feet, and the nausea of Traveling made the forest swirl before her. "I won't be here much longer," Jinnie stated.

"No." Ninehtah studied the crystal still hanging on its chain about Jinnie's neck.

"You had best give that crystal to me." She held out one hand, palm up. "It is not safe for you to wear it."

Untying the knot Kye had made, Jinnie lifted the chain and crystal over her head. "Kye gave it to me for protection," she explained.

Examining the crystal, Ninehtah nodded to herself. She threw it into the river. "That is a *guinya* stone. See the rocks?"

Ninehtah pointed at the rocks in the river, sparkling even as the moon set and the sun rose. "Notice how they spark as the water hits them? They hold a high concentration of *despada* energy. It is traceable. If you had Traveled wearing that crystal, Kye could have found you and attempted to bring you back."

Jinnie stared at the rocks, her bitterness distilling into anger. "I see," she whispered. She looked at Ninehtah. "Will you walk with me to the sea?"

"No, but I will accompany you to the mouth of the river. Come."

"Will I always Travel out of sync?"

"I cannot say for certain. The motion Kye created cannot easily be stopped, but I believe it will dissipate eventually. When it does, you should return to your normal pace of Traveling. I do know that, as a Traveler, you will continue to make a difference wherever you go. As you did here, for Brinadar. It may not be the alteration you wanted, or the modification you were intended to make, but it will be enough. The Universe has a way of righting itself."

"Oh, my God, Kye," said Jinnie, anguished. "What have you done?"

Ninehtah looked up at the lightening sky. "He has inadvertently given you freedom."

"What did you say?" Jinnie asked in disbelief.

"Travelers' lives extend two or three worlds ahead of us. With each bridge we cross, new bridges are formed. Your lives, however, have only extended to Yar. The next world to which you Travel will have nothing to bind you, nothing predetermined. You can choose your life, your name.

"As you move further from the source of disruption, further from Kye, you may begin a dual existence and extension again. Until then you are, in a sense, free."

Jinnie barely noticed the widening of the river or the smell of salt in the air as the forest thinned. She walked quietly, feeling numb.

"I cannot risk going farther," Ninehtah announced. "You must go to the edge of the sea. Its motion will ease your passage."

Stopping, Jinnie tried to smile. "Thank you for helping me to understand," she said.

"I wish I could do more to ease your sorrow," said Ninehtah. "Know this much: regret nothing. Each part of your journey is essential to the whole. The moment you are experiencing is as important as your destination."

Ninehtah stepped back. "Good-bye, Traveler. May you find your future."

Eight

Kye studied his reflection. *My eyes are clear and green,* he told himself. Removing his headdress, he turned his head from side to side. *My hair is clean, without feathers.*

He looked down at his hands, clenching them into fists. *I am not anywhere near the metamorphosis,* he thought. *Seshabah is mistaken.*

"Kye!" A Toranise lady he had danced with during the night clasped his shoulders from behind. "We're going to sail to Chatamer Woods for breakfast. Do join us."

"No. Thank you." Kye smoothed his shirt and stepped away from the mirror and the woman. He forced a smile. "Perhaps I'll join you later."

The woman pouted. It distorted her already unattractive features. Kye's need to find Hollany increased.

"Very well," the woman said. "We shall expect you later. And I," she brushed her fingers against Kye's hair, "will expect you later still."

She flounced from the Resting Room, and Kye released his breath. Her scent was distasteful, and her bold manner angered him. He wanted Hollany.

Kye opened the door slowly, checking the main hall. It was empty. The last of the Masquerade revelers had set sail. The evening of honor was over.

Moving swiftly, Kye went to the wharf and leapt aboard his boat. Casting off, he tried to sail down to the valley in too tight a circle. The boat rocked. Managing to keep his balance, Kye concentrated harder.

This time he circled wider, like a bird, descending slowly into the mists above his destination. As he sailed, Kye thought of Hollany.

Was she with the Daskiny Healer? Had she learned of his deceit?

Kye slowed his boat as it broke through the mists, revealing the valley below. He steered to the far end, heading for the house of the Daskiny Healer.

As he sailed, Kye scanned the area for Hollany, lifting his head high to catch her scent on the breeze. Nothing.

"Where are you, beloved?" he whispered aloud. "I need to hear your voice, smell your skin, touch your hair. Come to me, come to me, my *hollany*."

Kye reached the house and brought his boat to a halt, maneuvering it into a copse of *besta* trees. Their thin trunks gave way to the boat, and their long, graceful branches disguised its presence in the Daskiny valley.

Kye did not want to attract attention from the Dysans, particularly Elbanon. At the Masque, he had heard gossip about Brinadar and how she was still unmarked. As the evening progressed, it was also noted that Brinadar was missing from the party.

The Toranise men had wondered if Elbanon had come for her. A few looking uneasily toward the balconies.

She was right to leave him, the women had agreed, then moved on to Seshabah's costume change—wasn't it becoming? They had tired quickly of their search for the Traveler. Leave her to Kye, they insisted. Better still, leave Kye to us.

Kye had squired ladies about the dance floor repeatedly. Unwilling, always watching for Hollany, he had smiled and pretended to listen as the women flirted with the new champion of honor.

Kye climbed from his boat and marched to the back of the house. Without bothering to knock, he entered. His eyes instantly took in the emptiness of the single dark room.

"Hollany?"

The silence answered. A rodent darted across the room. Kye watched it.

Seshabah is wrong, he thought. *I am not in the metamorphosis. If I were, I would have done ...*

"This!" Kye sprang forward, snatching up the rodent and breaking its neck. He held the carcass up, triumphant, eyes glazed gold. A sound outside broke his trance. Kye's eyes snapped green. He looked at the carcass, throwing it away in disgust.

"Who's there?" Kye demanded.

"It is my house," said a quiet voice. "Who is in it?"

"I am the Toranise, Kye. We have spoken before."

Ninehtah opened the front door. Noticing the dead rodent, she did not enter the room, choosing instead to pick up a small basket and head to her garden. Kye followed her.

"Where is the Traveler?" he asked, keeping his voice calm. "Has she been to see you? Have you spoken to her?"

Ninehtah knelt beside her flowers. She carefully pinched a few leaves from a stem and placed them in her basket. "I have not seen your Traveler," she said. "If she is missing, perhaps she has Traveled already. Perhaps you should let her go."

"I can't!" Kye looked about the garden. He steadied himself.

"Has she been here?" he demanded.

Ninehtah looked up at Kye. "No."

Kye looked deep into the Daskiny's eyes, but he was unable to discern whether she was telling the truth. "Very well, Healer. I will find her. If she has Traveled, I will bring her back. She is wearing a crystal from a *guinya* stone."

"Ah, yes. I remember now." Ninehtah pretended to be busy. "You asked to read about the different energies available on Yar. You borrowed one of my books."

Ninehtah tapped her chin thoughtfully with a flower. "I believe you hoped to amplify the Traveler's natural energy with the *despada* energy of the *guinya* stone."

She shrugged. "It would make it easier to find her. I did not say if it would bring her back."

Ninehtah rested her hands in her lap. "Do you have the stone from which the crystal was cut?" she asked, hoping to slow Kye down and give Jinnie time to Travel.

"Yes, Healer. I keep it in my boat."

Ninehtah nodded. "No doubt its amplification of your inner self allowed you to win many tournaments."

Kye's jaw tightened. He took a step toward Ninehtah. "Do not think that you are immune to my authority because you are a Healer," he threatened her.

Ninehtah sensed the heat of Kye's metamorphosis. She didn't move.

Frustrated, Kye spun about and returned to his boat.

Ninehtah watched him as he set sail. He was heading for the coast. She went back to her gardening, hoping Jinnie had already Traveled.

In his boat, Kye reached under the seat and withdrew a stone. A piece of it had been chiseled away, but the *despada* energy still swirled inside. Tucking the stone into a pocket, Kye steered toward the inland sea.

If Hollany has Traveled, he thought, *I'll bring her back and pretend nothing unusual has happened. I'll tell her the Daskiny Healer said she was meant to return.*

"But what if she insists on meeting the Healer?" Kye said aloud. "What if the Healer lied, and they have already met?"

Kye sailed faster, tapping the *despada* energy of the stone. "I will deny everything for a lie. I love her. I haven't told her how much. That's all she needs to reassure her. I love her."

He sailed higher, eyes sweeping over the landscape as it changed from forest to scrub to sand. Far down the coastline, he saw a bright light, surfing at the mouth of the river, caught between the rocks.

Kye willed his boat to move faster and made it descend.

The river churned as it met the sea. Its current challenged the waves, and the motion interfered with Kye's sailing. He was forced to land on the riverbank and wade into the water.

The crystal's chain, lifted by the river's turmoil, had snagged on a sharp piece of rock. The crystal bobbed in the current. Kye pulled it free and held it against his chest.

"Hollany," he pleaded to the wind. "What have you done?"

Kye made his way back to the riverbank and sat down. The stone in his pocket interacted with its lost piece, creating a warm glow.

I can still call to her, thought Kye, *as I did before. But which direction would she have gone?*

He stood up quickly and launched his boat, sailing south to where he had first called to Hollany and where he had first pulled her from the sea.

* * *

Elbanon circled the valley once more. The dawn angered him after his long night of searching. At first he had thought he was hungry as he flew through the dark skies. Soon he realized he was looking for a person. Someone who had been important to him. Someone he missed.

The shadow of his wingspan crossed the road in front of Brinadar's cart. The Daskiny sitting beside her cringed.

"Be still," she commanded. Taking the feather from the shirt she wore, Brinadar held it above her head, holding it tightly in one fist.

Elbanon focused on the small movement, hovered for a moment, and swung away. From a great height, he watched the cart disappear beneath the trees.

Brinadar, he thought, recognizing her scent. *I love you still. Be well.*

* * *

Jinnie walked along the shoreline, anguished and angry. Her questions had been answered. All the pieces of the puzzle fit. Pulling off her hat, she tossed it into the surf. It bobbed for a moment, then disappeared.

"Like me," she whispered.

Jinnie looked north, hoping Brinadar was safe. Her gaze returned to the sea as the word 'safe' drew her thoughts to Griffin. Maybe she could get back to him. Not from Yar, not yet, perhaps not for a very long time, but eventually. Jinnie swiped at a tear. Whitecaps sailed the waves like surfers, cresting, crashing, drowning, surfacing.

A rush of dizziness made her sit down abruptly, not caring how the water soaked her legs.

"Hollany."

Jinnie tensed. She didn't turn to look at him. "Go away, Kye. I don't want to see you. I've read your diary." Jinnie lied to protect Ninehtah. "I know what you've done."

Kye knelt beside her. "Hollany, please. Please look at me. Let me explain."

Jinnie looked away instead, her hands clenching and unclenching the wet sand. "You really don't believe you've done anything wrong, do you?" she asked.

"How can it be wrong to love you?"

"Love me?" Jinnie faced him in a fury. "You almost destroyed me, as you destroyed so many other people, altering my life and theirs beyond restoration. How can you say you love me? How can you justify so much destruction?"

"I'm sorry," Kye said, his voice quiet. "There was a chance that Ninehtah was wrong, that your metabolism would stabilize once you were with me. There was a chance, and I took it because I love you. More than your Griffin."

"Never!" Jinnie wanted to punch him. "Never, even in a hundred lifetimes, could you love me as much as Griffin. He would have waited for me. He did wait for me. He loved me."

Jinnie pushed herself to her feet, pulling back as Kye stood up and reached for her.

"Why didn't you wait for me, Kye?" Jinnie demanded.

"Because I would have been a Dysan by the time you came to me. You wouldn't have loved me then."

Jinnie shook her head, all the horror, all the rage draining away from her. "I don't love you now."

"Don't say that!" Kye's sudden anger made Jinnie back up a step. He dropped his voice to a whisper. "Hollany. I love you."

"You don't love me, Kye. You love what I represent: power and achievement." Jinnie shook her head. "That's not love; that's ambition."

Kye struggled to control his anger, knowing he was losing a challenge he had hoped never to face. "I never meant to hurt you, Hollany. And I do love you."

Jinnie saw the pain in Kye's dark green eyes, the grief and despair, the complete desolation, and recognized it as her own.

"I'm not your *hollany*, Kye." Jinnie turned away. "I have to go now," she said.

"Hollany? Don't leave me."

"I have no choice. Please don't try to bring me back."

Jinnie felt the familiar disorientation, but no pain. She started down the beach again.

"Hollany!" Kye called after her. "I love you!"

Desperate, he took a step forward, fingering the *guinya* stone in his pocket. "Jinnie!"

Jinnie paused but did not look back. Her true name sounded distorted when Kye finally spoke it. She walked on.

The world seemed to tilt a little, but Jinnie kept walking. Now she seemed to be moving through a cloud. The sound of the ocean grew faint. Voices and faces passed her in the mist.

"I love you, Tessajihn."

"Let go of the past, look to the future."

"Beloved."

"I hope the best of life for you, Jinnie."

"The Universe has a way of righting itself."

Jinnie felt them pass through her like ghosts, taking her lives from her body until she had only memories. The mist thickened to a heavy fog.

* * *

The *despada* energy in the *guinya* stone caught the Dysan's attention. Elbanon descended in a spiral, recognized his enemy, and attacked from behind.

Kye's death was quick.

* * *

The fog pressed all around Jinnie. She shortened the length of her strides, and stretched out her right hand. After a few minutes, a light appeared ahead of her. Jinnie walked toward it.

The fog lessened to a mist again. The sand became grass, then some sort of pavement. She could smell flowers. Slowly the mist dissipated. Jinnie stopped.

It was spring. The sun shone in a clear blue sky. She was on a sidewalk, next to a small garden. Across a narrow street stood a white building with its windows open wide to the warmth of the day. A sign above the door read *Lianna's Café and Rest Stop, Visitors Welcome.*

Jinnie smoothed her hair, crossed the street, and entered the café.

The Traveler

The woman behind the counter smiled at her. "Morning," she said, her face friendly.

"Good morning." Jinnie took a seat at the counter. "I'm new here," she began uncertainly. "A visitor."

"Well, welcome, visitor," said the woman, pouring a glass of water and setting it in front of Jinnie. "My name's Lianna. What's yours?"

Jinnie recalled Ninehtah's words: "You can choose your life, your name."

"Krisen," she decided. "It means truest friend."

Epilogue

The Traveler stood up. She flexed her fingers. Before she could question herself further, she would use the Machine.

Going to the control panel, she entered the countdown sequence and picked up her travel bag. She felt like a passenger about to board an airplane.

"For a one-way trip," she murmured. There would be just enough power for the journey, if her calculations were correct. No return would be possible. Her destination didn't have the technology required.

The Machine hummed. A mechanical voice began to recite numbers.

The Traveler slung the strap of her bag over one shoulder and entered the Machine.

* * *

Jinnie stumbled forward, falling into snow. Its icy crust bit her hands. Where was she?

Voices ahead of her became familiar. Coarse, unpleasant. Dardidak!

Jinnie remained on her knees, crouching, trying to see between the tangled branches of bushes before her. Three Dardidak huddled not a dozen feet away. Their bows were drawn and strung.

Jinnie could just hear them. One of them had hit his target, and now they would wait.

They're waiting for me, Jinnie realized.

She looked up, beyond the Dardidak. In the distance, the white spires of a castle reached to touch a winter sky: Keldonabrieve.

She was back. Griffin would be in the tunnel. Wanting to weep with joy, Jinnie clenched her teeth. First, the Dardidak.

Moving stealthily behind the bushes, Jinnie found a better vantage point. She took the laser pistol from her bag. Its energy supply was limited. She had to aim to kill; the Dardidak were faster than they looked, fast and brutal. She would be, too.

Jinnie raised the pistol, targeted the first Dardidak's heart, and fired. Even as he crumpled, his companions were moving. Jinnie fired again; the second one fell lifting his bow.

The third Dardidak's arrow hissed by her cheek. Her laser struck him between the eyes. Done.

Remembering other Dardidak were certain to be close by, Jinnie broke cover and raced to the tunnel. Entering, she slowed her steps, adjusting to the darkness and the wet ice beneath her boots.

It can't be much more than a few hours since I left, she thought. *How far back into the tunnel was the fissure we hid in? Griffin would have to wait until sunset. The Dardidak are fearful of the setting sun.*

"Griffin?" Jinnie called softly.

Silence.

"Griffin, answer me!"

"Tessajihn?"

When he had woken and read Jinnie's words on the tunnel wall, Griffin had despaired. His mind had drifted in and out of sorrow as he waited for the safety of sunset and the unspeakable loneliness of a life without Tessajihn. Hearing her voice, he thought he was drifting again, dreaming.

Jinnie hurried to Griffin's side. He sat braced against the side of the tunnel where her words stained the rock. She knelt beside him. Relief made her cry as she opened the medical kit she had brought.

"You didn't leave me," Griffin whispered, reaching for Jinnie's hand and kissing her palm. "You're not a Traveler."

"I am." Jinnie leaned forward and kissed him, salting his lips with her tears. "I was. And I did leave you. I had no choice." She wiped at her cheeks as she gently pressed an antibiotic bandage onto Griffin's wound.

"I Traveled to worlds upon worlds that needed me to curb their insanity." Jinnie quieted, remembering.

Griffin kissed Tessajihn's hand again. "What kind of insanity?"

"Hate. Ignorance. Even love." Jinnie thought briefly of Kye. "Love is a kind of insanity, too," she whispered. "But mine is a happy madness."

"And so you'll stay with me now, my *jinnie*." Griffin didn't need to make it a question anymore.

"Yes. Now and always." Jinnie smiled. "You're my best-loved."

Jinnie felt a peacefulness that had eluded her everywhere but here. She remembered Ninehtah's words: "You will know, in the deepest part of your being, that you belong."

This is my final lifetime, thought Jinnie.

About the Author

Jenna Lindsey is the author of the fantasy novel *Quest for Evil: The Magic of the Key*. Although agoraphobic and hearing-impaired, Jenna hears her characters clearly and travels with them through her novels. Jenna and her husband, Jerry, live in Calgary, Alberta, with three impatient cats.

Manufactured By: RR Donnelley
Momence, IL USA
October, 2010